THE TEMPLAR LEGACY

Books by W.R. Park

The Shadow Master Series
The Shadow Master (a.k.a. Overlay)
The Prophecy (a.k.a. The Dacian Resurgence)
Santa Fe Sacrifice (a.k.a. Sacrificed)
The Templar Legacy (a.k.a. Carpe Diem)

Coming Soon!
The Shadow Master Series
Unlikely Assassin (a.k.a. This Time It's Personal)
The Night the Moon Died

Mathew Ward/Jimmy Black Mysteries
Fatal Incision
Phantom Hounds

Hunter Dougllas Novels
Coma
The Visitor

The Franciscan Trilogy
The Franciscan
The Alpha Search
The Missing Hair Shirt

Murder and Mummies on Route 66
The Talking Stones

For more information
visit: www.SpeakingVolumes.us

THE TEMPLAR LEGACY

W.R. PARK

SPEAKING VOLUMES, LLC
NAPLES, FLORIDA
2025

The Templar Legacy

Copyright © 2004 by W.R. Park

All rights reserved. No part of this book may be reproduced or transmitted in any form or by any means without written permission.

ISBN 979-8-89022-262-6

To the departed members of the Corinthian Athletic Association football team: Kevin, John, Joe, Danny, Donny, Jerry, Willis, and a few others whose names escape me. As the last man standing, thanks for the lasting memories. I miss every one of you guys.

The CAA only lost one game in three years. It was by six points on a Thanksgiving Day game. We later discovered that the opposing team's quarterback was a QB for Army and home on leave. Tough game!

Acknowledgments

I wish to thank Speaking Volumes for their faith in my work—and to bestselling authors James Rollins and Jon Land for their continuing encouragement to write. Write. Write. It finally paid off.

Prologue

ADAM AND MOLLY RANCE and their dear friends, Arturo and Tina Testaccio, Alvin L' Ami, and retired General Rubin Brock—had again survived one of their most intriguing missions. Brock left Washington, D.C. to be with his wife, Martha, in Arizona and write a spy novel. Rance, Arturo and Al vowed to retire for good this time, and if possible, enjoy a normal life—whatever that was. Rance, his wife, and dog, T.P., flew to a small castle that Rance had purchased several years ago on the southern coast of Spain, determined to disappear forever from those that would again call on his unique special ops problem-solving talent.

Two remarkable encounters from recent years were about to re-enter his life—and the lives of those he held dear.

The first took place when exploring the caverns below the newly purchased castle. Rance stumbled upon the last living remnants of the Knights Templar—Sebastian and Bertrand. After hearing their incredible tale, he promised to keep their secret and allow them to remain in the castle while it was being renovated—for as long as they lived.

A second event happened earlier this year in a subterranean tunnel leading to the Los Alamos government compound in New Mexico. Rance, under the influence of peyote, heard the spirit of an ancient Indian shaman speak to him of many things—including the legend of Blue Rabbit—who may or may not have helped save Rance's life.

CASTLE de MOLAY/SPAIN SIX MONTHS LATER

"TELL ME..." RANCE SAID. "I missed Brother Sebastian and Brother Bertrand at our welcome home party. Haven't seen them all day. Aren't they coming to join us?"

A look of gloom replaced Tome's bright smile. "Forgive me, but I have been putting off my sad story until later." Tome Puertollano was mayor of the small village of Tarego, a stone's throw from the castle. He motioned for his honored guest to follow him across the square into the small, cramped mayor's office. A collection of oil paintings and antiques occupied most of the space, except for an old desk piled with stacks of paper, files, and a single rickety chair.

Puertollano noted the look of surprise on his friend's face and explained, "My brother owned an antique store in Madrid. When he passed away last year, I inherited everything. All the paintings, rugs, and antique furniture came from Roberto's store." Tome anticipated Rance's question and raised his hand. "The castle furnishings were not a gift: your generous yearly payment for the restoration work on the castle was sufficient to pay for what you have." He grinned and added, "You enjoyed a discount, of course."

"Of course. Now tell me about Sebastian and Bertrand."

Gloom again crossed the mayor's features. "Gone. Both of them. Eighteen months ago, Brother Bertrand, the oldest, passed in his sleep. Not a month after Brother Sebastian completed the matching stairway in your castle, he too passed. We all knew that he was ill and broken-hearted over his long-time friend's death, but he continued working. He not only supervised the stonework, he did most of it with his own hands. It was a matter of pride with him. He wanted to pay you back in some small way for the kindness you afforded the two lost souls." Puertollano turned around in his swivel chair and searched for something under a wobbly pile of old files.

"Here it is," he said, placing a flat object the size of a small photo album in Rance's hands. "I was by Sebastian's side when he took his last breath. Before he went, he asked me to fetch that item," he jabbed a pudgy finger at the object wrapped in threadbare scarlet cloth, "from under his bed. He made me promise not to open what he wanted you to have. Then he had me say words in Latin and repeat them until I knew them by heart."

"They were...?"

"First he said... *'Causa finite ect.'* ...then... *'Carpe diem.'*"

Rance translated the Latin. "The cause is finished. Seize the day."

TWO HOURS LATER after an intensive castle tour, Rance was sitting up on their bed, pillows supporting his back. Dressed in a tan bare-midriff cotton sleeping top and skimpy matching briefs, Molly turned from the window to face her husband after watching the village lights extinguish. Walking over to the desk, she placed her hand on the unopened gift presented by the deceased Brother Sebastian. "What do you think about this—and the Templar's Latin message?"

"The first sentence... *'The cause is finished.'* ...is obvious. He had fulfilled his vow and acknowledged the end." Rance ran fingers through his light brown hair and gave thought to his next explanation. "As far as the second sentence is concerned, I'm not too sure what to think—and hesitant to open the package." He made a motion with his hands. "On second thought, bring it here. Let's have a quick look."

Mac slipped under the thick down bedcover and handed it over. Rance slowly unwrapped the fragile scarlet cloth, revealing a leather notebook embossed with the Knights Templar cross and oval seal. It was bound with a tattered white ribbon. Undoing the sash, he carefully opened the cover and exclaimed, "It's written in Latin."

Mac leaned across the bed for a better view and watched in fascination as Rance slowly turned page after page. The handwriting was beautiful, with ornate diagrams, including illustrations of knights wearing garments bearing the unmistakable Knights Templar cross, highlighted in red. Suddenly Rance flipped the book closed and looked into his wife's eyes. "There's a drawing in there of what appears to be a treasure map—and the headline's Latin title translates… *'Guardians Behold Our Keeping.'* "

Mac noticed a puzzled expression cross her husband's face. "Brother Sebastian," Rance paused and laid both hands on the leather cover, "said on his deathbed for me to, *'Seize the day.'* "

"Do you think he was encouraging you to seize the treasure they vowed to protect?" Mac asked in a voice just above a whisper.

"Either that—or he wanted me to seize the day and take over his responsibilities—perhaps returning whatever is hidden to their proper owners."

"Like the Holy Grail?"

"Like the Holy Grail—if it exists." He displayed an impish grin, his pronounced dimples deepening. "I realize that we've just concluded our last mission, and everyone has vowed to turn their backs on the past, but this is entirely different. Do you think that Arturo, Tina, and Lord L' Ami would like to join us on a treasure hunt?"

Mac's eyes sparkled with excitement. Her welcomed kiss and loving hug was all the answer he needed.

Exhausted from the long flight and lengthy celebration, they fell asleep in each other's arms. Less than an hour had passed when Rance sat straight up in bed, disturbing his sleepy-eyed spouse. Groggy, she asked, "What is it? Not another of those nightmares?"

"Can't you smell it?"

"Smell what?"

Rance flared his nostrils and took a deep breath. "The distinct scent of peyote."

"I wouldn't recognize the scent of peyote from that of barnyard fire smoke," she answered in a singsong voice.

"He was here," Rance thought aloud. "The ancient Indian from the Frijoles Canyon cave grinned at me." Running a hand through strands of hair, he shook his head and pointed to the middle of the room. "He and that giant Blue Rabbit stood side by side and both grinned at me. A bony finger was pointed at my nose and the ancient one spoke…"

"What did he say?" Mac was now wide-awake.

"The old man's eyes widened as he smiled, shook that finger, and as they both evaporated—said, *'Seize the day.'*"

Chapter One

TWO WEEKS LATER

"WHERE'S LORD L' AMI?" Arturo Testaccio, nicknamed, A.T., asked the host of Castle de Molay. Answering his own question, he said, "Searching for this little hamlet's last bottle of Jack Daniel's."

Rance had invited his two best friends,' Al and A.T.—along with A.T.'s new wife Tina, to visit his and Mac's new home—Castle de Molay. He lured them with mysterious hints about at an adventure of a lifetime. Not another government sponsored covert mission to save the world. Just pure adventure. They couldn't resist. All agreed. All had arrived. But Al L' Ami was now missing.

After unpacking and freshening up in their private rooms, complete with huge fireplace, four-poster bed, bearskin rugs, oil paintings, Spanish armor adorning the walls, and picturesque views of the Mediterranean Ocean—Mac had provided everyone a quick tour of the castle and grounds. Al had hung back at the stables, apparently admiring the horses.

Standing before two huge doors at the entrance of the castle, the couples turned when they heard approaching hoof beats and a shout, "I'll return shortly! Don't start without me!"

L' Ami had waved and steered his mount in the direction of the small village, Tarego. That was two hours ago. But it gave the married couples an opportunity to discuss domestic gossip, boring chit chat that would have driven the single member of the crew to drink. If he ever needed an excuse.

They were enjoying the cool ocean breeze while lounging on a rear turret when clattering hoof beats on the tiled patio drew their attention to the castle's front walkway. Down below, their smiling friend straddled a nervously prancing stallion while cradling an armful of flowers. "They're for the ladies! Let me cool off my pal here," he patted the horse's neck, "and rub him down. Then I'm all ears." He headed for the stable, reined in, and turned in the saddle. "And pour me a stiff one." He pointed over the hill toward town. "I wasn't successful. They never heard of Jack Daniel's."

Al's grin widened before he turned and cantered away. "However, my visit to town wasn't a total loss. Your friend, Mayor Puertollano, has a very interesting younger sister. Adriana has agreed to join us for dinner tonight at Café Madrid. She chose the restaurant. Insisted dinner was on her brother. He owns the place."

RANCE SAT IN A HIGH BACK CHAIR at the end of a long table that could, if necessary, seat two dozen guests. Mac and Al sat in the two closest chairs to his right, A.T. and Tina to his immediate left. His words echoed in the huge room overhung with high wooden rafters. Lowering his voice appeared to help as he explained how he met Brothers Bertrand and Sebastian—and their startling connection with the ancient Knights Templar brotherhood.

"I purchased the castle on a whim eight years ago, a place to escape and find solitude." His eyes found his two friends. "You both can relate, I'm sure."

Rance raised his pewter cup of wine. "This is what happened those eight years ago after entering my castle" Thus the first part of his story began.

"Sleeping on a borrowed cot was uncomfortable. One night I heard sounds coming from the ground floor. Creeping down the wide stone staircase from the master bedroom, I soon discovered the noise emanated from below a trapdoor in the back room that once served as a buttery. When I stomped on the door, the noise stopped. My neverending pounding and shouts did the trick. A bolt slipped from an inside lock, and when it slowly opened, I could hardly believe my eyes.

"Two old, bearded men, one in his eighties, the other in his late seventies, walked up the trapdoor steps wearing badly soiled, once white tunics, displaying a red Templar Cross on their chests. Being familiar with the Templar legends, that sight—in a Spanish castle—nearly bowled me over. I explained that I was the new owner, invited them into the only room with a chair and a bench, and served them wine. They told me their amazing and sad story."

Taking a deep breath, Rance continued. "They were the last two Knights Templar survivors that they were aware of."

"If I remember my history," L'Ami interrupted, "they died out in the thirteen-hundreds."

A.T. teased. "How old did you say they were?"

"Wait. Don't get ahead of me, you two" Rance warned. "The story's not over. Yes, in thirteen-o-seven, King Philip of France and the pope had all the Templars arrested on the trumped-up grounds of heresy—and seven years later the last Grand Master of the Knights Templar, de Molay, was burned at the stake. But he got his revenge, so the tale goes. While dying, he cursed both King Philip and Pope Clement to join him within a year. Clement died a month later and Philip IV seven months after that."

"Served them right," Tina chimed in. "Why was he burned?"

"Because they had become so powerful, both as warriors and in wealth, the king and pope feared their influence: so they conspired to eliminate the order. Based in France, only those Knights not rounded up and murdered were able to escape. It was rumored that as many as eighteen Templar ships loaded with treasure and valuable religious relics assigned to their care set sail for Portugal, Spain, and Scotland.

Stone churches in Ethiopia bear the mark of Templar mason builders. A two hundred-year-old legend speaks of Templars who buried a wealth of their fortune in a pit on Oak Island, Nova Scotia—and," he added with flair, "it's even speculated that the pit contains the Holy Grail."

"Oh, come now," Mac said with a soft guttural tone, "that's what you told me before—and it's still hard to believe."

"Hey, I'm only telling you what I read. My story's not finished. It appears, as Brother Sebastian explained…that is what the youngest Templar called himself…that down through the ages, the order survived. Their only purpose in life was to keep holy relics out of the hands of those that would use them for their own evil benefits." Raising a finger, he asked, "Don't you remember the rumor that Adolph Hitler thought he had possessed the lance that was believed to have pierced Christ's side? He was under the impression that with the lance's mystical powers—he could rule the world."

"Didn't help him any, did it?" Tina pointed out.

"No. But there are those that believe he was bamboozled. Someone had provided him with a fake relic. But that's another story."

Rance took a long swallow and continued. "All this time, Brother Bertrand, the older of the two, sat quietly listening to his friend explain their presence in the castle's underground and staring intently into my eyes. Made me downright uncomfortable, I'll tell you that.

"Down through the ages, as Sebastian explained, the holy assignment of protecting the whereabouts of the treasured relics and fortune was passed on to those who were deemed worthy and would take the oath to carry on the tradition formed centuries earlier. When one Templar died, another would come and take his place at the castle. A tunnel runs from a secret room under the castle to the ocean cliffs. Every few months a ship appears carrying provisions and occasionally a new recruit replacement to hide in the bowels of the castle."

He stopped a moment and thought. "Oh yes, Brother Sebastian said the castle was named Castle de Molay, after their last Grand Master. A crew of Templars built it in thirteen-eighteen on the foundation of a much older castle ruin."

"Today's Masons claim to be an offshoot of the Templars," A.T. reminded everyone.

"When I mentioned that to Brother Sebastian, he scoffed. Bertrand spit on the floor in disgust. Neither man thought that the Masons in any shape or form resembled the order, although Sebastian did offer that he believed they did good works, even if they were fraudulent in his eyes.

"It seems that it had been six months since a supply ship had arrived to bring them necessities. To survive, Sebastian had taken to leaving the castle every few nights to sneak into the village and steal food and drink. I assured him that I would provide for his and Brother Bertrand's welfare. The next day I invited Mayor Tome Puertollano to join me for lunch, told him about the two old men that had been living in the room under the castle, and with that, I then called the two brothers in to meet the mayor. After all was said and done, I struck a bargain with Puertollano. Every year I would send a bank draft for the upkeep of the two men—and in addition—sufficient sums to cover the cost of refurbishing Castle de Molay. It would provide jobs and income for the men of Tarego. The mayor was ecstatic. He planned to call a village meeting and make the announcement. A day and night-long celebration ensued. I slipped away so they couldn't parade me around again. Before I left that evening under the cover of darkness, Brother Sebastian thanked me for my kindness and vowed to help by supervising the masonry work. Brother Bertrand thanked me with tears in his eyes."

"What about the relics and treasure?" Al wanted to know.

Rance shook his head. "I never asked. They spent their lives vowing to either hide the treasure or keep its location a secret. I wasn't about to cheapen our new relationship by pressuring them to dishonor their vow. Besides, I wanted for nothing."

L' Ami stood to stretch his legs and paced around the table as he talked. "We're all sorry that your two knight friends are gone—but what does that have to do with us being here at your request? You promised us the adventure of a lifetime."

Al downed his wine, placed the empty cup in front of Rance, and went on. "I'll tell you this—and Arturo will back me up—being one of your sidekicks has been a strain. This old full-of-holes body has had a lifetime of Rance-led adventures."

"Have I ever led you two astray?" Rance pleaded with his hands. Both friends searched the rafters for a straight answer. The women were in hysterics.

Al took his seat and pointed to his cup. "Pour the wine, damn it, and tell us about this great adventure of yours. I can hardly wait. If that last bullet didn't kill me, nothing ever will."

Rance nodded to his wife as he walked around the table to fill everyone's cup. Mac went to the fireplace and pulled down on one of the fixed candleholders. A small hidden door sprung open: inside was a leather book wrapped in a threadbare crimson cloth. Turning, she held it high. Rance announced—"Ladies and gentlemen….let the adventure begin."

"CLAUDE, WE HAVE BEEN at this for three days now: nothin' we do stops the sea from fillin' the damned shaft." The small man with one squinty eye and a perpetual sneer pushed back a handful of long black hair from his forehead with a mud-encrusted hand. "We have found our efforts fruitless, as dozens before us have. Our angled shafts fill with seawater just as did the main shaft over two hundred years ago when the pit was discovered by the two boys."

Paschal sat back and let his feet dangle into the thirteen-foot wide shaft opening. "The rock slab discovered ninety feet down with the strange undecipherable hieroglyphic writing provided no clue as to the whereabouts of the Templar treasure believed to be buried here on Oak Island."

Exhausted and equally frustrated, he looked up at the man standing to his side. Before he could complain further, a finger shook angrily in his face. "Silence!" shouted the man with a shock of gray hair any male lion would surrender his female to acquire. His massive three- hundred-pound body shook with anger. Pursing full lips, he wiped them dry with a silk handkerchief and continued in a deep calm voice. "I have killed for the information to the treasure. Those Templars preparing for their supply voyage to the Spanish castle deceived me while screaming in agony. In the end, they gave us no more than what the world already knew—that a number of the Knights Templar ships escaped the French king's wrath centuries ago and one arrived in what is now called Nova Scotia."

"You don't believe that the Templars built this Money Pit, as legend has it?"

"Paschal, indeed, the Templars built this ingenious mysterious contraption. However, I think they salted the pit with bits and pieces of gold and jewelry discovered these two hundred years." He laughed until it appeared the weight of his body would topple him over. "It's a feat of engineering genius only they were capable of producing at the time." His voice rose to a roar. "They designed this mystery to confuse the greedy world for centuries to come. Oh, how they must have cheered over their accomplishment of deception."

Claude, the notorious Frenchman called the Bishop, smacked his associate on the side of the head. "Round up the rest of the idiots, Edmond, Maurice, Baudouin—and if Baudouin is drunk again—slit his throat and stuff his worthless carcass in the pit. Let some other adventurer discover the remains. It will add to the mystery of Oak Island and the Knights Templar buried treasure."

Paschal scrambled to his feet, limped toward his weary crew resting by the old dead oak, then turned. "Bishop. Next stop, Spain?"

The large man's eyes narrowed. "It's been a number of years since I scuttled the Templar's supply boat headed to the castle they described. Unfortunately, a slight run-in with French law prevented me, the Bishop, from pursuing the treasure until now. It's about time we paid a visit to their comrades in Spain—if they survived—don't you think?"

RANCE CONTINUED TO MESMERIZE HIS AUDIENCE with tales of the Knights Templar and their enormous treasure, which included ancient and historic religious relics. Stopping from time to time to sip from his wine cup, he continued—often referring to drawings in the leather-bound journal. "As I have said, the Templars began with a band of nine military and religious knights devoted to protecting pilgrims traveling on highways in the holy land. In time, they grew in numbers and garnered such power and wealth that they threatened both kings and the papacy."

"So de Molay was burned at the stake. A number of knights escaped along with much of their wealth and the relics placed in their keeping," Al reiterated. Leaning across the table, he tapped the old journal. "What does that have to say about the treasure?"

"Why….suddenly you're so impatient? I've never known you to be so." Rance grinned at the others.

A.T. picked up the cue. "I'll tell you why," he offered with a straight face. "Ever since he became Lord Alvin L 'Ami of the Manor, he has become extremely bossy—and bitchy, I might add." A.T. made a face in Al's direction.

L'Ami looked up at the rafters for help. Finding none, he confessed. "Okay everyone, I apologize for my short temper—but it always happens when I don't have my Jack Daniel's." He glanced over at Rance. "You know that."

"Perhaps this Adriana woman can cool your temper," Tina teased.

Al scoffed. "Tina, lovely lady. You have not seen Adriana. She has the opposite effect—bound to raise my temperature."

Now it was their leader whose patience had thinned. They were off the subject. "We have to be in Tarego for dinner in less than three hours. Can we get back to why we're all here?" Everyone nodded.

Before Rance had a chance to say a word, Tina asked a question. "Pardon me, but how did they acquire such wealth?"

"Legend tells of the Knights Templar embarking on a secret mission to excavate the Temple of Solomon ruins. They quickly found whatever they were searching for and returned home. Besides untold treasure, it's written they found the Holy Grail." Tina's eyes widened.

Raising a hand, he warned, "That's only a rumor, mind you." He smiled. "But it's intriguing, isn't it." A.T. motioned for Rance to speed things up.

"In addition, sons of wealthy families pledged their fortunes and property for the privilege of joining the growing band. What emerged was the beginning of the first world bank. They accepted deposits from kings and loaned funds to wage war. That's when the king of France and the pope devised a scheme to discredit the order—thus numerous arrests and de Molay's death by fire.

"The Paris Templars loaded their treasure on wagons and headed to the port city of La Rochelle. There they transferred it to ships and set sail for destinations unknown. An ancient map discovered years ago displayed a landmass that resembles Nova Scotia. Sketched on the map is a figure of a crowned knight." He held up the leather-bound journal and pointed to a faded page. "That map is reproduced here in the journal left in Brother Sebastian's keep."

"But I also noted another map as you flipped through pages," Al observed.

"Yes. "It's a version of a well-known map of the so called Money Pit on Oak Island. It's proof beyond doubt that the Templars designed and constructed the ingenious pit."

"This sounds too simple," Al noted. "You're not suggesting that all we have to do is go to Oak Island and dig up the treasure?" He laughed aloud and shot a quick glance at A.T. "Nothing has ever been simple for us."

"I'll drink to that," Arturo chimed in, raising his cup.

"If you two yahoos are through clowning around, I'll continue," Rance said. Both men nodded while stifling grins. In good fun, they enjoyed seeing how far they could push their friend's patience. But when the chips were down, they would be all business.

"I've studied all that has been written the last two hundred or so years on the subject of the Money Pit on Oak Island—and have come to a conclusion." Rance widened his grin. "It's an elaborate hoax—or at best, a grain of truth that has grown into a mountain-sized myth." A collective groan echoed off the rafters in the massive stone-walled room.

"Whoa," Rance said, raising a hand to settle his wife and friend's audible disappointment. "I didn't say there wasn't any treasure to be discovered—just that I didn't believe it would be found in the Money

Pit. It's my opinion that the wise old Templars concocted the hoax to throw others off the trail." He held up the Templar leather-bound journal and energetically waved it about. "There are a number of maps within, including mysterious writings and diagrams, which could direct us to any number of potential treasure troves."

No one said a word as he refilled his cup. "What I need is a little more time to decipher the content and form a plan." He watched both men roll their eyes and look skyward when he said the word, *plan*. Rance always had a plan. He had anticipated that response.

He pointed a finger at Al. "Since you're the odd man out—the only one without a partner—you're headed for Oak Island in the morning…"

"The night's young. There's Adriana…" Al groaned.

Rance cut him short. "She'll be here when you return," Rance said, trying to appear serious. "My suggestion to you—is to make the most of this evening."

L'Ami straightened his back in the solid wooden chair, stroked his salt 'n pepper beard, then leaned forward. "If you believe that this Oak Island thing is a hoax—why in the hell am I wasting time…and I might add, my own money going on a wild goose hunt?"

"I only said what I believe, based on the writings on the subject. Having said that, it's wise that one of us see the site first hand and make an on-site analysis. You are the obvious volunteer." Al slumped back in his chair and reluctantly nodded agreement. He knew that his friend was right.

Satisfied, Rance went on. Carefully turning to a page marked with a yellow sticker, he held up the journal. "This map shows a location in a remote area in Ethiopia." Another marked page displayed a sketch of Scotland. "Mac and I will investigate the Ethiopian site—A.T. and Tina will search the ruins of Scotland as indicated on the map. We'll all stay in touch by Global Phone and engage in a daily conference call—at least at first."

"I assume that our initial investigation is to merely nose around without arousing suspicion about our actual purpose," A.T. said, squeezing Tina's hand.

"Right as always, my friend. I've made a copy of each map and notes on all three locations that will provide us with a concept of what to be on the lookout for—based on the writings in the journal. At the outset, we're searching for evidence of a past Templar presence. Once we have established that fact, and with any additional support that may surface during our initial investigation, we'll meet back here in a week to gather our findings and formulate a workable strategy."

"We're perched overlooking the Mediterranean Ocean," Tina said. "Do you expect us to swim all the way to Scotland?"

Rance grinned and raised a toast to her question. "God save us all. A.T.'s brand of humor has rubbed off on his bride." Before the laughter had subsided, Rance answered, "I'll fly you, your husband, and the disgruntled Lord L' Ami, to Madrid's Barajas International Airport. From there, we all proceed on our merry way."

T.P., their nearly full-grown German shepherd stirred from his nap for the first time, whined, and looked up at his mistress with sad eyes. "I swear," Mac said, "he understands that he's being left behind." Reaching down to scratch his head, she added, "Mr. and Mrs. Benito will take good care of you while we're gone."

After the Benito family's Tarego house had burned down, and at the mayor's recommendation, Rance offered them the use of several rooms at the back of the castle, plus a handsome monthly salary. In return, Mrs. Benito would cook and keep house. Her husband, an excellent handyman, would care for the castle and grounds. So far, both the Benito and Rance family were happy with the arrangements.

Rance looked over at Al and said with a mischievous smile, "And we all hope that Adriana hadn't forgotten you by then." The only one not smiling was Lord Alvin L' Ami.

Arturo stood, and laying a hand on Tina's shoulder, announced his intent to shave, shower, and dress for dinner in town. He lowered his bald head, thought a moment, then sighed deeply. "This is the first time I can recall the three of us setting out on a mission without being on constant vigil for bad guys bent on our permanent demise." He placed an arm around Tina's shoulders and gave her a little squeeze. "This time we can relax and enjoy Rance's promised adventure."

Wishful thinking.

Chapter Two

MADRID'S BARAJAS INTERNATIONAL AIRPORT was fifteen kilometers from downtown and in the process of building a new terminal and adding two additional runways. When Rance filed his flight plan, authorities had neglected to alert him to possible landing and take-off confusion and questionable runway conditions. After circling for over forty-five minutes for clearance to land, Rance threatened the air control tower that if they did not provide him with a window within ten minutes, he would be forced to land on top of their new terminal building. He was low on fuel, he warned, with a grin toward his four passengers.

After securing the Lear Jet outside a private hangar, the treasure-seeking team proceeded to the nearest lounge for a drink and snacks. A.T. and Al went to their respective airline counters to purchase tickets to assigned destinations. Al's plane was scheduled to leave within the hour, and he made good use of his time by quickly downing two shots of Jack Daniel's. Arturo and Tina had a little more time to sit and chat with Rance and Mac. A.T. and Rance left the women alone to walk Al to his concourse. On the way back to the lounge, Rance peeled off from A.T. and walked into the gift shop to pick up a newspaper. He couldn't help but notice the tall gentleman dressed in black—with a body the size of a small mountain. Three men standing on tiptoes attempted unsuccessfully to peer over his spread elbows. Out of the corner of his eyes, Rance noticed that the black mountain was looking at a map of Spain and seemed to be muttering incoherently to himself in French. Rance paid the cashier and gave the stranger a final glance before catching up with Arturo who had waited patiently outside the shop. "The two of us together couldn't lift him," A.T. said, nodding in the direction of the gift shop.

"What do you think, Bishop?" Paschal asked, still on his tiptoes. "Which castle is it?"

"Dear little man, according to this map, at one time Spain boasted ten thousand castles—today, less than three thousand remain."

"Three thousand," Paschal moaned. "It'd take us the next three years to find the right one."

"Man of no imagination," Claude the Bishop scoffed. "We know that the Templar supply ship was destined for somewhere along the southern coast." He poked a thick finger at the map. "According to this map and my quick count, there are approximately eighteen within our search area."

Edmond, a beanpole of a man with long stringy shoulder-length brown hair and a sharply pointed chin, added his two cents. "What if'n their castle ain't listed?"

Ignoring the question, the Bishop folded the map and turned to his motley band and whispered. "You have your seat assignments for our flight to Seville. There, we'll rent a van, pick up some supplies, and proceed with our castle search along the Spanish coast. The Templar treasure has eluded seekers for over six hundred years. We're hard on the heels of the remaining knights who, with persuasion, will provide us with a key to riches." His belly shook uncontrollably. "We must all be patient."

Leaving the gift shop, the Bishop peered over his shoulder and reminded them—"Never forget Baudouin's fate."

KITCHEN DOORS SWUNG OPEN—and as she made her timed entrance into the dining room—the tall redhead spun like a ballerina. With flair, she bowed before the wide-eyed dinner guests, arms open wide. Large green eyes sparkling with mischief devoured the bearded man leading the parade. Readjusting the silver hairpin bedecked with garnets and diamonds that held her lengthy ponytail in place, she asked L' Ami, "Do you like my outfit? I designed it especially for you."

Al was wearing the crisp white shirt and dressy dyed-black overalls that he had worn at Arturo and Tina's wedding. The vision of his latest dream was clothed in an overall version of a culotte. In his best Sean Connery impression, he answered, "You look simply smashing, my dear."

Tina wore a petite emerald-colored, spaghetti-strap sheath that flattered her tiny figure and olive complexion. She flipped her short-cut black hair and glanced over at Mac. Mac's loose-fitting black silk pants with colorful splashes of flowers topped with a pale yellow ruffled blouse complimented her tall figure. Long and thick brunette hair framed her lovely face. Rance and Arturo's eyes met. They were both wearing the same color and cut of sport coat. Before leaving the castle, Mac suggested that her husband change his jacket since A.T. had appeared, wearing the same coat. Rance refused, saying, "I'll just tell everyone that he's my twin brother." Rance, who was six-foot-one and maintained a trim muscular build, possessed deep elongated dimples, denim-blue eyes, and light brown hair, and as he was fond of saying, with blond highlights. Arturo was five-foot-seven, powerfully built like a round bowling ball, and just as bald. For one reason or another, everyone was uncomfortably conscious of what they were wearing to dinner at Mayor Puertollano's Café Madrid.

"Introduce Adriana to your friends, silly man," the woman bubbling with enthusiasm suggested.

Still taken back by the redhead's entrance, Al stuttered. "Uh…everyone…this is Adriana Puertollano…the mayor's…"

Rance stepped forward and gently shook her hand. "You'll have to forgive our tongue-tied amigo." He leaned forward and whispered loud enough for all to hear. "It's his age, you see."

Before Al had an opportunity to defend himself, Rance introduced Mac, Tina, and A.T.

It was Adriana who came to Al's defense, by answering, "Age is a sign of maturity and experience." She winked at the man standing defenseless and continued. "…and he wears both sooo well."

Adriana stepped forward, hooked her arm in Al's, smiled and addressed her guests. "It's a pleasure to meet all of you—and I do hope that we become close friends as the night greets the dawn. The chef, an older brother, has prepared a feast you will not long forget—but first, the wine."

Indeed, Adriana charmed them all. Her flashing eyes, playful enthusiasm, and obvious intelligence won four more converts. Reluctantly, she answered the question concerning her status as an attractive unmarried woman. She explained that her parents had both become infirm due to an auto accident—and it was her place to care for them at their Madrid estate. She had spent the last nine years devoting her energies to their care while her three brothers went their separate ways. One, a wealthy art and antique dealer, recently passed away. The two others became restaurateurs. The oldest brother, Tome, also became mayor of Tarego. Considering her devotion to their parents, all three brothers, wealthy in their own right, agreed that Adriana should inherit the estate and all the financial holdings—including the title that came with an ancient land grant. Adriana was a member of Spanish royalty.

Rance kidded Adriana that her new male acquaintance was the lord of an Italian manor. "May I introduce you to Lord Alvin L' Ami," he said. Mac's elbow caught her husband just below his ribs.

SHE WAS TRUE TO HER WORD—rays of sun appeared in the east as Rance, Mac, Tina, and A.T. headed for the castle. Adriana and Al stood in the café's doorway waving good-bye. She playfully pulled on his beard and whispered in his ear. "My room is upstairs." Fluttering long lashes, she asked, "Would you like to join me in a nightcap and perhaps you'd like me to…?"

"Mr. L' Ami," the flight attendant said. "Please return your seat to the upright position. We're preparing to make our final descent into Halifax, Nova Scotia."

Al blinked his eyes and shook the dream from his mind. "Oh my… if only the dream could have lasted a few minutes more…" he whispered to himself. Smiling, he stretched his arms.

Believing the passenger was signaling for assistance, the attendant approached his seat. "Mr. L' Ami," is there anything you need?"

Fully awake now, he grinned and answered, "I've been well satisfied, thank you." Then added, "I'm in need of nothing—at least for a week." Puzzled, she walked back to her seat.

L 'Ami had flown into Boston, then boarded a small jet to Halifax. A rental was waiting for him for the forty-five minute drive to Mahone Bay. There, posing as an archeologist, he would hire a piloted boat for his trip to Oak Island. The Oak Island Resort and Spa at the western side of the one hundred and forty-acre island had a shuttle, but he preferred to arrive without fanfare. Booked for three nights, he doubted a fourth would be necessary.

Laying his head back, he closed his eyes and considered the wisdom of hiring a local guide to lead him to the area the world has come to know as The Money Pit.

"THERE'S A WORLD OF SAND down there," Mac observed, peering out of the copilot's window.

"We've been flying over the Sahara Desert for hours now: in a few minutes we'll be entering the Sudan. Another seventeen hundred kilometers and we land in Addis Ababa, Ethiopia. I have a Landcruiser reserved, along with a week's worth of supplies. From Addis Ababa we drive north five hundred kilometers over some rough mountainous terrain to Lalibela—then it's another four hundred kilometers to Axum."

"What's so special about those two cities?"

"According to what I've read, Lalibela is home to several churches displaying the *croix-patte*. That's the distinct Knights Templar cross. Legend has it that King Lalibela was destined for greatness from birth. After his mother had witnessed a swarm of bees circling his crib and flying away, she invoked the old belief that animals could predict the future of a worthy person. Harbay, Lalibela's half-brother, the King of Ethiopia, felt threatened by Prince Lalibela and had him poisoned. It is said that the prince lingered on death's doorstep for three days, during which time his spirit was transported to the three levels of heaven. There he was told of his destiny—and God provided him with exact details on how to build a group of churches the world had never seen."

"He survived? The churches—they're in Lalibela?"

"Don't get ahead of me, my dear," Rance said, tapping the fuel gage. "Plenty of fuel left. Yes, he survived. And yes, the churches are there. We'll see them in due time. In 1185, Prince Lalibela deposed his brother and became king. He immediately started building the rock-hewn churches. Legend also reports that a band of red-haired angels wearing cloaks displaying the *croix-patte* helped the king build his churches. In fact, on the roofs of churches hewn out of solid rock, the Templar crosses are visible."

Mac nearly jumped out of her seat. Interrupting her storyteller husband, she pointed out of the window. "Look. Look down there," she poked at the window. "There must be thousands of people walking across the desert. From what I can see from up here, the majority are children."

"It appears the Sudanese government has again abandoned them, or they're moving their village to a more hospitable location suitable for farming. An educated guess is that the government has turned a blind eye to its people's plight. It's sad, but this happens every few years. Before it's over, thousands will perish as the world turns the other way."

Mac slumped back in her chair and remained unusually silent for the remainder of the trip. As Rance circled the small airport, she looked over at her husband. "I've read about the genocide of those unfortunate people, and I remember on television seeing hundreds sitting under giant trees for shade. But, witnessing it in person…makes it too real."

Rance leaned over and lovingly patted her thigh. "I'm afraid you're in for an eye-opener this week. We're stepping back into history."

"YEA, ROSSLYN CHAPLE, AND CHAPEL are but a wee seven miles frae Edinburgh, where we stand. Take Stariton Junction A701 to Penicuik/Peebles. Follow A701 to the Roslin three-mile sign. Once in the village of Roslin ye'll see the chapel sign." The attendant handed over a map. "The Steading Bed and Breakfast—where ye're beddin', is one hundred meters frae the chapel. When ye see the two stoon pillars, pull in. They're guid people, they are. Kin to me, by the way. Tell 'em Billy Boy said hello."

Prepared to leave, Arturo picked up the map and keys to his rental Citroen Sax, but the little man behind the counter wasn't finished. "The chapel's noo called St. Matthew's Collegiate Episcopalian Church. There is a mass on Sunday: Tuesday and Friday they have a prayer service at noon. Rosslyn Chaple's off limits 'til they ken assess damage frae a collapsed wall." Having completed his duty, the attendant turned to his paperwork. Tina controlled her laughter. A.T. scowled.

A.T. drove while Tina read aloud from the Rosslyn Chaple and Chapel Guide Book she'd picked up from the traveler's display of Sites to See in Scotland. "We were right to begin our Scottish search here. According to the brochure, the Knights Templar stamp is all over the castle and chapel." She read silently, then said, "Listen to this. Legend suggests that the chapel is the hiding place of the Holy Grail, including a fragment of the holly rood—the cross of the crucifixion. Perhaps the true Stone of Destiny"

Tina glanced at her husband for his reaction. Staring straight ahead at the road, he said with a chill in his voice, "Go on."

Shrugging a shoulder at his indifference, she continued. "The chapel's said to represent Solomon's Temple—and displays encoded messages concerning its secrets. Another legend suggests that if you stand on a particular spot—doesn't say where—and blow a horn, a treasure will appear."

"The only treasure I want now is a cold beer, my love." A.T. responded. "We're only staying at The Steading because it's handy to the castle and chapel. The Roslin Glen Hotel would have been my choice, with its fine pub—or so the advertisement said." A.T. looked over for the first time. "What you say to getting a bite to eat at Roslin Glen—and a cool one before we drive on to our final digs? Maybe the locals can fill us in on what's really going on at Rosslyn Chaple."

"Fine with me. We should be getting close. Billy Boy said it wouldn't take us long." She returned to her reading. "There have been sightings of a phantom monk around the grounds—and a phantom hound that can be heard howling on dark stormy nights."

A.T. glanced up at the sky. "Looks like it could storm any minute. If you hear any howling, snuggle close. The hound you hear will be an Italian dog in heat. Oof." A sharp finger poked his ribs.

"Will you stop that," he whined. "You got that bad habit from Mac."

"Scotland's Robert the Bruce, who had been excommunicated, received with open arms, Templars who in the early fourteenth century escaped with their treasure when the king of Spain and pope had de Molay burned at the stake. Rosslyn Chapel's carvings are attributed to the Templar's handiwork. It's said that they devised a secret entrance to the tombs and relic treasure. An entrance yet to be discovered."

"WHAT'S YE' PLEASURE? Dewar's on draught, Belhaven Best, Guinness, Tennent's Larger, Dry Blackthorn Cider…"

"I'll try the cider," Tina interrupted.

"And it's a tall cold glass of Belhaven Best, for me," A.T. ordered. "It's not dinner time yet—but what can you put on the stove that's fast?"

"Ye're in luck mate. Cookie just finished makin' a dozen bacon sandwiches, she did. Hoo many dae ye want?" The stranger held up five fingers.

"If'en ye not stayin' here at the Roslin Glen, it must be The Steading where ye headed," the barkeep surmised. Tina nodded. "That's next to the castle and chapel," he said peering out the window at the approaching dark clouds. "Oooh," he whispered, making a screwed up face.

Tina finished her last bite of sandwich. "What do you mean…Oooh?"

Chapter Three

LORD L' AMI POKED HIS HEAD IN THE RESTAURANT door, hoping to catch a glimpse of its lovely hostess, Adriana Puertollano. Al was the first of the three teams to return from the fact-finding mission. His route to the castle took him through the small hamlet of Tarego, right past the mayor's restaurant. It was early afternoon: the employees were about preparing for the dinner crowd. For three days, his entire focus had been on the mission: now the focus of his attention was on the new love of his life, Adriana, Mayor Tome Puertollano's sister.

Sensing someone standing in the doorway, Adriana finished setting a table and spun around. Her eyes and smile widened, and her arms opened wide as she dashed into his welcome embrace. "It's so wonderful to see you again," she exclaimed, holding him at arm's length. Before Al had the opportunity to reply, she silenced him with a lingering kiss.

Stepping back to compose himself, he shyly said, "If that's the kind of greeting I'll receive—I'll leave and come back more often."

Playfully slapping him on his arm, she laughed, "Silly man. I'll greet you that way every day from now on—if you'll allow me." It was her turn to blush. She hadn't meant for her feelings to be known so soon in their budding relationship. But on second thought, she wasn't taking any chances of losing the man she had fallen for at first sight. He was so tall and handsome: she even liked his beard, even the ever-present overalls. Combined with that soft Sean Connery whisper and air of complete confidence, he had swept her off her feet and into his arms.

Her unexpected confession gave him the opening he had hoped for. Leaning over and cupping her face in his palms, he said, "My dear, your words please me…"

Before Al had a chance to complete his declaration of love, the kitchen door flew open. "Lord L' Ami!" Tome shouted, waving his arms about like a drowning man.

Brother, your timing couldn't be any worse. The frustrated sister looked to the heavens for patience.

Gently shoving his sister aside, the mayor/restaurateur grabbed the startled lord of his own villa and peered up into his eyes. "You must go to your friend's castle immediately. A very frantic housekeeper, Mrs. Benito, phoned to say that a group of men had just forced their way in, demanding a tour. Her husband, elderly as he is, is no match for a mountain of a man, as she called him, and his associates."

L' Ami's expression hardened. He must be the first back, otherwise Rance or A.T. would have intervened already. "The driver dropped me off here. I had intended to see Adriana, then walk to the castle."

Al turned to Adriana. "Your horse. Is he stabled out back? If you'll take care of my bags on the step outside—I can be at the castle in five minutes."

IN ONE FLUID MOTION, Al reigned in, leapt off, landed on two feet, and was up the front steps. Slipping in through the half open door, he hesitated and listened. Angry voices came from the direction of the downstairs Benito family apartments. Just ahead, sitting halfway up on the upstairs steps, Mrs. Benito with one hand to her mouth and the other, shaking badly, pointed in the direction of the voices. "They refuse to leave," she mumbled. "My poor husband, he could not stop them. He tried…"

Al touched his lips, nodded, and walked slowly to the stone steps leading down. Edmond, Maurice, and Paschal had Mr. Benito surrounded, his back to the wall. Mrs. Benito's *mountain of a man* stood before them, a white silk handkerchief to his lips. "But my good man," the Bishop said with a false smile, "we are going to tour this castle—with or without your help. You may as well do our bidding—or we may be forced to acquire the help of your frail wife." He tapped Paschal on the shoulder. "Why don't you go upstairs and…"

"Only one person will do the forcing around here. Me." Al said with conviction. "And we'll begin by releasing Mr. Benito." Stepping forward, he raised his voice. "Now!"

As the Bishop's men turned to attack the intruder, Al's knife was in his hand, and the tip of the sharp blade pricked the fat man's triple chin. Claude gasped in surprise and stood tall in a failed attempt to relieve the point's pressure. The stranger's powerful grip on his upper arm was painful. The Bishop's eyes glared at his men: through gritted teeth he demanded they stand down. This crazy bearded man would slit his throat without giving a moment's thought. That, he was certain of.

Never letting up on the pressure of the blade, Al motioned toward the stairway with his head. "You three. Up the stairs. And no funny business if you want your partner here to survive."

A powerful shove twisted the large man's body. The point of the blade was now at the base of his spine. "I'm well aware of where to insert the blade so you'll never walk again—if you live," the crazy man warned. "One false move and it's over." Letting Claude feel the knife's pressure, he added, "And tell the three stooges not to stop until they're on the outside lawn." Holding the large man's collar and guiding him upstairs with his left hand, Al's right hand maintained the point's pressure in the precise spot to do the most damage. No stranger to peril, he obviously knew his business and was unafraid of the overwhelming odds. Four against one. A formidable foe, to say the least, the Bishop discerned.

Taking one step at a time, the fat man struggled up the ancient carved stone steps, afraid not to move steadily, fearful of the blade's sharp point pricking his lower back. "Look here," he said in a strained voice just above a whisper, "this is all a misunderstanding. Ouch!"

L' Ami was in no mood for excuses. He had heard enough to know that the uninvited castle guests meant no good. If he hadn't arrived when he did…well, he didn't want to think about that just now. First, he wanted them out of Rance and Mac's home. Then he'd ask questions. And demand answers.

With expressions of amazement, the Benito's held each other tightly, watching the parade of intruders. L' Ami kicked the huge wooden door open with his boot and roughly shoved the captive mass of humanity onto the stone entry. Below the steps, standing on the well-manicured lawn, stood the Bishop's angry men. One, the man called Paschal, held a pistol in his hand, aiming at the two standing on the top steps. "Boss. Step aside. I'll shoot the bastard."

Al slipped behind the Bishop and well out of sight. Flinching from the prick of the blade, Claude shouted to be heard over the roar of a low flying aircraft. "Don't be a fool! You'll either get me shot or stabbed!"

"Step aside, boss. I can't miss from here. I'll teach that…" A shot rang out. Paschal yelled in pain, grabbed his upper arm, and fell to his knees. Al grinned as he peeked around the mountain shielding him and past the three accomplices. Coming on a run across the far lawn, waving his pistol, was the human Italian bowling ball, Arturo Testaccio. Further behind, struggling with two sets of baggage was a tiny woman with short black hair.

L' Ami stepped back and gave the Bishop a hard kick to the backside. As the man struggled to control his shifting weight from plummeting him down the steps, Al shouted for all to hear. "That's one of my partners. The one with the pistol and a deadly aim. That plane you heard landing behind the castle is the owner of this pile of rocks—and if you think we're tough—you don't want to cross Adam Rance."

Arturo grabbed the wounded man by the collar and lifted him to his feet. "You, fatso," he ordered the Bishop, "get this piece of shit to the hospital. And whatever you four did, I'd suggest you hightail it out of sight before the third member of our wrecking crew arrives. Turning to his red-faced wife, he calmly asked, "Need some help with the bags, my dear?"

Moments later, Rance rushed through the door, Mac close behind. Mr. Benito had briefly explained the forceful intrusion of the four strangers. From the landing above the steps, he could see four men hustling away in the distance. Hands on hips, he faced his two best friends. "What in the hell went on here? And who in the hell are those men?" he asked, pointing a finger at the fleeing foursome.

L' Ami slapped A.T. on the back, leaned over and picked up Tina's bag, kicked his friend's baggage on the ground, and said, "I'll explain everything over four fingers of JD that I brought back from Canada."

"SO YOU HAVE NO IDEA WHAT THOSE MEN WERE AFTER?" Rance asked with a puzzled expression. "Poor Mr. and Mrs. Benito are still in shock and not much help. I'm sorry they had to endure such an experience."

"Maybe we should invite the Benitos to have dinner with us tonight at Tome's place in town," Mac suggested.

"Good idea. Why don't you go ask them to be ready in three hours. We all need a bit of rest and time to freshen up before we head for Tarego."

"I wonder if that gal…what's her name? Adriana. I wonder if she'll still remember Romeo here," A.T. nodded at Al, and laughed.

"We, like Al, stopped off at the restaurant to make reservations and enjoy a glass of *vino rosso*. Once Tome told us about the stressful phone call, Tina and I hustled toward the castle. When I saw Al and the fat guy faced by the one with the gun—I dropped the bags—and came on the run." Arturo patted his wife on the hand and apologized, "Sorry about the bags. But I knew you'd understand." Tina looked the other way, ignoring her husband. Everyone laughed at A.T.'s hurtful expression.

"The mountain of flesh, the one they called boss, said that it was all a misunderstanding," Al said. "Misunderstanding, my ass. They were after something in this castle and were going to rough up the Benitos to find what they came after. I'll bet a new pair of overalls on it."

"By the way, Al," Tina interrupted, "you had better phone Adriana and tell her you're all right. She appeared very concerned."

A.T. pointed at his friend. "Just look at that shit-eating grin. Our confirmed bachelor has been bitten by the Spanish love bug." He ducked a handful of pistachios.

Rance leaned back in his chair and raised his martini. "Well, you two dispatched fatso and friends: here's to an enjoyable dinner. I'm sure we all have much to report about our exploratory visits to Nova Scotia, Scotland, and Ethiopia. Mac and I will see you all in three hours. We'll take the horses to town. The Benitos can use the carriage."

"We have a jet and horses," Arturo mumbled under his breath. "What we need is a Hummer."

"A red one," Tina added.

Chapter Four

MR. AND MRS. BENITO CHOSE TO SIT with town folk that they had known for years, which was just as well, since their employers and friends had much to discuss in the private room Adriana had arranged. Several bottles of fine wine complimented homemade bread dipped in olive oil with a dash of red vinegar and topped with freshly grated cheese. The castle's recent invasion was the talk of the moment. Adriana sat to Al's left and laughed at jokes the others had heard a hundred times. Once she had left to check on appetizers, L' Ami clicked his glass.

"This might be asking too much—but it would be a great favor to me if you would consider Adriana in this night's debriefing. It's not like we're on another covert operation to save the world. I cannot insult Adriana by asking her to leave while we eat and discuss our recent assignments. She means the world to me. More than you'll ever know. Love's been a long time coming for me—now that it's here, I'm not letting Adriana go." Silence. No one said a word. "Do you all understand?" All eyes searched Rance for an answer.

Rance's stone-faced expression hadn't changed. He finished the last of his wine and poured another, all the while, refusing to look into his friend's eyes. *This is the showdown that I had hoped would never come,* Alvin L' Ami thought to himself—trying to read something positive in Rance's blank expression. He did not want their friendship to end this way. They had been through too much together. The three of them. But Adriana was a once-in-a-life-time chance for him. He would take his lumps if it came to that. He could not let her go. He wouldn't!

Rance took a long sip of wine and a deep breath. He glanced at each person at the table and then locked eyes with a defiant friend who had saved his life on more than one occasion. Raising his glass and holding it out to Al, he made his decision. "First it was me," he nodded to Mac. "Then it was A.T.," he said, smiling at Tina. "Now, damn-it-all, it's about time you joined the group with a love of your own. You've been the fifth wheel far too long. We," he said, circling his glass around the table, "couldn't be happier for you and Adriana—though I can't see what she sees in an old bushy overall-wearing curmudgeon." Everyone applauded as they witnessed the look of relief cross their friend's face.

Adriana swept into the room to see what all the fuss was about. Al glanced up and mouthed the words, *I'll tell you later.* And he did have a doozy of a story to relate. Later, she would spend the early morning listening in fascination about the exploits of the three friends. To indoctrinate Adriana into the group, during dinner, Rance disclosed the story of the Knights Templar and the recent missions they had just returned from.

With a full stomach and a slight wine-buzz, Rance nodded to the beaming L' Ami. "Al, you first. What did you learn on your visit to Oak Island? Find some treasure?"

"After arriving and checking into the Oak Island Resort and Spa, I decided to gather all the numerous pamphlets scattered around the lobby that dealt with the mystery of The Money Pit. Lounging in my king-size bed, sparingly sipping a glass of JD, I set about reading all I could about the target of my mission. Inquiring at the front desk about the availability of a local guide, I was told that the Triton Alliance, the company that owns the land around the pit, had recently cordoned off the area."

Listening intently, Adriana placed a hand on Al's and asked, "Did someone find the treasure?"

"No, my dear. Someone found a body."

"Are you talking about the body found two hundred years ago?" Arturo chimed in.

"No. A body with its throat slit. A male body was discovered two days before I arrived by two young girls who were digging in the pit on a college hazing dare. I managed to invite an assistant coroner to join me for a drink. He was staying at the resort until the investigation was complete. Apparently the deceased was, what he termed, a fresh body. Less than a week old, as best as they could determine. Examining his clothes, they found no identification—except a laundry mark with the name *Baudouin* stenciled on the inside coat label." L' Ami raised a finger. "One other thing. The dead man, from the amount of alcohol absorbed by his vitals, was drunk at the time he was murdered."

"Baudouin is a French name," Tina said. "Either that, or he was wearing a Frenchman's borrowed coat."

"Those four yahoos today at the castle were French. No mistaking that accent. The large one was well educated: the other three were speaking gutter-French," Al observed.

Rance slapped his forehead with his palm. "Now I know where I had seen that fat man. He and two of the other men were in the Madrid Barajas International Airport Gift Shop. Fatso was draped in black like a monk and reading a map of Spain."

"I'm sure that's just a coincidence," Mac said. "I mean the dead Frenchman on Oak Island and the Frenchmen who frightened poor Mr. and Mrs. Benito..."

Arturo and Al exchanged quick glances and spoke at the same time, "You'll never convince Rance of coincidences."

Rance scowled as if in pain. "Agreed. It's a long-shot that the two episodes are related—but...one never knows." The scowl deepened. "When you consider the possibility of the Templar treasure buried on Oak Island—and the two Templar Knights who lived in the bowels of the castle… A dead Frenchman and a group of Frenchmen bent on searching the de Molay Castle—it's not that much of a long-shot."

A.T. looked around the table. "I believe we all agree."

"Before we leave the castle again on an extended mission, I'll have a talk with our friend, Mayor Puertollano. I'm sure he can recommend a number of men with weapons we can hire to guard the castle and the Benitos 24/7." Pointing at Al, he finished by saying, "That's settled. What else did you learn?"

"It's a foregone conclusion by the locals—as we had already determined. The treasure is a hoax. They play up the possibility to encourage tourism."

Rance, assuming Al had completed his debriefing, turned to face Arturo and Tina. "I'm not through," L' Ami said with a wave of both hands. "There's more. A new possibility." Commanding everyone's attention, he continued. "A man named Fred Nolan owns the north central part of the island—and is a treasure hunter in his own right. It's said that he has a map with lines intersecting a position where a large sandstone boulder and cone-shaped granite rocks where found. Lines connecting the rocks make a giant cross. The second morning, during a light drizzle and heavy fog—I took a walk along a low-lying ridge to inspect the boulder he calls *The Headstone*. The weather was in my favor, because there were armed guards stationed in a circle around the perimeter of the headstone and rocks. You couldn't see your hand in front of your face. On my knees, I crept up to the boulder to see for myself what was so special about the object of Nolan's fascination. I was lucky to find it in that pea soup. There was little sense in attempting to eyeball the boulder—but I did manage to use the Braille system to see if I could feel any manmade markings."

"Did you?" the wide-eyed hostess interrupted. She was completely absorbed in Al's account. Much to her delight, her interest would be satisfied as the night progressed.

"Not really. Sandstone has a rough surface, and without a clear and closer examination, there was no way to say for certain."

"How do you suggest we proceed in the future with Oak Island?" Rance asked.

"That night, in the bar, where I conducted most of my business," he grinned, "I made friends with two of Nolan's excavation guards. Nolan was called away on an underwater project he had financed and would be away for about a month. All work on the headstone and cross is now at a standstill. He will not allow them to proceed without his personal supervision." Refreshing his glass, Al added, "To answer your question. We have time to devote our immediate attention to the Scotland and Ethiopian locations. Then come back to Oak Island—if necessary." Al leaned back to relax and hear A.T. and Tina's experience.

Rance sent a silent message to Arturo to begin. "First of all," A.T. said, "I learned that I like Belhaven Best beer."

Tina rolled her eyes and shrugged her shoulders at Rance, then spoke directly to Adriana. "You'll soon learn that these three have a warped sense of humor—even when their lives are hanging by a thread. It's not easy to become accustomed to—believe me. Mac can verify to that." Mac nodded in the affirmative.

"Are we through giving away company secrets?" A.T. asked with a smug look. "Can I continue now...?"

"Don't leave out the part about the ghost," Tina interjected.

"Ghost?" Mac whispered aloud.

"Yes. The barkeep at the Roslin Glen Hotel told us about a phantom monk that appears on stormy nights accompanied by a howling dog," Tina explained, with a wink and an impish grin.

"A.T., get on with it," Rance said, "and leave out the howling monk."

"Dog," Mac reminded him. "Howling dog."

"I'll be the one howling in another minute—if my Italian friend doesn't continue," Rance warned.

"See," Tina said, looking directly at Adriana.

Ignoring his wife's attempt at humor, A.T. recognized the look of frustration in Rance's expression: he had witnessed it often enough and began again. "There's little doubt that Rosslyn Chaple has the Templar stamp all over it. Discarding all the romantic legends," he glared at Tina, "the evidence of Templar involvement is obvious…from ancient text to mysterious carvings, to secret sealed vaults."

"Workers are in the process of completing years of refurbishment on the chapel," Tina added.

"That's why we were unable to do a complete search of the chapel itself…"

Tina interrupted again. "Complete search? My dear understating husband, it would take months to conduct a thorough search…"

"Adriana, please excuse my wife. She still misses her days as an Italian undercover agent—and has a tendency to *overstate* most situations." Arturo took a sip of wine and smiled. "Actually, she's partially correct—and I have a suggestion, Rance. There's far too much Templar evidence in and around the castle/chapel grounds to ignore."

"Are you going to tell them about the seventh Earl of Rosslyn?" Tina asked.

Arturo placed both hands on his bald dome and shook it from side to side. Adriana laughed at the look on the Italian's face. Everyone joined in, except Rance. With a rolling of his hand, Rance urged A.T. to go on.

Glancing at his wife, as if to ask permission to continue, he paused: Tina nodded with a forced smile. "As I said, there was no way to adequately investigate references in Sebastian's book—and compare them with what little we were able to discern in such a short visit. And, of course, we were further limited by workers shooing us out of their way."

"Tell them about Commander Peter Loughborough," Tina insisted. "He's the typical Italian male—never gets to the point without being prodded."

Arturo leaned across his wife and swiped her glass of wine. "That's all for you, my dear." She snatched it back and stuck out her tongue.

"Loughborough, the seventh Earl of Rosslyn Chaple, was the officer in charge of security at Windsor Castle when a gatecrasher broke into Prince William's twenty-first birthday party. The foreman on the chapel site told us that the earl normally bans the general public from the grounds unless they have special authorization."

A.T. looked at Tina out of the corner of his eye. She peered at the ceiling hung with vines and wine bottles. "Well, anyway, here's my suggestion. Earl Loughborough will rent out the castle for fifteen hundred pounds a week. Next week, the restoration crew takes a month leave—and we discovered that the castle grounds have not been reserved during that period. It's rumored that he needs money to resume work. They are running out of Historic Scotland funds. We could rent the place and all advance on the pile of rocks and mortar—and search at our heart's content."

"Sound idea, A.T.," Rance said. "How do we contact this earl?"

"We. He. Already did," Tina announced, nudging her husband, and pointing at her empty glass. "It's all paid for, signed, sealed and delivered."

"I knew you'd agree, Master." Arturo said nonchalantly.

Rance opened his mouth, but Mac beat him to it. "Let's go back a minute—to the headstone and domed rocks on Oak Island—and crossing lines. Rance, there was a faded diagram on a page in the middle of your… Sebastian's Knights Templar journal. You must remember."

Closing his eyes for a moment, Rance visualized the page. "You're right. There is a diagram that fits Al's description. I'll check it out once we're back at the castle." Nodding to the two Italians, he said, "Good job, you two. As usual, A.T.'s way ahead of me."

As much as she hated to miss a word, Adriana had slipped out to check on a special dessert, raisin-cream ice cream. Her sudden noisy reappearance startled the group. Pointing at the entrance to the main dining room, she excitedly stammered, "The four men you mentioned…forced their way…into your castle. They are out there…and…harassing Mr. and Mrs. Benito."

L' Ami beat Rance and Arturo through the door, the three women close behind. The Bishop stood at the end of the Benito table. His size alone threatened those sitting across from each other. As Al reached out for the big man's collar, he motioned to the three men at a far table. Rance and A.T. followed his movement and stepped in their direction.

A hard yank did little to move the mountain of flesh. The Bishop, unaware of the person who had grabbed him from behind, swung his arm to swat the intruder. "I'm talking to these fine citizens—be off with you," he growled from deep within his bulk.

Al elongated the knuckles of his right hand and delivered a crushing corkscrew blow to the kidney that would have downed a horse. A loud grunt whipped everyone's head in their direction. The Bishop's knees buckled slightly as he placed a beefy hand to his right side. Turning, his eyes were on fire with anger. "You!"

"Yes. Me. Get your fat ass away from our friends."

Claude motioned to his associates to come to his aid, then turned his attention to the bearded man facing him. Edmond, Maurice, and Paschal leapt to their feet, but were blocked by the man who had shot Paschal, and another that was a stranger. "Where's your gun now, bastard?" Paschal squeaked, as he waved a long knife in A.T.'s face.

The two men had worked together for so long that they knew each other's moves like a choreographed dance. Arturo stepped back. Rance turned to walk away, then suddenly spun on one foot: the other lashed out and knocked the knife from Paschal's hand. A.T., taking advantage of surprise, buried a shoulder into Maurice's chest, propelling him into Edmond. Both men fell backward, sprawled over their chairs. Rance's right palm struck Paschal in the middle of his chest, knocking the wind from his lungs. He collapsed in his chair.

Momentarily distracted, L' Ami foolishly turned toward the action in the corner of the main room, providing Claude, the Bishop, the opportunity to step behind and wrap his huge arms around his intended victim. The first powerful squeeze nearly took Al's breath away. Snapping his head back to crush Claude's nose fell far short of the mark. The mountain of a man was too tall, and his bulk kept L' Ami's head well out of range. Claude laughed as he steadily squeezed the life out of the man whose feet had left the floor. Al's two friends rushed to his rescue—but as they found out, it wasn't necessary. Just before he felt darkness overcoming him and a rib on the verge of snapping—he heard a sound like a loud ancient gong in a Hindu temple.

Mr. and Mrs. Benito and their friends frantically scrambled out of their chairs as Claude's body toppled over and crushed the table beneath his weight. Collecting his senses and bending over in an effort to ease the pain of his ribs, L' Ami looked up to see his smiling Adriana, holding a large frying pan above her head. "No one's hurting *my* man—

and getting away with it," she said calmly, with more than a hint of pride.

As Rance and A.T. tended to their friend, and Mac and Tina congratulated the heroine of the evening—Mayor Puertollano rushed into the room banishing a meat cleaver. "What's going on here?" he demanded to know. "What's that man doing on my table—and who are those three in the corner?"

Adriana took charge. "Brother, these are the four men who accosted the poor Benito family and forced their way into Mr. Rance's Castle de Molay. When I stepped out to check on dessert, I noticed the fat one harassing the Benitos and their guests." She shook the frying pan at the prone figure. "As for the fat man sleeping on your table—I'll take credit for that." She extended her chin defiantly, waiting for her brother's reply.

Rance stepped close and relieved Adriana of the weapon, handing it over to her brother. "Here," he said with a grin, "your sister's dangerous when in a mood to cook." He turned to L' Ami. "Al, better keep that in mind."

Both Mac and Tina, said, "See," reminding Adriana of the warped sense of humor warning.

"Tome, better send for your police and get these four a cell for the night," Rance suggested. "No. Better yet, provide them with quarters for the next few days. And it would be a good idea if you contacted Madrid to see if they're wanted by the authorities. In the morning, I'll stop by your office to discuss security for the castle while we're away."

Rubbing his ribs, L' Ami asked, "Did I hear that dessert was about to be served?"

"Yes, my poor injured darling," Adriana whispered in his ear. "Allow me help you to our table." She glanced up at her two new girlfriends and winked. "How did you ever manage to survive without me?"

After Tarego's five-man police force arrived and escorted the dazed Bishop and his three associates to the jail, the private party resumed their discussion over the most delicious ice cream anyone had ever tasted.

"Adriana, you were marvelous out there," Rance said. "And I must concur with her astute observation—'How did you ever manage to survive without me?' I must admit, I too have often asked myself that very same question."

"Well, that makes three of us," Arturo added, with a wine salute in Adriana's direction. L' Ami remained silent, sighed heavily, and removed a drop of dessert from the edge of his beard.

"Okay, back to business—and Mac's and my visit to the Ethiopian town of Lalibela."

Mac was shaking her head. "What's the matter, my dear?" Rance asked, knowing full well what her gesture meant.

"The landing," she said. "The landing almost ended our trip." She looked at her husband and shook her head again. "Obviously, there was no landing field—just a bumpy flat field with a scattering of rocks. No. Let me change rocks to boulders."

"Now who's exaggerating?"

Mac continued. "Oh, the rocks…boulders were not the major obstacle—nor the fact that the makeshift landing strip was short. It was the herd of camels…"

"Camels?" came the joint murmur.

"Yes. Camels. Just as the wheels touched down, a dozen camels appeared from behind a stand of tall brush and walked lazily across our path."

"Camel road kill," A.T. laughed. "An Ethiopian Bar-B-Q favorite." Tina nudged him in the ribs and shook a finger in his face.

"Thank you, Tina," Mac said. "It was no laughing matter. Later, when you two are alone, remind him that no one likes a smart ass—especially an Italian smart ass." Now everyone was in hysterics.

"What happened?" Adriana asked with a serious expression.

"Well, Sky King here managed to avoid the largest of the rocks and boulders but remained on target for the camels. Suddenly, one…must have been the seventh camel in line—spotted a clump of fresh grass. When he, or she, stopped, those behind stopped as well. We taxied right between the two groups—and cut engines within a few yards of a giant boulder."

"Ye of little faith, my dear. All in a day's work," Rance chuckled.

L' Ami smiled at the love of his life. "You didn't know that my father was a pilot, did you?" The others groaned. They've heard it before. Adriana shook her head, no. "Yes. He worked in a stable—and piled it here and piled it there."

Adriana sat expressionless, then stood up to leave. "Where are you going now?" Al asked her.

"To go get my frying pan. I'm convinced that I'm going to need it."

Mac laughed. "I like her more and more." Tina agreed.

"If I have everyone's permission," Rance said, with the look of an impatient man. "We were within a short walking distance of the main dirt street. Townsfolk who had heard the approaching jet aircraft peered at us from open windows of their brick huts. Some were carved out of red volcanic rock."

"I must assume that you saw the churches excavated at street level. They were also carved out of the same red rock," Adriana offered.

Surprised that she was aware of the fact, Rance continued with a puzzled expression. "Yes. The roofs of the churches were street level—

as you mentioned—featuring carvings of the *croix-pattee,* Templar cross. We were met by one of the priests and escorted into a cave that led into a huge domed cavern. A doorway and carved stairway led to a complex of narrow subterranean tunnels. In time, we exited onto the pathway leading to the main church—*Beta Giorghis*—the Church of St. George."

"When Rance and the priest stepped into the darkened stairway leading to the tunnels, I pretended to remove a pebble from my boot, providing time to quickly survey the large cavern room," Mac added. "Only a few lanterns lit the surrounding area, but sufficient for me to see what appeared to be numerous grottoes leading in every direction. In addition, in the maze of underground tunnels, I saw what I would believe to be crypts. What I wouldn't give to search every inch, given time."

"If we can distract dozens of priests and deacons from their daily duties," Rance speculated, "we'll find the time to do a thorough search. We saw enough Templar imprints to warrant a return visit—after turning Rosslyn Chaple upside down."

"If I might offer a suggestion," Adriana said, raising her hand like a timid school girl. "Three weeks from now, a month-long religious celebration will take place outside of the town of Gondar—the closest settlement to Lalibela. *Timkay* ceremony, the climax to the event, will be held at a medieval castle and its huge baptismal pool. Pilgrims will arrive from all throughout Ethiopia." Shrugging one shoulder, she continued. "It's possible that the area around the sights of interest in Lalibela will be void of villagers—and only a token guard on duty."

Everyone sat around the table in silence. Amazed at the attractive hostess' timely knowledge of Ethiopia. L' Ami appeared thunderstruck. Rance was the first to gather himself. "You must excuse our gaping mouths—but you've taken us by surprise. First, I must say that your suggestion *will* be acted upon. Second, if you don't mind me asking—how in the hell did you acquire such knowledge?" All eyes and ears were on Adriana.

She sat forward in her chair, stretched both arms out straight, and placed her palms on the tabletop. With a sly smile and a flip of her long red hair, she explained. "The last years of caring for my infirm parents provided time for me to concentrate on the love of my life," she glanced at Al, "*first* love of my life. I had the opportunity to obtain a PhD in ancient civilizations and languages from The College of Madrid." She looked deeply into Rance's eyes. "The fact is—I'm thoroughly familiar with the history and legends of all the places you've discussed thus far—including that of the Knights Templar. And if asked, I could recommend several other locations that might also be of interest." Crossing her arms, she sat back and smiled.

Pointing at his friend, Al, Rance laughed and downed his half-full glass of wine. "Man, you've got your hands full with this one." Taking Rance's comment two ways,

L' Ami cocked his head and grinned.

Then Rance offered an uncharacteristic suggestion—one, that a year ago when involved with government clandestine ops, he would not have even given consideration. "Adriana. Do you think you could tear yourself away from brother Tome's restaurant to join our band of treasure hunters? Your knowledge of ancient history and languages could be invaluable. It would complement what I've failed to learn and recall.

"That is if you could learn to endure our warped sense of humor—and that bearded letch sitting next to you."

"On one condition," she said, her expression turning serious. "Only if I can bring my frying pan with me."

Customers in the main dining room turned their heads toward the private room, wondering what the hoots, laughter, and applause were all about.

L' Ami tapped Rance on the shoulder as they were leaving the restaurant for de Molay Castle. Nudging Rance aside, Al informed him that he would be staying in town tonight. Adriana had whispered to him that there was a subject that needed their immediate attention. "I'll meet you at the mayor's office in the morning, then Adriana and I will join you on the way back to the castle." Al squeezed his friend's arm. "And thanks for inviting Adriana to come with us. You have no idea how much that pleased both of us."

"Oh, yes I do."

IT WAS THREE-THIRTY IN THE MORNING when Rance's Global Phone rang. "Yea, this better be good—who ever this is? And it better not be Rubin Brock…"

"It's Al. Sorry for the early wake up, but I couldn't wait to tell you and the others," came an excited explanation.

Rance lay his head back down and closed his eyes. What he heard had him on his feet, shaking his sleepy-eyed wife. "Yea, yea, I'll alert everyone. Congratulations. See you at ten in Puertollano's office."

With her palm soothing her forehead, Mac asked, "Who was that at this time in the morning? I heard the name, Rubin Brock. Don't tell me he has another assignment for us."

"No, that was L' Ami. He and Adriana are getting married in the morning."

Mac sat straight up in bed. "Wonderful!" she shouted, then considered the hasty decision. "Did he say why they are going this route so soon?" She quickly added, "Not that I'm saying they shouldn't. I think it's great. She's a great girl—and you know how I feel about Al."

"He said that Adriana told him that they were both adults and that she wasn't at all prudish—but sharing a bed in the same castle with her new friends and not being married—just didn't seem right." Rance laughed. "Al jumped at the chance to say yes."

"So *he* believes that she proposed to him?"

"That's the way I'd look at it," he answered with a sly expression, knowing he was heading for deep water.

"Mayor Puertollano will issue the marriage certificate—and also being Tarego's magistrate—he will perform the ceremony. I'm to be the witness."

Mac was shaking her long thick strands of hair. "You won't be the only witness. I'll be there, too. And do you think that you can keep A.T. and Tina away once you tell them? No way. Wild horses couldn't make us miss *this* occasion. It's settled?"

"Settled."

Chapter Five

WHILE THE GULFSTREAM JET CRUISED at thirty-three thousand feet on autopilot, the three females, heads together, grouped around the front table gossiping about the morning's wedding. At the back, A.T. and Al were gathered around a map of Scotland, gulping beer, and listening to Rance discuss plans for the Rosslyn Chaple and Chapel grounds search. "We'll be flying over the West European Basin, avoiding the English Channel, and England proper. Edinburgh Airport is less than ten miles from the castle. Isn't that about right, Arturo?"

"*Si*, Captain. But the first stop must be at the Roslin Glen Hotel pub so I can introduce you two reprobates to a draft of Belhaven Best brew. It'll make ye sleep like a bloody Scottish babe."

Arturo turned his attention to the newlywed. "You seem unusually quiet my friend. Did you forget to pack a supply of Jack Daniel's?"

"No. It's not that," Al answered, sneaking a glance at his lovely bride seated at the front of the cabin. "It's just that I've never been married before. Truthfully, it seems a bit scary…"

"You were pushed off a cliff…fell out of a helicopter into the ocean without a chute…blown up in a mud hut in the Sahara…knifed on numerous occasions…and two years ago you were gut shot and nearly died," Rance reminded him. "And now you're admitting that you are afraid of the woman who obviously adores you? Though none of us can fathom why." A.T.'s bald head bobbed up and down in silent agreement.

"Very amusing," L' Ami growled, then kept his remarks to himself as the women stood and walked to meet their mates.

"What's on the agenda, guys?" Mac asked, taking a seat across from her husband. "Solved the riddle of the Knights Templar and

Rosslyn Chaple? Located the treasure as yet?" She smiled innocently and added, "Remember, my dear—*carpe diem*."

"That reminds me of a Valentine card I once read. The verse went, 'I love you more today than yesterday…because yesterday you annoyed me to no end.' " The toe of Mac's boot said hello to Rance's left shin. Everyone laughed, except the target.

Rubbing his shin and ignoring the laughter, Rance asked A.T., "This tale about a secret vault rumored to house religious relics under Templar protection—is it a viable possibility?"

Tina answered for him. "According to the foreman at the chapel site, yes. In time, and with the owner's permission, they will attempt to scan for such possible locations."

"Another reason we need to stop at the Rosslyn Glen Hotel," Al said, "is to pick up a large package waiting our arrival. At least I hope that my contact located the equipment and shipped it express."

"What is waiting for us at this hotel?" Adriana asked.

"It's the latest gadget in electronic scanning technology, I'm told."

"Do you know how to operate this new…scanner?" Adriana asked, plopping down on Al's knee. Wincing and holding his breath for a second or two, he thought to himself. *Damn. She's feels heavier than she looks.* But he knew better than to think out loud.

"I wished you hadn't asked him that," A.T. mumbled, eyeing Rance sheepishly. "Our fearless leader here is a wiz at reading and understanding instructions…" Pausing, he had an afterthought, "…If they remembered to include the instructions."

Adriana withdrew from Al's knee and frowned at the look of relief on his face. "If I remember correctly, a Father Richard Augustus Hay wrote a journal describing a series of cave-like vaults, in which the bodies of the Earls of Rosslyn were buried in their full armor. The only problem is that the good father did not disclose the locations. In fact, the grounds of Rosslyn Glen are full of caves—including tunnels that connect with the Chapel."

Mac made a whistling sound. "It's a good thing we have the run of the grounds for several weeks. Sounds like we're going to need every bit of it."

"Too bad we don't have something that would provide us with a clue," Tina mused.

"Some say there's a clue in a ballad of Rosabelle written by Sir Walter Scott," Adriana said, still frowning at her husband's earlier expression. Closing her eyes, she went on. "If I can remember it all." She shook her head. "Here's one version:

> O LISTEN, listen, ladies gay! No haughty feat of arms I tell.
> Soft is the note and sad the lay. That mourns the lovely Rosabelle.
> Moor, moor the barge, ye gallant crew! And, gentle ladye, deign to stay!
> Rest thee in Castle Ravensheuch. Nor tempt the stormy firth to-day.
> The blackening wave is edged with white. To inch and rock the sea-mews fly.
> The fishers have heard the water-sprite. Whose screams forebode that wreck is nigh.
> Last night the gifted Seer did view. A wet shroud swathed round ladye gay.
> Then stay thee, Fair, in Ravensheuch. Why cross the gloomy firth to-day?
> 'Tis not because Lord Lindesay's heir. To-night at Roslin leads the ball.
> But that my ladye-mother there. Sits lonely in her castle-hall.
> 'Tis not because the ring they ride. And Lindesay at the ring rides well.
> But that my sire the wine will chide. If 'tis not fill'd by Rosabelle.
> O'er Roslin all that dreary night. A wondrous blaze was seen to gleam.

'Twas broader than the watch-fire's light. And redder than the bright moonbeam.

It glared on Roslin's castled rock. It ruddied all the copse wood glen.

'Twas seen from Dryden's groves of oak. And seen from cavern'd Hawthorn den.

Seem'd all on fire that chapel proud. Where Roslin's chiefs un-coffin'd lie.

Each baron, for a sable shroud. Sheath'd in his iron panoply.

Seem'd all on fire within, around. Deep sacristy and altar's pale.

Shone every pillar foliage-bound. And glimmer'd all the dead men's mail.

Blazed battlement and pinnet high. Blazed every rose-carved buttress fair.

So still they blaze when fate is nigh. The lordly line of high Saint Clair.

There are twenty of Roslin's barons bold. Lie buried within that proud chapelle.

Each one the holy vault doth hold. But the sea holds lovely Rosabelle.

And each Saint Clair was buried there. With candle, with book, and with knell.

But the sea-caves rung, and the wild winds sung. The dirge of lovely Rosabelle.

Mac cheered and clapped her hands. "Husband, it appears that you're no longer the only one among us with a photographic memory. Well done, sister."

Adriana took a deep breath and a sip of her husband's drink. "Whew, didn't think I'd get through it all," she said, grinning at the shocked expression on her husband's face. "It's been awhile since I read Sir Walter's poem."

"Well done is right," Rance said. "There could be a clue in there somewhere. Would you mind writing it down? I'll make copies for everyone so we can all study the meaning—and some night soon over nightcaps—we'll dissect Sir Walter's words."

"Oh what a tangled web we weave—when we practice to deceive," A.T. recited.

"I'm impressed, my husband," Tina said. "I'm also surprised that Italy's finest ex-investigator had time to read Sir Walter Scott."

"Only on those long and lonely night stakeouts. One needed something to pass the time," he answered with a straight face and a wink in Rance's direction.

"*Ivanhoe*," L' Ami exclaimed.

"What," A.T. replied.

"That's the extent of my knowledge of Scott's work. He wrote *Ivanhoe*."

"What's this reference to Castle Ravensheuch?" Mac wanted to know. "We're headed for Rosslyn Chaple. Among other lines, that part has me confused."

"I believe both castles are one in the same," Rance said, standing and stretching. "It's time for me to make a heading correction. We'll be on the ground in less than an hour." He disappeared into the cockpit, A.T. close behind, settling into the copilot's seat.

Rance's Global Phone rang. "Would you handle that, A.T.? I'm a little busy right now. It's time to contact Edinburgh Airport tower and alert them that we're coming in."

Arturo picked up the phone, opened the line, and listened to a frantic-sounding message. A.T. listened with his left hand, the other massaged his bald crown. Looking sharply at the pilot, he thanked the caller, closed the phone, and sat silently until the look on Rance's face said, '*Well?*'

"That was Mayor Puertollano. It seems that the fat man and his three reprobates escaped confinement several hours after we took off."

"Better call and check in with the Benitos. They have twenty-four hour protection—but I wouldn't put anything past those four," Rance suggested.

"I'll do that, but Tome said they were last seen hijacking the bus to Madrid. He alerted the Spanish authorities, but word's come back that the bus hasn't been sighted yet. It's as though they dropped off the face of the earth, he said."

"We should be so lucky. I don't think we've seen the last of 'em." Rance adjusted the earphone and poked a thumb over his shoulder. "Tell our passengers to fasten seatbelts. We're going down."

"Do wish you would use other words—other than, 'We're going down'." A.T. said, heading out of the cabin.

Five minutes later he rejoined the pilot as the airport landing strip came into view. Looking to his left, he glanced at Rance and pointed out of the window on his side. "What in the hell is that? Looks like a pregnant whale."

Rance peered over his friend's shoulder. "That's the Super Transport AIRBUS. And you're right: it does look like a pregnant whale."

"NOW THERE, MR. AND MRS. TESTACCIO, ye're back already—and ye 'ought a passel of friends," exclaimed the Rosslyn Glen Hotel barkeep. "Be it a round of Belhaven Best for gents and ladies alike?"

Everyone looked at each other with nods all around. When in Rome. "You guessed it right, mate. And you sure have a good memory."

"It's not often I 'ave a customer who ken put away six pints an' four bacon sandwiches in one sittin'..." He cocked his head at Tina and observed. "...and with such a good looker by his side.

"Besides, I knows ye comin' by the village gossip. Heard ya chartered the Rosslyn ground for a time."

"So much for a stealth arrival," Rance muttered under his breath.

"Don't know about all of you," L' Ami said, "but bacon sandwiches would go good with the brew."

On his last draw, the barkeep's hand froze on the tap's lever. "Well if I live an' breath—if it ain't Sir Sean Connery, himself. Whit an honor to be fillin' ye cup, Sir." Al's physical mannerisms, looks, and voice, mirrored that of the famous Scott. For all the barkeep knew, Connery, wearing a beard and wig, was in disguise.

A.T. slapped his friend on the back. "Oh, at times he thinks he's Sir Sean—but actually—he's just as famous. This here's Lord and Lady L' Ami." That cost the Italian clown another elbow in the ribs.

"Lord and Lady L' Ami?" Adriana said with a confused look.

"Long story, my dear," Al said, placing an arm around his wife's waist. "When we get back to my estate in Italy, it will all become clear. However, it has one drawback." He placed a hand on A.T.'s neck and gave it a playful squeeze. "This comedian owns the adjoining estate."

Tina took Adriana by the elbow and moved her away from the group, whispering, "That means you, and I—for self-defense—must agree to band together to survive their constant bantering or it will drive us both nuts." Mac placed a hand over her mouth.

Chapter Six

THE SUN WAS WELL BELOW THE HORIZON when the three teams of treasure seekers left the tavern and drove away, heading for their temporary home. Rosslyn Chaple. Rance stopped the rented SUV before the chain barring entrance to the one-lane road leading to the castle. A sign hung from a link that read: NOT OPEN TO THE PUBLIC. TRESSPASSERS WILL BE PROSECUTED. Stepping out of the vehicle, A.T. unhooked the chain and waved Rance through. Replacing the chain, Arturo commented on what he could see of the surrounding area. "The gravel on the road appears to have a red tint—and the stone walls on either side of the drive and entranceway look weather-beaten—by thousands of Scottish winters."

Rance pointed ahead. "Look to the left, it's the castle entrance and looks like it could collapse any minute and suddenly end our search of the castle house—our new home for the next few weeks."

"Even in the dim light and headlights," Mac observed as she leaned toward the windshield, "the castle seems to be built out of a stone with a pink hue." She pointed a finger in the direction of the roof. "Isn't that a dark gray slate roof?" Everyone looked to their left.

"There are four…no five chimneys that I can see. I'll bet that in the winter, all five fireplaces are roaring away," Al said. "That old stone house would get mighty cold at night."

Adriana squeezed her husband's arm. "All the more need to snuggle close, my lord."

A.T. nudged his wife. "These newlyweds are more than I can take. We had better place them in the farthest bedroom or we won't get any sleep. Perhaps the dungeon would be perfect."

"Some place where the only ones they'll keep awake will be the ghosts," Rance chimed in, receiving a deep frown from Mac.

A.T. removed the key to the front door from his breast pocket and handed it to Tina. "Why don't you girls go in and turn on the lights while we strong men carry in the bags and electronic equipment."

"And prepare the drinks," L 'Ami suggested. "Adriana's knapsack is full of wine bottles—and of course—Black Jack D for me."

The party looked like six peas in a pod wearing light khaki jackets over matching cargo pants. Mac and Adriana wore their long hair tied back into pony tails. Tina's was too short, cropped the way it was. Tomorrow they would leisurely investigate the castle grounds and visit Rosslyn Chapel. And later that evening they would change into black turtleneck tops and slacks to begin their search in earnest. Full from their feast of bacon sandwiches and tankards of ale—topped off with glasses of wine to help them relax—they turned into bed early.

"AH LASSIE, YER BEAUTY MAKES AN AULD KNIGHT'S HEART SING."

"What…? Who are you?" Tina asked, sitting up in bed, the corner of the sheet tucked under her chin. Startled to hear his voice, she turned to witness her husband's even breathing. He was sound asleep. The man standing at the foot of their bed, dressed in full armor, and speaking aloud, had not stirred Arturo from deep slumber.

Straightening a white tunic emblazoned with a large red cross, he widened his grin, displaying two rows of sturdy-looking teeth. Removing his helmet, revealing a shock of curly reddish-blond locks that matched a full but trimmed beard, he nodded at the sleeping man. "Yer man cannae hear me, Lassie. Dinnae no' feart o' me. Ye bring back memories o' m' lady wi' ye short dark hair—an' she wis a wee bit o' a lassie like ye. Yer in my keep while ye in m' castle. Neither de'il nor man ken harm ye wi' me roond."

Placing one hand on a sheathed sword, the knight donned his helmet, then crossed his arms, and dissolved into a shadow. Tina heard a faint whisper from the darkness. "I, Sir William, will guide ye true."

"WHAT'S WRONG, TINA?" Mac asked. "You've been unusually quiet this morning. Have a sleepless night? Those sandwiches did weigh heavily on *my* stomach."

"She's acted that way ever since waking up," Arturo said. "When I opened my eyes and felt across the bed, she wasn't there. Wrapped in a blanket, she stood by the open window staring out at the chapel grounds. Can't believe that an Italian woman could be so quiet." Tina remained silent.

After a breakfast of eggs and toast, the group retired to the dark paneled drawing room to sip tea and discuss the day's activity. The three women sat cross-legged on a large blue sofa facing a white framed fireplace. Two matching plush chairs guarding each end of the sofa held A.T. and Arturo. Rance occupied a small desk directly behind the sofa, a map of the Rosslyn grounds spread on the desktop. The heavy furniture rested on timeworn wooden flooring. An equally frayed red Persian carpet covered the remainder of the dimly lit room. Cracked and peeled oil paintings graced the walls. Everyone appeared to fall under Tina Testaccio's quiet spell as they sipped tea and absorbed the depressing atmosphere of the musty smelling room.

Tina gasped as she turned to look in Rance's direction. "What is it?" her husband said. "Rance always looks that way in the morning, my love. But he's not that ugly."

Pointing a shaky finger over Rance's head, she exclaimed, "That…that's Sir William."

They all stared at the large oval painting of a knight in full battle armor on the far wall behind Rance. The bearded man held his helmet under one arm, the other placed on the neck of a large gray horse.

"What makes you think his name is Sir William?" Mac asked.

"That's what he said last night," Tina whispered. Her olive complexion appeared to blanch. She gripped her cup with both hands as her palms became moist from perspiration.

"Him? Last night?'" A.T. said, displaying a confused expression.

Tina nodded and stood, then walked to the painting. She remained silent while gazing up at the handsome knight above her head. Turning, she forced her words. "Yes. Last night as you lay sleeping…that knight," she poked a thumb over her shoulder, "stood by the foot of our bed. Don't ask me how. And no, it wasn't a dream. I was as wide awake as I am now."

Intrigued, Adriana asked in a calm voice, "Did he speak to you?"

Uncomfortable with relaying her bizarre experience, she told them what a man dressed as a Templar Knight had said. "As he dissolved into the shadows, his last words were, 'I, Sir William, will guide ye true.' "

Tina stood as though her shoes were nailed to the floor, waiting for a flood of doubts, which, much to her relief, never came. Mac, along with the three men, had known Tina long enough to realize that hallucinations did not fit her no-nonsense persona. If she said she saw the strange aberration—it happened. They did not understand the implications, but on the other hand, they did not doubt her experience.

Rance was the first to break the silence. "I've been around long enough," he gestured to his two covert ex-special ops partners, "as you guys have—to know that we no longer doubt anything. Including the supernatural.

"Tina, it appears that Sir William has taken a liking to you—most likely because you reminded him of his dear departed wife. He also pledged to keep you safe and guide your search—if that's the way his words can be interpreted."

"I just hope that Sir William's words apply to all of us," L' Ami added. "Tina, next time he talks to you, bring that up. Good ghost or not, it gives me the willies."

"I wonder which Sir William he is," Adriana said, taking a closer look at the painting. "There have been a number of Sir William St. Clair (Sinclair) knights in the family. There's no name on the painting. He could be the William who built the chapel and died in 1484—or his grandson—or another…there was even a William who was a hermit…"

"There are seventeen knights buried in the chapel that we know about," Rance interrupted. All laid to rest in full battle armor."

"Sounds very uncomfortable," A.T. said with a grin.

"This isn't a laughing matter," Tina said, her dark eyes flashing disapproval. Arturo shrugged his shoulders and decided the best thing to do was remain silent.

Mac wandered to a window at the back of the house. Changing the subject, she asked, "Have any of you looked out the back windows at the terrain outside of this stone mausoleum? We're perched on the edge of a forested gorge—and it's deep, too."

"Yes," Al agreed. "Adriana and I took a short walk outside before you guys came down for breakfast. Mac's right. The castle must have been built to repel enemies approaching from below."

"We didn't walk far," Adriana said, "but from what we could see as the early morning haze lifted—the grounds around the castle and chapel are beautiful—green pastures and clusters of ancient evergreens."

Rance rustled the map on the desk. "Okay. Enough of the mysterious Templar and the beauty of the Scottish landscape. We'll see all that needs to be seen over the weeks to come—if it takes us that long to find what we've come for—once we figure out what *that* is." Nodding to Tina, he added, "And I imagine we'll hear more from Sir William." Tina had no comment. She looked into her husband's eyes, then smiled an apology for snapping at him earlier.

All three wives sitting on the large sofa, legs tucked under, turned to face Rance. "I've indicated three sections on the map with a red marker—one for each team. Adriana, because of her research, is familiar with the chapel. She and Al will spend the day in Rosslyn Chapel. A.T., you and Tina thoroughly search this castle house and the surrounding grounds. Mac and I will head for the outer glen and river that meanders around the castle and chapel—including Wallace Cave.

"We'll spend the full day in our assigned sections, then tomorrow and the next day we swap sections until each team has had the opportunity to investigate all three sections. Keep copious notes as each evening's debriefing will be short—covering only information of immediate importance. Tonight and tomorrow night we'll relax and have dinner at one of Roslin's best restaurants…"

A.T.'s coughing fit interrupted Rance's dinner suggestion.

"Okay," Rance said with a scowl aimed at his Italian partner. "Perhaps we can take the short drive into Edinburgh for a change of scene." For the first time this morning, he displayed a wide grin. "You remember the old saying: 'All work and no play—makes for a dull life.' Or whatever it said." Everyone laughed at his loss of words.

"Words of wisdom from the man with the photographic mind," Al scoffed.

"If everyone has had their fill of humor, come, and study this map, then be on your way. We meet back here at two o'clock for a few hours nap: remember we work under cover of darkness tonight. After our rest, we head to Roslin Glen Hotel for a bit of dinner, refreshment, and our debriefing—saving Edinburgh's best for the third night. Agreed?" There was a round of nods and a clinking of empty tea cups.

"IS RANCE ALWAYS THAT INTENSE?'" Adriana asked Al as they strolled across an immaculately manicured lawn toward Rosslyn Chapel.

"Only when preparing for a mission. Rance has an uncanny way of focusing all of his attention on the job at hand." He placed his arm around his new bride's waist and pulled her to his side. "And that ability to block out all distractions is responsible for the success of our many missions together—Rance, A.T., and yours truly."

"I witnessed what he did to those men in my brother's restaurant. He had fire in those blue eyes."

"You have to remember that they were threatening your dinner guests and his neighbors—and the ones who had harassed the Benitos at Castle de Molay," Al reminded her.

Adriana stopped and stepped back. "And I also saw what Arturo did to that one man—and how you attacked that big brute."

With a sheepish expression he reminded her of how she laid low the man who had wrapped his huge arms around his body, attempting to squeeze the life out of him. "You weren't so bad yourself, my feisty Spanish flower.

"Mac's a martial arts expert now, just like her husband, and helped destroy the Dacian She-Wolves two years ago." He thought better of the comparison and corrected himself. "No. Mac's good—-but I've not seen anyone as deadly as Rance. Tina has years of training and experience with Italian Special Intelligence—as has Arturo—plus, he's as powerful as a bull. I have my own talents that have contributed to our trio's success through the years. And now we have your fiery spirit..."

L' Ami hugged her close. "The six of us make an unbeatable team. I couldn't be happier."

Adriana's eyes softened as she whispered. "We had better get in the chapel, my love...before I drag you back to the castle and place you on the rack of love."

Al gave the castle a fleeting glance but shook his head. "Remember what I said about focusing on the mission?" Placing a hand on her back, he gave her a gentle nudge toward the chapel doors and said, "You're *my* distraction."

"SIR SEAN, THE BARKEEP CALLED." Al turned his head as the thirsty and hungry searchers entered the Roslin Glen Pub.

"Yer fan beckons ye, m' lord. Ne'er keep a guid man waitin'," Arturo said in his best Scottish accent. "Better see whit aye wants or oor brew will be flat. Humor him. Maybe the drinks will be on the hoose."

"Rance, grab a table and gag the Italian while I see what the barkeep has in mind. And I'll send over a round of Belhaven Best."

Before another tease could roll off A.T.'s tongue, Tina gave his arm a tug and led him away, following the others to an oversized booth tucked into a dimly lit corner of the pub. Mac had picked up a dinner menu from an empty table and looked relieved. "By god, they have more on the menu than just bacon sandwiches," she announced to all.

Rance had his eyes glued on the barkeep and L' Ami. Al listened intently as the other man talked up a storm, his words emphasized with animated gestures. Approaching the table, both Rance and A.T. recognized the concerned expression on their friend's face. They had seen that look before. Something was wrong. Al stripped off his short sleeve khaki jacket, revealing a khaki-dyed bib overall—his favorite garment—and with a menacing whisper said, "They're here."

"Who's here?" Tina asked.

"Remember the four bozos that harassed the Benitos at the castle and restaurant—then crashed out of the Tarego jail and stole a bus? Well, they're here."

Rance's head snapped right, then left. "Where are they?"

"They're not here now. The barkeep, Charlie, said they came in earlier this morning and started asking questions about the tourists staying at the Rosslyn Chaple. Good man, Charlie. He wouldn't volunteer any information. Shut up tighter than a clam.

"Said one was a big man dressed in a black suit who was perspiring profusely. His name was named Claude—but the other three called him Bishop. He dabbed his jowly face with a silk handkerchief the entire time he was here, Charlie said. The one called Paschal was a tiny man whose sneer and squinty eye unnerved Charlie. A tall slim guy with long shoulder length mousy brown hair and a perpetual grin was called Edmond. Maurice, the fourth man was of average height with a small forehead, short cropped bleached blond hair, no neck, and a scar over his left eyebrow. Charlie said Maurice never showed any expression—but grunted behind thin tight lips. He was the scariest-looking of the four men. All spoke with a French accent."

"Damn, your new friend Charlie is an observant man," A.T. noted.

"That's what I said," Al added. "He's been tending bar here for eighteen years. Comes with the territory and experience, he said."

"Charlie has earned a healthy tip this night," Rance observed, waving a *thank you* at the grinning barkeep. Furrowing his brow, he shook his head as though answering a silent question.

Picking up on her husband's mood, Mac asked, "What is it, honey?"

"Probably nothing. It's just that I have had the feeling several times today that we were being watched. Old habits never die, I guess. Yet..."

"An old habit that has saved our skin on many an occasion," A.T. said. "Listen to your intuition now—especially since we've learned about the Bishop and his three weasels."

Rance nodded agreement. "But right now, let's enjoy the brew and food. Mac, what's on the menu for tonight?"

Mac gave the menu a serious inspection. Her facial expressions gave away her distaste for what she read. "Well, if you want to eat like the Scotts, it's Haggis all around, followed by black blood pudding." she laughed as she stuck out her tongue and gagged.

"Haggis?" Tina hissed. "Sounds delicious."

"If you like a pregnant sausage," Arturo said, holding his nose.

"Just what is a Haggis?" Mac asked, looking at her husband for an answer.

"It looks like a bloated sausage the size of a deflated soccer ball—stuffed with minced heart, lungs, sheep or calf's liver, mixed with suet, onions, oatmeal—and boiled in an animal's stomach for several hours." He smiled at Mac and asked, "You heard enough to make a dining decision?"

"We all have," Tina echoed everyone's sentiments. "Read on."

"Well, there's a soup called Cullen Skink." She made another face. "It's smoked haddock with potatoes and cream."

"Continue," L' Ami suggested.

"How about this? Smoked Scottish salmon or succulent lamb. That's how the menu describes it. They both come with newborn potatoes and freshly picked vegetables."

The males chose the salmon: the females selected lamb. Small talk was the order of the evening and over tankards of ale. After the table was cleared, Rance got everyone's attention by rapping his knuckles on the tabletop. "Let's keep it to loud whisper for our first day's debriefing. A.T., you and Tina are on. What if anything did you find interesting in the stone house?"

The two Italians glanced at each other. Tina nodded to her husband to begin. "When we arrived last night, most of the surroundings were bathed in shadows. I'm sure you all noticed the difference when you investigated your section of the map. No doubt that the castle itself is in ruins—with the exception of the stone house."

"Many of the standing ancient stone walls and turrets appear to be biding their turn, waiting to collapse and join their brothers. That turret guarding the entrance to the house looks ready to take the plunge the next time a butterfly decides to perch there," Tina added.

Arturo took over again. "From where we parked the SUV, all we could see of the stone house was two or three stories. Remember, Mac noted this morning that we were perched on the edge of a deep gorge. We discovered—after looking under all the rugs—my special-agent wife's suggestion…"

"That's ex-special agent," Tina reminded him. "And *your* reason for having throw rugs—is something to shove dirt under."

"If you're referring to the time I dropped a flower pot and swept the spilled dirt under the rug…"

"I know. I've heard your excuse a dozen times now," Tina countered.

Everyone except Rance appeared amused by the playful banter. "Can we get back to whatever it was you found under the rug?"

A.T. scowled at his long-time friend. "Well, I was in a hurry," he said, refusing to give Tina the last word, but then complied. "When I picked up the tapestry rug in the front foyer—I discovered a trapdoor. It led to well-worn stone steps leading down to five more floors."

Tina took over. "If you walk outside and peer over the edge, you can see remnants of the castle clinging to the side of the gorge among vines, bushes, and clumps of bright yellow and orange daylilies. Sixty feet below is a forest of trees."

"Rosslyn Chaple was destroyed several times," Adriana interjected. "The stone house was added in 1622." She began to laugh. "In 1447, the castle was badly damaged by fire. Princess Elizabeth Douglas asked a serving maid to retrieve a puppy from under a bed. Using a candle to light the way, the maid caught the bed afire, and the flames spread."

"That all may be true," A.T. agreed, "but it's obvious that they utilized the bottom room of the house as a dungeon—or as the Scotts would say—donjon. That's about all we found of initial interest in our preliminary search. We want to snoop around both the musty attic and donjon tonight. Especially the donjon."

"Al. What if anything did you and Adriana find of interest in the chapel?" Rance asked. "I know that we've come to the Rosslyn grounds without a solid clue as to what we're looking for—other than a sense that something's here that will further our search for Sebastian and Bertrand's Templar treasure."

"Rosslyn Chapel itself is a treasure," Adriana said, smiling at her husband. "I've studied the chapel for years in books—but witnessing it in person—took my breath away."

Coldly, Rance replied. "We're not interested in its beauty, Adriana. We need to know what the chapel can tell us."

Mac dug her fingernails into his thigh, upset with his patronizing tone. He painfully got the message. First glancing briefly at Al, he turned his attention to Adriana. "Sorry if I was short with you just then. I didn't mean to infer that you were not contributing to this mission. Please accept my apology." He looked at his wife and added, "Or I may never walk again."

Adriana very graciously smiled and said, "No offense taken. But I assure you that the chapel hides a world of secrets and in itself tells a medieval tale of ancient history and knowledge." She caught Al's eye: he nodded agreement because he understood what she was about to suggest. "Rosslyn Chapel is a wondrous piece of sculptured architecture, unlike any other that I'm aware of. Of course, due to the overhanging protective steel roof and skeleton framed scaffolding reconstruction workers left in place for their return from vacation—much of the original outside design cannot be recognized. Especially several dozen spirals surrounding the building. It is both my and my husband's recommendation that two people could never adequately investigate the premises. That would be a waste of precious time. Therefore, we need everyone to converge on the building for a search if we're to be effective. While the inside beauty will mesmerize us all—we need to pay particular attention to numerous vaults, tunnels, and yet uncovered hidden passageways."

"Agreed," Rance said. "But let's stay on plan. That way we will all be familiar with the chapel—then on the fourth night—all three teams will converge as you suggest.

"That reminds me. Al, did you think to bring your miniature bug finder? The one you used to check for bugs in the Moscow hotel when we first met with Generals Brock and Rutskoy to plan kidnapping the Russian president."

Adriana, not fully aware of Rance, A.T. and Al's covert adventures, raised both eyebrows and stared at her husband, who innocently inspected the tavern's ceiling. Ignoring her wondering stare, he answered, "Always take it with me when on a mission. What do you have in mind?"

"Considering we have company, as your friend Charlie explained, when we get back to the castle house—sweep it clean for any devices the Bishop and his crew may have left behind."

"Speaking of *mission*," A.T. said, "this is the first mission we've undertaken without any government's involvement. It's kind of relaxing for a change."

"Yes, and one where we don't get paid—and we're using our own money," L' Ami reminded him with a grin.

"Unless we find the Templar's treasure," Rance reminded them.

"I believe it's our turn," Mac said, getting back to business. "Do you want to take it, or me?"

"Be my guest, my dear. But first," Rance held up his hand to get Charlie's attention, then made a circling motion, ordering another round of tankards. "Our throats are going dry. Proceed."

"When the light mist lifted from the grounds, the world around us burst into color. Tina's daylilies were everywhere. Grass, trees, and bushes were a brilliant deep green. Birds were in their best form, singing our welcome. Ruins of the castle appeared to be alive with…"

"My dear wife," Rance said with some annoyance, "you sound like a tour guide: get to the meat of our search." Arrival of the ordered round of drinks tempered Mac's reply, but not her expression of irritation. It was Rance's turn to inspect the ceiling.

"There were three areas of interest," she said smiling while giving her husband the evil eye. "First is the availability of the River Esk winding through the property. It could be the body of water mentioned in Scott's poem—and not the ocean as one would suspect. Hundreds of years ago, the present meandering stream could have been a raging river.

"Second is Wallace's cave. Sir William Wallace, one of Scotland's greatest heroes, is said to have hid in that cave after an English sheriff killed his sweetheart—and Wallace killed the sheriff."

"You've read the brochure, I see," Rance said, then winced when she playfully dug her nails in again. "Ouch! You're gone from bruising my ribs with your elbow—to stabbing me with your lethal claws."

Adriana looked at Tina and said, "There's another William to think about," then changed her mind. "No, that William was not a Templar knight. Your William wore the Templar symbol."

"My William?" Tina answered, not at all amused that the apparition had singled her out.

"Well, anyway…" Mac interrupted, to get back on track. "We found the cave in question just above a muddy bank on the side of sandstone cliffs. It was nearly invisible overgrown with a tangle of sturdy vines."

"Tonight, Mac and I plan to enter with the use of ropes and an electric lantern," Rance said, picking up the pace of the debriefing.

"I'm also interested in investigating the larger of the waterfalls cascading from the cliffs. It's a natural spot for a hidden cave hollowed out by the constant pressure of the water over untold hundreds of years."

"That's about it for us," Mac said, taking a sip from her tankard.

"Appears that nothing out of the ordinary can be considered of interest with the exception of A.T.'s discovery of the floors below the trapdoor," L' Ami said.

After finishing their drinks in relaxed conversation, they left, leaving Charlie an eye-popping tip. It was time to change into their black duds, and for the next three hours they would search unnoticed, assisted by the cover of darkness—always alert to the possibility of the Bishop and his men lurking in the area.

While slipping into their black garments, Adriana again interrogated her husband about the covert history of his friends, and why Rance appeared to be so uptight.

"Let me take your last question, first," Al said. "It's difficult to change old habits overnight. All our past missions were life or death assignments—with no option for error. Two years ago, I nearly lost my life due to an unforeseen incident. You've seen the scar. The three of us have worked together for so long and so close—we know how each of us will react in different situations. It's second nature. We don't have to think. We react. Now enter three females. After Mac single-handedly trounced three burly mercenaries, Rance grew comfortable with her on a mission. She then went undercover to bring down a group bent on taking over world governments—nearly losing her life in the effort. Obviously, that's always in the back of his mind. He's aware of Tina's talents, but it's not the same. You, my dear, are an unknown entity."

"So he's comfortable with you and A.T.—but uncertain about the three wives? Is that it?"

"That's not quite it. But close. It's just that Rance is having difficulty in adapting to our slower way of doing things. He has, believe it or not, mellowed since meeting and marrying Molly. Her name was Molly MacWinter—thus the nickname, Mac."

"Mellowed?"

"Yes, mellowed," Al laughed. "Now I'll tell you about the adventures we've shared in just the past three years. Including the kidnapping of the Russian president." By the expression on her face, he knew he had her full attention. "It will provide you with an idea of our past together." The fiery Spanish redhead would soon develop a new appreciation for her husband and his friends.

Chapter Seven

"I COULD HAVE TAKEN OUT THE BEARDED ONE," Paschal whispered, brushing long black strands from his good eye. He's the bastard that took you out, Bishop."

"Let me correct you, my sneering friend," Bishop said with a calm voice and placing a hand with pudgy fingers on the shorter man's head. "It was that Spanish bitch that *took me out*—as you so eloquently say it.

"I do not want any of you knuckleheads to harm a hair on any of their heads. We need them to do the work of discovering the Templar treasure for us. Then you can have their heads for all I care—leaving the bearded one and his bride to me. For now, we merely stay out of sight and observe." Claude, the Bishop, laughed: his enormous girth shook beneath his oversized black cape. "Since it is unrealistic for me to remain out of sight—unless disguised as a mountainside—you three must do."

"But Bishop," Edmond the beanpole of the group said, his long shoulder-length stringy hair moving with each jerky gesture. Stroking an overly sharp chin with long boney fingers, he asked, "Can't we play with 'em a bit—just for fun?" His cackle sounded like an old woman's voice.

Paschal laughed saying, "Edmond dressed in a black robe would make a spooky ghostly monk—like the one in the castle legend." Maurice, who seldom smiled, displayed a morbid grin, and nodded a head that appeared to sit on his shoulders, then rubbed his short-cropped bleached blond stubble. A scar hovering over his left eye turned blood red.

"I can tell from Maurice's telltale scar that he's excited about the prospect of Edmond's devilish idea of fun," Claude the Bishop mused. "All right, have your little amusement—but if you are caught—you may pay for it with your lives." His features darkened. "From what we witnessed when they ran us off the grounds of de Molay Castle and how easily they handled us in the restaurant—this group is not accustomed to taking prisoners."

"FEEL THAT COLD BREEZE? We must be close to the bottom floor," A.T. said. The dark dampness closed in as he looked over his shoulder at Tina. "You hold your lantern low, and I'll hold mine high. That way we'll illuminate the entire donjon."

Handcrafted stone steps were well-worn, indicating a steady use of the bottom room. A.T. fought his way through a sticky web of spiders, shuddering as he attempted to control his fear of the creepy crawlers. It reminded him of the time, three years ago to be exact, when with broom in hand, he swept away web after web in the secret tunnel below the Russian president's bedroom. He hated the damn things now—just as much as he did then.

"Guess the maid missed this room," Tina said with a smile, her eyes darting from every visible nook and cranny of what her husband called a donjon.

"Watch your step," Arturo warned as he walked across the uneven stone floor. He stood in the middle of the room and with lantern held high, made a full circle. Shadows shimmered in all directions. "You can see—there and there," he pointed, "where the tools of the torturer's trade were fixed to the stone walls."

Looking into Tina's eyes, he whispered, "I have a strange feeling about this place."

MAC GRABBED RANCE'S ARM THE MINUTE SHE HEARD IT. "You didn't hear that, did you?"

"Do you mean the sound of a howling dog?"

She hesitated, then answered, "Yes."

"No," he said, moving on toward the pitch black cave entrance.

"Good," Mac swallowed hard and said, "Neither did I."

They had walked in complete darkness with the exception of a dim haze reflecting off a pale moon. Black high-top waterproof boots came in handy while sloshing through the muddy shallow stream toward the waterfall that caught Rance's imagination. They stood below and to the right of the cascading falls: a fine mist clung to their clothes like tiny pearls. Looking up, the full moon appeared to rest on the crest of the hill. A strong breeze stirred a branch of a dead tree, its shadow black against the background of silver.

Mac gasped and nudged her husband's shoulder. "No," he said, acknowledging her obvious concern. "I definitely did not see the black silhouette of a robe-clad monk cross the moon's surface."

"Good," she responded with a shaky voice, "neither did I." She hesitated and continued. "It's part of the castle's legend—and not real. Right?"

Unconcerned, Rance answered, "It's our imaginations. Here," he said, pushing her in front of him—"you go first."

There was just enough of the moon's reflection to see the *why me first?* expression on Mac's face. "It's slippery, my love," Rance warned her. "From behind, I can guide you up and over the edge of the small cave next to the falls." She bought his logic and proceeded, using hanging vines and clinging shrubs as climbing grips.

Once inside, Rance widened the lantern's beam, and the slimy muddy surface of the cave loomed before them. Spray from the waterfall kept the interior in a constant damp condition. All sorts of crawling bugs scurried away from the bright beam. Roots from trees and shrubs above hung down, penetrating the cave's ceiling. To their left, they could see water as it tumbled past the opening of the small cave. Holding the lantern high and to the right, it was apparent the cave only extended into the cliff about eight feet. The only exit, with the exception of the way they had entered, was to the left where the water flowed. Rance decided to investigate the possibility of a larger cave, perhaps hidden behind the falls. Motioning for Mac to follow, he cautiously moved forward.

"Woops. Watch your footing!" Rance shouted to be heard over the fall's roar, catching hold of a hanging root. "The cave floor slants downward the closer we get to the waterfall. Use the roots to steady yourself.

"Step on the large ledge, but again, it's slippery." Heavy mist had washed the surface clean: mud was replaced by equally slippery moss.

Rance held the lantern out into the falls and moved it to his right, away from the opening. "Just as I thought. There's a rock cave carved out behind the cascading falls." Teetering on the edge, he stretched as far as he could to see how far the beam would shine and what it looked like behind the falls.

"There's a small rocky ledge that leads into the cave," he noted as he uncoiled a rope from around his waist. "I'll tie this around me: you grip the end firmly. There's nothing to securely anchor it here. If I begin to fall, yank me back. If my weight's too much, and you're in danger of slipping yourself—release me. Save yourself. I'll just get a good dunking."

"I wouldn't argue that you couldn't benefit from a good dunking, but I'm not letting you fall. Move out and be careful."

Rance chuckled to himself, knowing full well what she meant by, 'You could benefit from a good dunking.' He had been too short with the group, especially with Adriana, and would make it up to her.

His first step was nearly disastrous: the rocky ledge was slimier than he thought. Soaked to the skin from the spray, he edged himself closer to the cave opening. Holding onto an equally slimy wall with one hand while hanging onto the lantern made it difficult. Spying what appeared to be a solid ledge void of moss, he took the chance and leapt, landing safely.

Shouting again to be heard, he said, "I'm secure! Tie yourself off and come ahead! I'll shine the lantern your way!" Within three tense minutes, Mac jumped safely into Rance's arms.

To her amazement, he suddenly slapped the palm of his hand on his forehead, then shook his head. "I'm becoming my worst enemy."

"We all realize that, darling—but what is it this time?"

"It's impossible to go back the way we came. There's no way to jump from here," he pointed, "back up there. The distance is too great and the rocks too slippery. No. Unless we find another way—we are…"

"Don't say it. I have faith in my addlebrained husband. You'll find a way out. In the mean time, let's investigate what looks like a very large cave."

Lifting the lantern high over his head gave them a good view of the cave's interior. "The cave seems to be weeping," Mac observed. "The tears of Lady Rosabelle, no doubt."

"Now you're letting your imagination get the best of you…"

"No more than the howling dog we didn't hear—and the silhouette of a mad monk we didn't see."

"Let's concentrate on the cave and allow spirits to do their ghostly deeds," Rance suggested, leading the way over a stack of boulders. "As if we weren't wet enough—the constant dripping of Rosabelle tears—will not allow us to dry off."

"That's *Lady* Rosabelle. Give her her due."

"I guess, since it's Lord Alvin L' Ami—then it must be Lady Adriana L' Ami."

"No," Mac reminded him. "It's Sir Lord and Lady L' Ami."

Keeping up the playful banter as they climbed over rocks, Rance added, "I guess that since you're the Lady of Castle de Molay—you want a title as well. When will it ever end?" he moaned, then stopped in his tracks, holding up a hand.

"Over there, in the far left hand corner of that alcove—there's a large dark shadow. See it? Could be a tunnel or a shaft."

On closer inspection, it was a vertical shaft. Picking up a small rock, Rance dropped it over the edge. They listened. It did not take long to hear it strike bottom. "No water. That's a plus when I go down," he said. "There's plenty of rope…"

"When *you* go down? You're not leaving me up with a rabid hound and a mad monk while you have all the fun. I have strength enough to go hand-over-hand. There may be horizontal shafts to search. No, I'll be right behind you."

Her tone of voice told Rance there would be no talking her out of following him. "Okay. I'll make a loop and secure the line over one of those large boulders. When I reach bottom and find your shaft, I'll signal for you to follow. If I don't find it, I'm coming back up. Agreed?"

Rance shouted from below. "Mac! You were right. At the bottom, there are two horizontal shafts going in opposite directions. The main vertical shaft widens with room for three men abreast. Come down slow. But first check the loop around the boulder: make certain it hasn't worked itself loose. Be careful. Your gloves will give you traction on the line."

"THAT COLUMN IS CALLED THE APPRENTICE COLUMN," Adriana said. "A master mason started building the column, then was called away. When he returned to Rosslyn Chapel, the creation was complete. His lowly apprentice had carved that beautiful spiraling marble lace work you see winding around the column from the bottom to the top. Angered that the helper had upstaged the master—the master promptly beat him to death."

"Nice folks, these Knights Templar."

"See those carvings above?" she pointed. "It's suggested that since they appear to depict American southwestern cactus and American Indian sweet corn—some say it proves that the Templar ships arrived in the new world—two hundred years before Columbus discovered America."

Adriana noticed Al's fascination with the apprentice column. "There is also a suggestion that a holy relic—perhaps the Holy Grail—is hidden within that very column."

"Or the bones of the apprentice," Al answered, unmoved by her hint of treasure. "Once we set up our electronic x-ray-vision equipment, we'll know. Until then, what next, my love?"

"Well, the chapel is said to represent Solomon's Temple, the place where it's speculated the Templars discovered Solomon's treasure—the source of their original wealth. One legend says that if you stand in the right spot within the chapel and blow a horn, a treasure will be revealed."

L' Ami patted his breast pocket. "I only play a harmonica: will that do?"

Attempting to stifle a grin, Adriana was slowly becoming used to the trio's dry humor one-liners. Rance was the worst. She reasoned it was self-defense, a way of dealing with a past life-and-death profession. She assumed correctly. Humor had kept them sane. Well, almost.

"I love the feeling of the dimly lit chapel and the surrounding carvings," Adriana whispered, laying a hand on the small altar. "Wouldn't it have been wonderful if we could have been married here?"

"You don't think your mayor brother had the authority? Are you implying that we're illegal?" Al teased. "I've already checked the marriage certificate twice for a date of expiration." Knowing he was skating on thin ice, he quickly disappeared behind the massive marble pulpit saying, "There's a stone stairway over here."

I'm going to have to enlist Mac to show me some of her martial arts moves Adriana thought to herself as she went in search of her husband.

Al had to stoop in sections of the damp and musty smelling tunnels that spread out in several directions from a large dark and light-colored stone carved room. He counted eight tunnels in all. "We're going to need a large bag of bread crumbs so we don't get lost." This time the attempted humor was lost on his Spanish bride.

"That's why we recommended that all three teams converge on the chapel," she reminded him. "Now about that marriage expiration date…"

"Look down this tunnel," he said excitedly, hoping to change the subject. Sometimes after one makes a stupid remark, there's no safe way of stepping out of the frying pan. "Aren't those grave markers? There must be over a dozen."

ADRIANA AND AL WERE THE LAST TEAM TO ARRIVE back at the castle house and slip into bed for a much needed rest. They had had a full first day. L' Ami's stomach was already rumbling: he was ready for breakfast, but that was five hours away. He leaned over to kiss his new bride goodnight, but she was already asleep. *Hope she's not dreaming of an expired wedding certificate.*

"HAS ANYONE SEEN MAC OR RANCE this morning?" Tina asked, pouring coffee for the group. "It was Mac's turn to cook breakfast."

Al looked at Adriana and shook his head. "I believe we were the last ones in. We haven't seen either one. Did anyone notice if they took an early jog? Normally, they both enjoy an early morning exercise."

"*Si signor*, he's always teaching her new moves…"

L' Ami laughed at his Italian friend's observation. "If he keeps it up—she'll be as good as the master."

"Mac's already better: she's female," Adriana said, surprised at her own attempt at dry humor.

Arturo's eyebrows lifted as he glanced at her husband. "She's becoming as dangerous with her tongue as with her frying pan."

"That's what happens when you let 'em vote and obtain a driver's license, my friend. Or, at least that's what *you* told me," Al countered.

Tina stared at A.T., then suppressed a grin. "Hey, you bushy-faced overall-wearing lord of the manor—don't get me in any more trouble than I'm normally in with the misses. *Capisce?*"

Tina, worried about her two tardy friends, slipped upstairs and knocked on their door before slowly opening it and whispering their names. The room was empty.

"Now I'm really worried," she said, returning to the small kitchen. "They're not upstairs, and their bed is still made up. We haven't seen them this morning. If they went somewhere—I feel certain that they would have left us a note."

"Settle down, wife of mine—they both can take care of themselves," A.T. declared, and offered to make breakfast. "If they don't materialize after smelling my special Italian eggs…"

"From Italian chickens no doubt," Al interjected.

A pot holder hit L' Ami in the face. "You volunteering this morning?" Arturo asked. "If not, just sit there and feed your face. Or better yet, go outside and holler for Rance and Mac. Maybe they're in shouting distance."

"If they're not here after breakfast," Tina said, "I'm for tracing their footsteps into that far glen—towards the waterfall that piqued their interested. You're all invited to join me."

A final cup of coffee in the drawing room did nothing to quell Tina's concern for the still missing team. A.T. could sense her nervousness. Her investigative intuition was seldom wrong. "Okay," he said, standing and walking to the door, "I'm becoming a mite antsy myself. Wherever they went, they should have returned by now."

"Agreed, my friend," Al said, motioning the girls forward. "We have four no-goods—the Bishop and his ugly accomplices nosing about—that Charlie warned us about. No telling what they've been up to."

HAVING OBSERVED SEVERAL recently dislodged rocks at the foot of the cave entrance, the search party climbed the slippery cliff and into the cave. The short right-hand passageway ended abruptly, so they turned left toward the sound of rushing water. Carefully edging themselves along the right-hand wall, they decided that Tina was the obvious candidate to make the leap, rope around her waist, to the rock ledge below. Arturo would follow. The two would make an initial search of the large cavern. Al and Adriana would remain where they were as back up—and as an anchor with the rope in hand—in case that was the only available exit. No one could make a reverse leap back the way Tina and A.T. had jumped.

Arturo shouted out Rance's name. Silence. Except for the constant roar of the cascading waterfall. "This is one huge cavern," Tina observed, scampering over huge boulders.

"By the shape of the cavern and tossed-about rocks and house-size boulders, the waterfall must have flowed through here hundreds of years ago—perhaps, thousands of years ago." Glancing around, A.T. added, "I see no evidence that Rance and Mac were here." He called out again.

Tina climbed the largest boulder resting in the center of the cavern and peered about. "Shine your light there," she pointed, "to your immediate left—about twelve feet from the far left-hand wall."

Following her directions, he moved quickly, a bright beam leading the way. Over his shoulder, he shouted, "I can see a rope tied around a boulder!"

Picking up the end of the rope hanging over the edge of a darkened pit, he turned as Tina rushed to his side. Holding up the end, he said with a concerned frown, "This rope's been cut."

Suddenly a light flashed up from below, followed by a loud angry shout. "Where in the hell have you been—you Italian slacker—and what took you so damned long? I hope you brought some coffee with you."

"Rance!" Tina yelled.

"And me, too," Mac shouted back.

Arturo Testaccio flipped the rope end aside, walked away grumbling, then returned. "You're damned lucky Mac's down there with you—you ungrateful Yank—or as far as I'm concerned, you could rot in that hole." He flashed his beam in Rance's smiling face and added with gusto, "I'm sick and tired of saving your worthless skinny butt."

Rance tied a rock on the fallen end of the rope and stepping back, hurled it to his friend. "Make a square knot—Boy Scout—and pull us up."

Grinning at Mac, he said, "I'd better go first. After you're up, the little Italian imp might do as he threatened and leave me down here."

Once out, they each tied L' Ami's extended rope around their waist, slipped into the pooling water at the edge of the flowing stream, and swam the short distance to the upper ledge where Al and Adriana pulled them out.

Rance and Mac were famished. They promised to explain what happened over coffee and breakfast. Mac and Tina embraced and A.T. smacked his longtime friend on the shoulder. Nothing needed to be said.

"Rance had faith that you'd come in search," Mac explained, pouring her second cup of coffee. "I wasn't so sure," she interjected with a sheepish expression.

"When the rope fell from above—and I saw the end—there wasn't a doubt it was cut," Rance took over the explanation. "We couldn't see who was at the pit's edge, but whoever it was, knew we were down there."

"I don't need but one guess," Al said. "It was those bozos we were warned about."

"That would be my guess, too," Rance agreed. "At some point I'm certain our paths will cross—then it's our turn."

Mac took over by adding, "We tried a number of times to climb out, but the pit was wider at the top than the bottom, with the exception of the base of the pit. And there were no handholds. Rance attempted it three times by placing his hands on one side of the shaft and his feet on the other—bridge style. He'd get about twelve feet, slowly inching his way up, then fall just as the shaft widened."

"Did the pit lead anywhere?" Adriana asked.

"There appeared to be an attempt to dig two horizontal shafts, but they, whoever they were, gave up after six feet," Rance answered, then went on. "Before we leave, that cavern bears exploring. There could be other pits and shafts elsewhere in that huge room."

"Well, thank heaven you both are safe," Adriana sighed. "I can see that this is going to be an exciting adventure. New to me, at least."

Tell them about the howling dog—and the black-clad mad monk," Mac said, her voice trailing off.

All eyes were on Rance, his face fixed in dismay. He hadn't thought twice about the two events until now and wished that Mac had forgotten them. "Just the wind and a shadow from a large tree limb. Nothing more to report," was all the attention he was going to give it.

Without another word, Rance picked up his cup, strolled into the drawing room, then stood by the window overlooking the deep ravine. One by one, they followed and sat in the plush sofa and chairs waiting for Rance to rejoin them. "What's he doing?" Adriana whispered in Al's ear.

"From the faraway look in his eyes before he went silent—I'd say he was formulating a *plan*. A.T. and I have witnessed that same blank expression—too many times in the past." Overhearing the reply, Arturo nodded agreement at Adriana.

"Al. Is the portable seismographic-dipolar equipment operational?"

"As in the past, this is not a covert mission where we have clearance to utilize government satellites—and it's not necessary—unless you want to penetrate a half-mile or so below the surface. Shock-producing planting rods should suffice. What do you have in mind?"

"It's just a hunch, but there's a good chance those numerous undiscovered tunnels lead from the chapel and castle to that large cavern created by the waterfall."

Placing his empty cup on the desk, Rance stood behind the wooden straight-backed chair, firmly planted both hands on the back, and explained. "Mac and I could use a few hours rest. Tina and Adriana—take the SUV—gather up a few groceries and in general, snoop around town. I'm particularly interested in the names and locations of watering holes besides Charlie's tavern. And stay clear of the Bishop and any of his goons—if you spot 'em."

"And you want A.T. and I to do what with the earth dipolar?" Al asked.

"Take the equipment to the ridge above and behind the waterfall and do your thing. See if my instinct is right."

"Why do you want Tina and Adriana to check out taverns?" Mac asked.

"Because, dear wife, tonight an old Scott is going fishing for French fish in those watering holes. In disguise, I'll seek out those who are on our tails—not to mention—cut our lifeline in the pit. We need to know as much about them as they do, or think they do, about us. I've got a plan about how to do that, too."

"I scanned the castle house last night for bugs," Al said, "or should I say early this morning before Adriana, and I hit the sack. We're clean."

Rance pulled the chair out, sat down, and made a steeple with his fingers. "Change of plans…"

"Here it comes," Arturo grumbled. L' Ami snickered.

Ignoring the Italian grump, Rance continued. "Originally, the search schedule was for each team to rotate our three target positions, but on second thought, that would be unproductive. Redundant. Adriana's the chapel expert. No one can do a better job of leading the rest of us in thoroughly searching that area of the Rosslyn grounds." Adriana's smile widened.

"A.T. and Tina have searched every inch of the castle house. In time, they will introduce us to all the spiders and their webs. And from the look on A.T.'s face, he's found something interesting. Hold it 'til later, friend. Before we leave for good, we'll all investigate the waterfall cavern for additional pits and shafts—and tunnels—if my hunch is correct."

Rance stood and held his hand out to Mac. "You all have a good morning. Lady Molly Rance of Castle de Molay and I have a date with a soft feather mattress."

WALLACE'S WAYSIDE TAVERN is as large as Charlie's establishment, but that's where any similarity ends. Tables packed with thirsty patrons are crammed together, making it hard to navigate the slim aisles, and the noise decimal is acutely higher. These are no tourists staying at a hotel enjoying a comfortable evening of food, drink, and conversation. This tavern is where the working-class comes to unwind from a long exhausting day in the fields and warehouses. Fake William Wallace relics hang along each wall and behind the bar manned by a large muscular individual sporting a perpetual grin. He laughs aloud at everyone's jokes while wiping beer foam-soaked hands on an apron that has yet to take a tumble in a washing machine. His equally muscular barmaid manages somehow to twist and turn and slip and slide between the tables without spilling the tankards on a wide tray held high. All eyes are on her ample cleavage, waiting for the small white buttons of a well-worn blouse to pop loose, and watch in fascination at the possibility of an avalanche of flesh.

"Oh sorry, dreary," the old white-haired bearded man apologized for bumping into her as she made her way from the back of the room. Lifting his colorful knit cap that matched his wooly trousers, he backpedaled in a drunken wobble, and like a pinball, bumped into a table of four men. Unable to control his movements, he fell, knocking the squinty-eyed man over and onto the floor.

Angrily struggling to push the old Scott aside, the man shouted to his friends. "Get this drunken old bastard off me!"

With a grunt, the man with bleached blond hair reached down and lifted the old man like a rag doll. As he was about to pitch him in the air, a heavy hand smacked his shoulder. "We dinnae ne'er treat oor elderly like that, Frenchman—poot the auld one doon." A rather large Scott with huge, calloused hands loomed over the man Charlie identified as Maurice.

Not one to back down from a fight, Maurice thought about flinging the old man into the arms of his intimidator, when the Bishop's hand gripped his wrist, and shook his head…no. Angry with the circumstances, the scar over Maurice's eye reddened. Turning his head away from the tall man, he grunted in protest and dropped the wide-eyed old man to the floor. Dusting himself off to retain what little dignity remained, the old Scott shuffled toward the door, lifting his cap in a salute to the man that had come to his rescue.

Two blocks away, the old man ducked into the backseat of a SUV parked by the curb. "Is it working?" he asked the bearded man sitting next to him.

"Like a charm," L' Ami said, showing Rance a small handheld gadget resembling a cell phone. "We can hear them as clear as a bell, and we'll be able to track their movements from the miniature screen. At least whoever it was you planted the bug on."

"From Charlie's description, I'd say it was Paschal. Believe he was the one Arturo shot back at de Molay Castle."

"Rance, what happened in there?" Mac asked.

"When I stumbled over Paschal, driving him ass over teakettle, I managed to implant a flat tiny bug onto the inside of his leather belt—

at the middle of his back. He'll never feel it there, and if he's like most men, when he takes his pants off—he'll leave his belt in the loops."

"Al, what's the range?" Tina asked.

"This one's more sophisticated than the one Rance had in Moscow. The range is up to eight miles—and if atmospheric conditions are tolerable—add another mile."

"That means not only do we have the capability to eavesdrop on these guys," A.T. said, "but we'll have a pretty good idea where they're laying their bones at night and during the day."

"And most importantly, we'll know when they're approaching the castle and chapel grounds," Rance pointed out, tilting his head as if to hear an inner thought.

"What did you just think of?" Mac asked, recognizing the expression.

"Two flaws in our thinking. *One*: We can only track Paschal, not the other three. *Two*: If Paschal has another pair of pants with another belt, we lose contact."

"Friend, does Paschal look like someone who owns a second pair of pants?" A.T. said, shaking his head doubtfully.

"We can't pursue the Templar treasure while wasting our time watching for and listening to Claude and the three blind mice—nor can we ignore them entirely," Rance said, removing his makeup.

Rance turned to Mac. "Why don't you and Tina share duties of keeping track of what's said and their ongoing location. Adriana will have her hands full with chapel analysis." Mac and Tina nodded at each other.

"Thanks. Let's go back to the castle house and get a much needed full night's rest—and we'll all attack the dungeon after Arturo and Al leave before dawn and scope out more hidden tunnels." The men groaned their disapproval.

Chapter Eight

"WE HAVE TUNNELS ALL OVER THE PLACE," Arturo exclaimed, tossing his rain slicker over a bust of some ancient nobleman. "We quit. The morning mist is turning into a downpour."

"There better be some coffee left," Al said sternly, yet smiling at his nodding wife. Adriana pointed to his muddy boots, shook her head, and wagged a finger in his face. "Oops. I forgot I'm no longer a free man and must abide by civilized rules. No mud in the house...uh, castle."

"What time did you two leave this morning?" Rance asked with a twinkle of mischief in his eyes. "Whatever time it was—we appreciate you not waking us up. Right, darling?"

Al raised a finger at his friend to emphasize a point, but before he could get the words out, Adriana shoved a breakfast pastry in his open mouth and a cup of coffee in his hand. Also annoyed by the early morning soggy assignment, Arturo saw a glimmer of humor in the sight and chuckled to himself. Turning to Tina, he pointed to her earplug. "Anything new on the radio?"

"No. Guess they're late risers."

"Maybe they have more sense than to traipse around in the rain and mud," L' Ami offered, staring hard at Rance—who was ignoring him.

"According to the image locator, they must be staying at the Bed and Breakfast inn attached to Wallace's Wayside Tavern," Mac explained. "The beeping signal hasn't moved since we sat in the car last night—and nothing of significance to report regarding their conversation—except for a few more cuss words I'd never heard before."

"Mac, if you and Tina are uncomfortable listening to their trash talk—the three of us," Rance gestured to himself and the other two, "can take over the…"

Both ladies made a sour face, and Mac spoke up first. "I'm sure I also speak for my Italian sister. We appreciate your male sensitivity gesture—but we can handle whatever spills out of their garbage-filled mouths."

Pouring a shot of JD in her husband's coffee cup, Adriana asked, "Where did you discover the tunnels?"

"In addition to what we found yesterday, there were several extending from the chapel toward the castle house and in the direction of the glen and waterfall area."

"And the tunnel heading toward the castle house was much deeper than the others," A.T. explained. "It appears to angle down—perhaps to the level of the dungeon below."

"You anticipated as much," Tina said.

"Yes. There's a portion of one wall that appears not to be as old as the surrounding bricks and aged plaster. Al's equipment will tell us more."

"Speaking about the electronic equipment," Al noted, "we had no choice but to return to the castle house when the rain increased. We were in the vicinity of the cliff above the waterfall when I made the decision to retreat. This equipment is too sensitive to risk shorting out. But, a tunnel, or better still, tunnels, were definitely below our feet."

"Since you girls were afraid of melting in the Scottish sunshine," Rance teased, "we had better—after breakfast—begin in the dungeon."

A.T. barked at Rance and tilted his head at Mac. "It's a damned good thing you brought your bodyguard along with you."

Tina waved her arms about and shushed everyone. "The bad guys are stirring," she said, pointing to her radio receiver ear plug.

"Who's talking and what are they saying?" A.T. asked.

"It's Claude—from the sound of his voice—he appears to be very upset. He's angry with Paschal. Something about Paschal holding them up." She pushed the plug in tight with a finger. "Paschal's complaining that his pants are stained with spilled beer…and…oh hell…he put them in the inn's washing machine. I can hear it chugging away…"

"What now?" Al asked, concerned with the surprise look on Tina's face.

Removing the plug, she flipped it to him saying, "That idiot Frenchman, he must have put the belt in the machine along with the pants. Your device has stopped transmitting—and we've lost visual target contact on the monitor."

Al looked at Rance and shrugged a shoulder. "Water will do it every time, boss. Sorry."

"Fortunes of war. We've had far worse setbacks," Rance yawned. "We'll just have to be all the more vigilant. Right now, I'm more interested in what's in A.T.'s donjon."

"IT WASN'T MY FAULT that old geezer fell into my lap last night, Bishop," Paschal moaned. "That was my favorite pair of pants."

"Your only pair—you fool," the Bishop scolded. "Their daily search is probably underway by now. You cost us valuable time." Pointing a finger in the tiny man's face, he warned, "I remind you of Baudouin's fate." Paschal lowered his head. Edmond chuckled under his breath.

"It's imperative that we be in place to observe their progress—and over the next few days plant our electronic bugs throughout the buildings, ruins, and grounds." Claude's eyes flashed with excitement. "So many, that they'll think they've been infested. They may accidentally discover one or more, but that's okay. It's no secret that we're here. By now, they're fully aware of that fact. These people are not fools. Far from it. But they won't find them all—and we only need one to pick up what we need to know. Then we act." Edmond's grin widened.

ADRIANA SHIVERED AS SHE GLANCED AROUND the dungeon. "It's so damp, and the remnant of torture chain hooks on the walls...."

"They give us all the willies, darlin'," Al assured her. "This morning's rain has increased the level of dampness. But it won't affect my trusty portable penetrating sonic-wave detector."

"Isn't there a more technical name for that unit?" A.T. asked.

"Yea. But it's too technical sounding. Confusing. My name for it is simple enough for even *you* to understand."

A.T.'s eyes rolled in Rance's direction. Picking up on his Italian friend's frustration, he said, "L' Ami, get that contraption up and running—and Arturo, which wall do you want him to scan first?"

A.T. bumped Al aside, walked to the far right hand wall, and tapped a spot with his finger. "Start here and move a few feet in either direction. If you look close, you can just make out the difference in texture and rock color. This area," he said, brushing a palm over a five-by-five section of the wall, "if I'm correct, is not as old as the surrounding wall. It looks as though there may have been a passage here at one time. A doorway perhaps. One that at some point in time was sealed closed."

"Arturo, open that metal box by your foot and flip the switches to activate the batteries. Rance, keep an eye on the monitor inside. When I move this six-foot-long wand from right to left—watch for a change in shades of gray. Sound waves emanating from minute holes in the bar will penetrate the wall. Dark gray will indicate a thickness of about three feet. That's where I have it set for now. We can change the depth later if need be. If we hit a spot more than three feet thick—a light gray tone will appear."

A.T. flipped the switches and added his two cents. "And next, we'll try it on his lordship's noggin to see if there's any gray matter still functioning."

Al held the wand vertically, nodded at the three women and said, "Excuse me, ladies," then gave the baldheaded fireplug a typical Italian salute using the back of his hand and chin.

Adriana turned to her new friends and said with a disgusted tone, "They don't ever stop, do they?"

Mac raised a brow and answered her remark. "Don't say we didn't warn you."

"Can we please…?" Rance groaned impatiently, pointing to the wall.

Slowly, Al moved the long vibrating wand from right to left. "Solid gray," Rance observed.

Strong vibration forced Al to use both hands as he worked his way left. "Nothing yet…no, wait…we're beginning to see a change in tone. Keep moving. Slower," Rance suggested.

"There!" Arturo exclaimed, watching the monitor. "Just as I suspected. The area you're passing over now is not as thick. Keep going. See how wide the opening is."

Al continued. "He's right," Rance said. "We're back to solid gray now."

"That does not necessarily tell us what we want to know," Al said, staring at the grinning Italian. "Sorry to bust your bubble, mate. It could be that there's just a difference in wall thickness. To be certain, I need to adjust the sonic depth. There should be packed earth behind this entire wall. We're well below the ground surface. I'll adjust both the sonic power and depth of the probe to seven feet—then we'll see if there's space behind the light gray area—or solid dirt." He glanced over to his smiling wife and winked.

The process was repeated. "Solid gray as before," Rance announced.

Moments passed and A.T. pumped his arm. "I knew it! Nothing but light gray." He smacked Rance on the shoulder. "There's your tunnel."

"Time for an assessment meeting," Rance announced, walking over to the huge wooden table used by a past owner as a wine tasting table, complete with dozens of rickety wooden straight back chairs. To the far left were the remnants of several worm-eaten wine racks. Motioning with his head, he said, "From a torture chamber to a wine cellar—perfect chilling conditions for both activities."

Adriana whispered to her husband, "And he has ice water in his veins." Al pretended not to hear and hoped Mac had not.

Everyone occupied an uncomfortable wobbly chair. "We need to accomplish three tasks simultaneously," Rance said. *One*—chip a hole just large enough for someone to crawl into the sealed passageway. Later we'll reseal the wall to hide the evidence of our damage. *Two*—discover where this passageway exits within the chapel. *Three*—be on the lookout for the Bishop and his goons."

"There's a small shack on the far side of the chapel where the workmen store their tools," Arturo said. "I'm sure there's a sledgehammer that will fit my hands."

"Excellent. A.T., go now: retrieve your hammer while I explain steps two and three. I'll crawl into the passageway. Al and Adriana will enter the chapel and wait for my signal—and search for the exit. It too, is probably sealed at that end."

"How will we be in contact with you?" Adriana asked.

"It's all in your husband's bag of tricks." Rance stood and walked to where Al had set down several canvas bags. He held up a miniature featherweight wireless ear pod receiver with a short fiber optic mike. "We have a set for each of us. This way, we can all stay in touch."

He nodded to Mac and Tina. "This brings me to the third phase of this morning's activity. We need lookouts placed in strategic positions—watching for any breach of the grounds by the bad guys."

"I was wondering if you were going to include us," Mac said sarcastically. Then added with a smile, "You know how *you* are."

Ignoring the comment, he continued. "There are two non-glare high-powered army binoculars with your names on them. Tina, did you climb trees when you were little?"

"I was always mother's tomboy—why?"

"There's a stand of tall oak trees on the ridge beyond Rosslyn Chapel. Someone hidden and perched among the thick branches—with the aid of binoculars—could scan for miles. That's your assignment.

"Mac, you'll camp in the attic of the castle house. There's a small window facing the approach by way of the winding road. You'll be able to observe anyone coming at us from that direction."

"That still makes us vulnerable to an approach from the castle house ravine—as well as a section of the far glen—which is Tina's blind spot," L' Ami reminded him.

"Once the wall is open and Rance is inside the passageway, I'll solve that problem," Arturo said, bounding down the worn stone steps with sledgehammer in hand. "I cannot fathom any one of the Bishop's bunch, much less the fat SOB himself, climbing up that steep ravine. I'll perch myself atop the castle ruins facing the glen and keep an eye out."

"Will you need a boost up the ruined wall?" Al asked with a grin. A.T. squinted and shook the hammer in his friend's direction. Adriana glanced at Mac for help. Mac looked away and shook her head. There was no changing the three musketeers after all these years.

"Any questions?" Rance asked. No response.

"Good. A.T., *take down that wall*," he pointed, anticipating a chorus of groans, but could not help himself. "Everyone, don your ear pods—Tina, Mac, pick up your binoculars. Al, switch on the transmitter. Let's stay in touch. And good hunting." Rance paused. "Don't know why I said that. It just sounded good." This time they all groaned.

"I'M INSIDE. THE SPIDERS HAVE FOUND A HOME," Rance said, speaking into a thin black curved cable protruding from his right ear to the corner of his mouth. "A.T., with your love of the furry webmakes—this should have been your assignment."

A shiver ran down Arturo's spine. "I wouldn't spoil your sense of adventure, old friend. I'm out of here, heading for the old ruins behind the chapel."

"Everyone in place?" Rance asked. One by one, they all responded in the positive.

Aiming the beam straight ahead, he illuminated the entire narrow passageway beneath the ground from the castle house to the chapel. "This tunnel was crudely carved out of rock and earth—although the flooring is packed solid," he said, providing a walking narrative of his surroundings. "Just up ahead, there's a small fracture in the concave ceiling. Nothing much. Merely a slight cave-in. Years of heavy rain seeped through a small fissure. I'm surprised that there's not more damage."

"Is the tunnel straight, or curving left or right?" Al asked. "And how far do you estimate you've come?"

"I paced off the distance from the castle house door to the chapel's side door earlier this morning. It took me two hundred and forty-two long strides. Thus far, I've walked eight strides—so I'm approximately one-third of the way to you and Adriana."

Skirting around a pile of rocks and fallen dirt, Rance asked, "How about our spotters—all clear?" Three voices acknowledged all was clear. No sign of the French quartet. "Good. No telling when the snakes will raise their ugly heads."

"We're on the bottom level of the chapel in the area of the Templar graves," Adriana said, glanced over at her husband and shrugged both shoulders. This was all new to her. Her adrenalin level was at its peak.

Rance coughed and took a deep breath. "Thick must, dampness, and lack of fresh air are smothering," he complained. "Now the tunnel is slanting down a bit and I'm forced to stoop lower than before."

"Must be hard on an old man's back," A.T. broke in.

"The old man just passed another small collapse in the tunnel wall. But as before, it's nothing to be concerned about." He coughed again. "Now I'm two-thirds through. Al, try tapping on the wall. The sound may give me an idea of your location. When I come to a dead end, I'll ask you to stop, and I'll begin tapping with my crowbar."

Stepping over and around horizontal coffin-like raised sculptures of knights in full battle armor, Al tapped the white stone wall facing the direction of the tunnel with a small hammer. He glanced behind him and addressed Adriana. "I hope I don't wake any of them?"

"That's not funny," she said with a scowl. "Not funny one bit." There was no place to hide, so he turned and continued a steady tap.

"Remember, we all can hear you guys," Rance warned. "If you two love birds are through bickering—maybe it's time to listen for my taps. Al, I'm to the end of the tunnel and can't wait to get out of here. There appears to be a sealed door of some kind. Stop and listen for me." He began tapping. Lightly at first, then much harder. He wanted out in the worst way. It was becoming harder and harder to breathe.

"Turn your mike off, Rance," Al suggested. "We can hear your tapping as it's amplified from your side—not on this side of the wall. But leave your earpiece in to hear me."

Rance pushed the toggle button and proceeded to tap. "Nothing here," Al said. "We'll move further into the chamber where there's a small private altar. From the carvings of a large Templar cross, I'd say it was a burial altar for services of those knights whose likenesses decorate the stone floor."

Al and Adriana walked into a small chapel-like room decorated in similar fashion to the main chapel above. Flowers were carved into the low barrel ceiling: weight bearing marble pillars displayed delicately engraved designs and numerous duplicate carvings of the Green Man face mask seen just below the south window in the upstairs chapel. "The ugly gargoyle-looking faces—you call the Green Man—dominate throughout the room," L' Ami observed, pausing in the wide doorframe.

Adriana, about to lecture her husband on the various carvings, spun around and placed a well-manicured finger to her lips. "There," she pointed to the left-hand wall, "do you hear that?"

"Faintly."

Pressing an ear to the wall six feet behind the small stone altar, she said, "Rance, we can hear you. Tap harder."

Moving a few steps to her right, she nodded to Al. "You're in front of us, Rance—just behind this wall."

"There's a faint indentation in the form of an entry on my side," Rance replied. "What do you see on your side?"

"The same thing," Al said, "but it appears to be part of an elaborate design—with no visible levels—just a series of those ugly face masks the size of half a bowling ball."

L' Ami studied the masks and their placement: two rows, one seven feet up from the stone floor and the second at floor level. Then two more the size of half a tennis ball—one above, one below. He touched his forehead with the small hammer. "Hold onto your britches, my friend. An idea is forming. If I'm correct, you'll be with us in a matter of minutes."

He placed a palm on the mask to his far left. "Honey, when I say push—push this one's face in as hard as you can while I push the one to my right."

Adriana stood with arms by her side, eyebrows raised. "Please. Just do it. There has to be a mechanism here somewhere to release pins holding the entrance solid. See those two small masks?" he pointed to the one above and below. "If I'm right, they are two balls, that when pins are released, will allow the wall entrance to swivel open.

"Don't look at me that way. I saw this once in a movie." He gestured to the face before her and motioned with a nod to push.

They all heard Rance exclaim, "God help us all. He saw it at the movies."

"No snide remarks from the peanut gallery—or I'll seal up the other end of that tunnel—and the rest of us will head to Charlie's for liquid refreshment. Now honey, push."

They both grunted. Nothing happened. No sound or movement of any kind. "Okay. Let's try once more."

For the next five minutes they pushed the round grimacing face mask in every combination. Not a sound, except for their heavy breathing. "Try one at a time, alternating one mask after another. Perhaps a pattern is the key," Rance offered a suggestion.

"Wait," they heard Mac interrupt. "Where did you say the masks were placed on the wall?"

"Across the top, about two feet down from the ceiling—and across the bottom, about two feet above the floor," Adriana answered. "Plus, one in the middle of the wall."

"And where is the carved Templar cross you mentioned earlier?" Mac asked.

"On the opposite wall," Al answered.

"This is a long shot, but worth a try. There could be a T design representing a crucifix. Push the two outside masks, then the middle one, and the one just below the middle mask."

Al and Adriana glanced at each other. Al said, "Why not?"

Adriana shoved hard on the left mask. Al did the same with his, then repeated the effort by pushing the middle mask. When he pushed on the bottom mask, it moved slightly. He pushed harder. As it slid inside, the other three masks disappeared as well. Simultaneously, they heard a soft scraping sound. "Must have been the pins," Al deduced. "Well, I'll be damned," he added. "Mac, you're a genius."

"That's what she got from living with me," Rance chimed in. "Good work, partner." Mac remained silent, but he could imagine her wry smile.

"Now you two on the other side. Put your shoulders to the right side of the wall, and I'll do the same on the opposite side. Ready? On three. Three!"

The wall creaked and dust flew, but the slab only nudged slightly. "Three again!" Rance shouted. This time it opened a few inches.

"On the count of three once more," Al whispered in this mike, "but if you shout again in our ears, I'll put your ear pod where the sun doesn't shine, old friend."

"Sorry," Rance apologized. "I forgot I turned it back on. Uuuh." He squeezed his trim six-foot-one frame through the opening, shaking the dust from his hair. "Howdy, you' all. We're gonna have ta stop meetin' like this." Adriana turned her back and studied the Templar cross.

"Ignore him," Tina suggested. "Mac does."

Dust flew as Rance smacked his hands together. "Well, we learned two things this morning. *One*, the castle house dungeon tunnel exits into the small underground chapel. For what purpose? That's anyone's guess at this point…"

A.T., perched atop a ruined outside castle wall interjected a thought. "Maybe that's how my lovely wife's ghost, Sir William, came to our bedroom the other night."

"I can see you from where I'm wedged in a large fork in a tree. You better thank your Italian saints that I'm not cradling a sniper rifle in the crook of my arm, wise guy. From here, I could pick off that pesky fly buzzing around your shiny bald head."

"I don't like these damned ear pods, Rance. They shouldn't be authorized for wifely use." A.T. covered his head with both hands and added, "She's not kidding about picking off the fly. Tina was Italy's Olympic sharpshooter gold medal winner a few years back."

"What is the other thing we learned this morning?" Adriana asked, tired of all the interruptions.

"*Two*," Rance said, holding up two fingers. "We learned that those squinting ugly faces may be the device that could open secret—yet to be discovered—burial or treasure vaults that…"

A scream forced everyone to wince and tear off, then replace, their ear pods. "That was Mac's voice," Rance said, holding his earpiece tight. "Mac. Mac, are you all right? What's wrong?" Silence.

Squeezing back through the wall opening, he shouted over his shoulder, "Everyone except Tina—head for the castle house. Now!" Dashing back through the tunnel, he could hear Al and Adriana's footsteps at his heels.

It took him more time than he would have liked to reach the dungeon, then sprinted up the steps. As he passed the open castle house door, ready to head for the top floor where Mac was stationed, he heard a loud angry roar coming from outside. Changing direction, he burst through the door, ready to face whoever threatened Mac. Turning to his left, he saw Mac sitting on the grass at the edge of the deep ravine, an expression of surprise on her face. At first glance, she appeared unharmed.

Standing two feet away from his wife was a man with no neck, cropped bleached blond hair, and with both hands made into fists. His face was a bloody mess. He grunted aloud and raised his arms over his head, ready to charge his foe. Arturo lowered his head and sprang forward, burying his shiny dome into the man's midsection. The blow was so powerful, it lifted him off his feet and propelled him over the edge. A.T. stood, hands on hips, watching the man called Maurice bounce off a ledge of castle ruins and tumble into the darkened thick forest of trees below. Ignoring his audience of friends, he offered his hand to Mac, saying, "That one was for you, my dear."

"His bloody nose and lip was for me. The bastard!" Mac said in anger.

Seeing his wife all in one piece was a relief, to say the least. Rance held out one hand to Mac and the other to his friend. "It seems I'm always in debt to you, A.T."

Chapter Nine

"BISHOP, WHAT DID THE DOCTOR SAY? And how long will Maurice have to stay in the hospital?" Paschal asked, not that he really cared. He'd resented that they were now short-handed ever since Maurice was caught on the castle grounds and tossed into a ravine.

Claude bared his teeth in a false grin. "Why Paschal, Maurice would appreciate your concern for his welfare. He was examined by the hospital staff physician. Besides a broken nose, split lip, a deep gash along his hairline, two painful broken ribs—one on each side—and a mild concussion that will keep him under close surveillance overnight, your dear friend is no worse for wear."

"It might improve his looks," Edmond said with a chuckle.

"Wouldn't hurt him one bit," Paschal agreed.

"Enough nonsense," Claude said, smacking his palm on the small table in the tavern's dark corner. Lowering his voice, he asked, "Paschal, how many bugs were you three able to plant around the castle grounds before that idiot was caught?"

Wiping the beer foam from his lips with a sleeve, Paschal glanced at Edmond. "We're not sure that Maurice had the opportunity in the castle house—since that idiot went for the tall babe. Don't know what he was thinking when…"

"He was thinking with his crotch," Edmond interrupted.

"Yeah," Paschal said. "And it was a good thing that short bald-headed bastard got to him first. From the deadly look on her husband's face, if he had grabbed Maurice, Bishop would have visited him in the morgue."

"Back to my question," Claude demanded.

"We only had time to plant three before that woman screamed. Neither of us was going to stick around after that. He looked at Edmond. "He managed to plant a large bug in the waterfall cavern—and I placed one in the chapel's main room—and a second under an altar in a small room that the bearded one and his woman were searching."

Waving for another round of drinks, he went on. "They discovered a secret panel that led to a tunnel from the chapel to the castle house. It was left open after they all fled, using the tunnel as a shortcut to get to the castle house after they heard the scream in their ear pods. That's how they all kept in touch, Bishop."

Claude downed his tankard and nodded thanks to the barmaid for the ordered round. "I said it before. These people are no dummies. I don't know who they are—but they *are* dangerous—and there's little doubt that they are pros."

"You want I should call for reinforcements, Bishop? Paschal asked.

"No. Not just yet. We need to man the receiver day and night and see what we can pick up from their conversations in the chapel, and cave, if they go there. You two take turns. Maurice's no good 'til he's up and around."

Bishop made a chapel steeple with his fingers, touched his many chins, and with a sinister tone, said, "No. We'll play a waiting game. Out of sight—but not out of ear shot. We'll call in hired mercenaries when we're ready to eliminate those six after we have what we came for: the location of the Templar treasure."

"THE CASTLE HOUSE IS CLEAN," Al assured the group assembled in the drawing room.

"That clown wasn't snooping around by himself," Rance surmised. "We just didn't see the others. Sweep the chapel—top to bottom."

Rance nodded to A.T. "Why don't you join him."

Arturo gently punched L' Ami on his arm. "Good idea. I haven't had the opportunity to see or search the chapel in any detail. This will provide me the time. Let's go, Fuzzy."

Al raised both brows and caught his wife's eye. "This shouldn't take too long—and after I plant this wise ass Italian in one of the crypts…"

Adriana cut him short and with a straight face, warned, "I wouldn't do that if I were you. Unless you believe you can take care of his widow as well as your charming petite wife. That's the tradition in my family."

Arturo stopped in mid-stride, eyes widening, his face turning crimson as everyone had a hardy laugh. "Damn!" he muttered before slamming the door. "She's turned into one of us."

Before entering the chapel, Al placed a finger to his lips. "We don't know if bugs were planted in there—so let's play it cool. If they're listening, they'll be aware that we're inside and moving around. So let's give them something to listen to." Reaching for the door handle, he continued. "How long did you plead with Tina to marry an overweight baldheaded has-been?" Al deftly dodged a well aimed boot.

Inside, the two friends split up. While Al quietly swept the main chapel with his portable device, A.T. wandered around gawking at the incredible workmanship. "It's beyond me to grasp how such delicate carving could be accomplished. Of course, I said that about Mike's work at the Vatican."

"Mike's work?" Al shouted from the far corner.

"Yeah! You heard of Michael Angelo. All we Italians are on a first name basis." L' Ami refused to enter the game. He had found Paschal's first planted bug. Wildly waving his arms, he attracted A.T.'s attention. Pointing to the electronic snooper hidden behind the lacework of the Apprentice Column, he shook his head, and again placed a finger to his lips. A.T. understood the silent message. For now, it was better to leave it in place and not alert the Bishop and his men.

Al strolled under every arched entry and exit—crawled beneath small and large altars and overhanging ledges—without further success. The main floor of the chapel was clean with the exception of the one bug hidden in the decorative column. Commanding his friend's attention, he pointed to the stairway to the bottom floor where they had discovered the tunnel to the castle house. A.T. nodded and led the way.

Arturo motioned for Al to follow, then he placed a hand on the still-open tunnel entrance, and with his head indicated that the Frenchman should lend a shoulder and help close the pivoting stone. Once sealed, Al went about his bug search. A.T. set about investigating the numerous crypts with carvings of the lord knights lying prone above their ancient bones.

In a matter of minutes L' Ami discovered another bug and turned to find A.T., sitting on the chest of a dignified knight, cleaning his finger nails. Breaking his rule of silence, he shouted, "Hey! Italian. Have some respect for your elders. That better not be Sir William you're desecrating—or he may come calling on you tonight and not your wife..." He made a slashing motion with his finger across his throat. "...and even after all these years, I bet his sword's as sharp as ever."

A.T. leapt up, turned, and brushed the dust from his pants and from Sir William's shield—then bent low and whispered, "No offense intended, my lord."

"I hope he heard you and forgave your insult—if not you're in deep do-do," Al chuckled. Motioning Arturo to the far corner of the stairway alcove, he said in a soft voice, "The idiots are not too innovative. Found a bug under the lip of that small altar. There are only two planted. One upstairs and one down. There may be others scattered about, but the castle house is clean, and we know that the chapel is only slightly dirty. Let's head back."

When they entered the castle house foyer, Arturo found six modern folding chairs and a large folding table leaning against the wall next to the entrance. He frowned at Al, whose eyes were fixed on the foyer table. A half-dozen bottles of wine, a large wicker basket, and an open canvas bag filled with napkins and a tablecloth sat atop the table. "Someone having a picnic?" Arturo asked the bug man.

"How observant: you'd make a great investigator some day," came a voice from the drawing room—followed by female giggles. Stepping into the foyer, Rance gave orders. "Al, you carry the table. A.T. the chairs. I'll handle the food basket and carryall. The ladies will carry two bottles each."

A.T. hooked three chairs under each arm and bowed his head to Rance. "Where to...master?"

"Head to the middle of the glen, just west of the castle wall ruins. Find a nice level spot—minding cow or sheep dungs." He turned to Al. "With your electronic gadget—will you be able to detect a long distance eavesdropping device aimed in our direction?" Al picked up the table and nodded, yes.

"Good. We're going to have a picnic, enjoy fine wine, tasty food, the day, and devise a plan to smoke out the enemy before we search any further."

L' Ami balanced the table atop his head and followed Arturo into the grassy glen. "It's about time we saw some action," he said with a grin. Then added, "A.T. will get all he bargained for this evening when Sir William comes to defend his honor."

Holding two bottles by their necks, Tina ran to catch up to her husband. "What does he mean, 'when Sir William comes to defend his honor.' ?"

As strong as he was, Arturo struggled with the six chairs. They were heavier than they looked. Avoiding Tina's searching eyes, he explained. "Don't pay any mind to the ramblings of a man on his honeymoon. He'll say most anything to get attention."

"If I don't get a straight answer, you don't get any wine, big boy. You know how sensitive I am about Sir William."

A.T. swerved, bumping Al with his hip. Al staggered and nearly dropped the table. "That's what you get—big mouth," Arturo growled.

"It was nothing," A.T. said to Tina. "I happened to sit on top of one of the carved prone statues of one of the knights to dislodge a small grain of sand that had wedged its way under my thumb nail. Nothing that would make your Sir William angry. Hell. I don't even know if it was his grave." Throwing the chairs to the ground, he shouted to the stragglers. "This is as good a place as any. And you, wife, this is one hell of a dumb argument."

"DID YOU MAKE THE CALL last night?" Bishop asked Paschal.

"Yeah. But you said that there was no need for reinforcements right now," Paschal answered with a scowl at his other two associates.

"We could handle those amateurs ourselves, boss," Edmond complained with a bitter tone.

Bishop motioned to Maurice, who had not grunted a word in days. "Just ask your partner there. That short Italian ball of muscle made a believer of him." Maurice glared out of the eye without the gauze patch.

"Who do we have coming, and when will they arrive?" Bishop turned again to his second in command, Paschal.

"Six of the nastiest and toughest former IRA thugs that Ireland ever produced. Their active days are numbered and they're willin' to hire out to the highest bidder. They should show their ugly faces sometime midday tomorrow." Paschal met the eyes of Edmond and Maurice, then flashed them on his boss. "No disrespect—but I don't like the idea of outsiders knowin' our business. Hell, they might…"

"Give me more credit, doubting Paschal," Bishop interrupted with a dramatic wave of his hand. "Your dirty half-dozen will not be made privy as to *why* they are targeting those within the castle—only that they are to eliminate the three couples. No more. That way if something unforeseen happens—we remain as white as the driven snow." Bishop laughed so hard he nearly slipped off the chair struggling under his weight. "And then we eliminate the eliminators.

"Why, my good fellow, I might even decide to wrap my person in white rather than black." Paschal and Edmond joined in the laughter. Maurice clamped his teeth shut. Had he felt Bishop's joke was the slightest bit humorous, he would not have even ventured a small grin. It would have been too painful.

WARMED BY BOTH SUN AND WINE, laughter and good cheer bounced off the dirty gray ruined walls of the extended castle grounds within throwing distance of their table. The picnic was a success and lifted the spirits of the six friends whose recent days were weighted with intrigue. Arturo was his old self, telling jokes and playing the court jester. Even Lord L' Ami laughed at the jokes he had often heard.

It was agreed that they would go to town that evening to visit Roslin Glen Hotel's tavern, schmooze with their barkeep friend, Charlie, enjoy a few bottles of Belhaven Best, and have a leisurely dinner. They deserved the pressure-free evening, considering their plan to draw out Bishop and his men. The ladies decided to wear dresses and shelve the khaki working outfits. "Okay." Rance said, rubbing his palms together. "What say we gentlemen strut our stuff in *our* finest wardrobe?"

Al laughed. "Well said, fearless leader. I plan to wear my black dress overalls with a crisp new Scottish plaid shirt."

"Are they the same overalls you had dyed black for Tina's and my wedding?" A.T. asked with raised eyebrows. "What happened to that great looking blue silk shirt you used to wear for special occasions?"

L' Ami's face formed a pained expression. "You've got a short memory old friend. I was wearing that shirt waiting for Antonio to return to the villa the night that she attempted to kill you and Tina—and she gut-shot me before I broke her miserable She-Wolf neck."

Silence. Adriana, aware of the incident that had nearly taken Al's life last year, squeezed his arm. The other couples exchanged glances and shrugged their shoulders: no one wanted to relive the moment. A.T. shook his head at his friend: it was a silent *I'm sorry* message.

"Well, I don't know about you ladies, but I'm looking forward to dressing up this evening," Mac said, breaking the awkward moment. Standing, she began to gather the assorted empty bottles and leftovers. Within seconds, Tina and Adriana lent helping hands. Their husbands folded the chairs and table. A happy, relaxed gang headed toward the castle house to rest and freshen up for their big evening on the town. Rance's mind wandered ahead. Would the Bishop and his cutthroats come out from under the rocks? He'd talk with Arturo and Al, reminding them of the danger lurking in the shadows.

As usual, the three gents were dressed and sitting in the drawing room waiting for their wives. Rance had just finished his warning when three bouquets of spring flowers appeared in the arched doorway. Each woman wore a full skirted silk flowered dress. Mac was in yellow, Tina in purple, and Adriana in red. Like a Broadway musical, they flowed through the arch, bowed, twirled so the skirts bellowed full—stood side by side—kicked their right legs high. In a flash turned their backs and like can-can girls of Paris, bent over as they flipped their skirts to reveal matching flowered panties.

Three male mouths fell agape. Once the initial shock flew, they bent over in hysterics. "Damn!" A.T. shouted. "That was worth the price of admission."

"You should set that routine to music," L' Ami choked, wiping a tear from his eye.

"Now we know why you three were taking so long. You were practicing the can-can," Rance added, still laughing.

Separating, the women searched out their respective husbands to compliment them on their attire. Mac fawned over Rance's brown plaid sport coat, light tan mock turtle shirt, and lightweight brown corduroy slacks. Tina was all smiles as she recalled the tweed sport coat, rust-colored shirt, and slacks Arturo had worn the night that they had met for the first time in seven years. "I like the black and white plaid shirt. It goes well with your black dress overalls," Adriana said, giving Al a butterfly kiss.

"And I like the red flowered panties," he whispered back.

"Oh, someone shoot me," A.T. groaned. "I need a drink."

CHARLIE ANNOUNCED THE FIRST ROUND OF DRINKS was on the house in honor of his new friend Sir Sean Connery. Taking advantage of Lord Alvin L' Ami's new-found benefactor, a round of Belhaven Best was delivered to the back table. This was an evening to enjoy, but much was yet to be discussed, and now was good a time as any. According to Rance—how they were going to smoke out Bishop and company was at the top of the agenda. They now knew where two of the bugs were planted in the chapel. Tonight in whispers they would plan the announcement of a major discovery to lure the Bishop into a trap.

"Okay," Arturo said, raising an eyebrow in Rance's direction and signaling for another round. "What devious scheme do you have in mind to smoke out the bad guys?"

Savoring the last drop and shoving his empty tankard to the edge of the table, Rance answered just above a whisper. "Tomorrow, we all make a full assault on the chapel: figuratively, we turn the place upside down. Make a lot of noise above and below. About noon time, Tina shouts she's discovered a secret compartment hidden under Sir William's shield."

"You mean the shield that covers his prone statue covering the tomb?" Tina asked.

"The one and only. We come on the run. His statue is close to the bug under the small altar—so there's no doubt the Bishop will hear."

"And just what will we discover?" Adriana asked with anticipation.

"How about a map that shows the location of a treasure consisting of ancient relics and gold coins?" There were grins and nods all around. "That should appeal to their greed, don't you think? Enough to stir them into action: perhaps they'll make their move that evening. We'll announce an early bedtime so we're well rested and ready to leave the castle grounds in search of the treasure the next morning."

"And we'll be ready for the bastards," A.T. added.

RANCE AND MAC SEARCHED THE WEST CORNER of the main chapel: Al and Adriana took the east side. Arturo and Tina rummaged in the underground chapel where the small altar and the prone statues of the knights were located close by. Hours passed. It was noon. Suddenly, Tina shouted, "I've found something! I've found something! There's a secret compartment under the shield over one of the knight's statue."

A.T. confirmed the find. "You guys: she's found it. Looks like an old sheepskin map."

"Looks stiff," Al said, peering over his friend's shoulder.

Rance wedged his way in between. "Careful when you open it: it could crack."

A.T. ran his finger over a blank slice of sheepskin they had purchased the previous night in town before heading back to the castle house. "Rance, it's written in Latin. What's it say?"

Taking the sheepskin from Arturo, he played his part. "It's smudged—but there's no doubt it shows the location to some sort of treasure." He paused as if to study it further. "See here," he pointed. "That's the Knights Templar symbol. And this line mentions a cache of religious relics." Another brief pause. "And something here. It's hard to make out the words—but looks like that there's a chest of gold coins stashed with the relics."

"That's proof enough for me," L' Ami said excitedly, raising his voice while facing the altar. "Let's pack up and head for the booty."

"No," Rance countered. "We need more time to study this old map in relation to current maps of the area—then make transportation arrangements. No. We'll retire early tonight and head out before sunup. I'll stash the map behind Sir William's portrait in the drawing room. It'll be safe there."

BISHOP AND HIS MEN HAD HEARD IT ALL. Excited, they could feel gold coins weighing down their pockets. Not to mention what they would get in ransom for the holy relics, perhaps in a bidding war with international collectors.

Paschal made his call to the mercenaries. "Their orders are to snatch the sheepskin map from behind the portrait of the knight—then eliminate all six occupants of the castle house."

Edmond laughed. "Or, whichever comes first."

Paschal continued. "After it's done, we're to meet the IRA men on the outskirts of town. There's an old, abandoned sheep shearing station," he grinned, "appropriate enough—three miles off the main road coming in from Edinburgh. Maurice and Edmond will come in through the loading doors, guns blazing. You, boss, and I will come in the front door moments later, so as not to get caught in a crossfire. We relieve the bodies of the map and head for our reward."

Bishop and his men had no idea that they had been set up for a fall—and Rance and his team had no idea that they would be dealing with six hardened and well-armed IRA mercenaries.

SPREAD OUT, SIX SHADOWS DASHED TOWARD THE CASTLE HOUSE. Dressed in black, carrying machine pistols, they noted with interest that all the lights were out in the target's roost. Flattening themselves against the outside stone walls, weapons upright, one motioned to the far right-hand window. A single nightlight glowed dimly in what the castle house floor plan indicated would be the drawing room. A giant of a man, obviously the leader of the assassination team, pointed to himself and gestured to another, a much smaller man—then pointed to the window with the light indicating that they would get the map. A beefy finger pointed upstairs and swept the finger to the remaining four men. They were to eradicate those sleeping upstairs.

Placing a hand on the latch and a shoulder on the door, he twisted and shoved. The unlocked door inched open. Turning, he showed a row of brown stained teeth. This was going to be easy: nodding to the others, he slowly slipped inside. The big man moved like an athlete. Crepe soles tread quietly. Two men moved to their right as four headed in single file, weapons at the ready, toward the left and the stairs leading up to the sleeping quarters.

Suddenly, dazzling bright lights and loud blasts of Beethoven's Fifth Symphony startled the intruders. Momentarily blinded and confused, the attackers froze, except one. The trigger finger of the last man walking single file twitched, nearly cutting the third man in half. Several slugs passed through the body, tearing into the second man's back. Two of Bishop's assassins were down. Four to go.

Unable to get off a shot, or he'd take out the remaining two by the stairs, their leader hesitated. Rance leapt up from behind a bookcase to the right of the portrait and spun on one foot, the other sweeping the weapon from the big man's hands. As the smaller man turned to assist his boss, A.T., rushing from a crouched position behind the couch, buried his head in the man's stomach, driving him into the wall with a bone-crushing sound. The man's neck had snapped, and Arturo lay prone, dizzy from the impact.

When the trigger-happy assassin sprayed two team members, it had surprised the lead man, who had nearly reached the top of the stairs. He then turned from the carnage over his shoulder to face those above. Taking him by surprise, Al's boot caught him under the nose, driving the bone deep into his skull. He crumpled like an accordion. Dead.

Heads snapped toward a resounding noise coming from the arched kitchen doorway, followed by a spray of bullets hitting the tin ceiling. Al smiled as he made his way, stepping across the three bodies on the stairs. He recognized the sound. He had heard the same sound when Adriana cold-cocked the Bishop with her frying pan in her brother's restaurant.

In shock from what he had just witnessed, the big man, the only one of the mercenary team of six still standing, flexed his muscles and snarled at Rance. Whipping a pistol from a belt holster, he waved it about, threatening Rance's life. "No!" shouted a female voice to his right. "That one will kill you with ease. It would take me one minute longer."

Arturo was still shaking his head to clear the cobwebs when he looked up in dismay at Tina taunting the mountain of a man. She stood legs apart: her arms were spread out, fingers making a *come to me* gesture. "Put the gun away big boy or I'll whip your ass."

A.T. held his breath as Rance backed away, concerned he'd pull the trigger. The lone assassin roared with laughter. "When I've shot these two," he quickly glanced at Rance and Arturo, "and the others—your ass will be mine, sweet cheeks. And then we'll have some real Irish fun."

His brows furrowed. A creaking sound from behind caught his attention. As he slowly turned his head, the portrait of Sir William with its heavy frame came crashing down, the top of the frame splintering as it hit the top of his head. Stunned, but still on his feet, the weapon fell from his hand.

Rance moved in for the kill, but stopped when Tina shouted, "No! I'll take care of this pile of Irish manure—as I said I would."

Their hesitation provided the opportunity for the big man to collect his wits. He lunged for the pistol and was bringing it up to arms length when Tina crouched, slipped a small Italian dagger from an ankle holster, and underhanded, flung the blade. Falling to his knees, he clutched his throat where the dagger was lodged. His eyes bulged in disbelief. Blood bubbled from a mouth omitting a deep gurgling sound. Rance placed a boot on his shoulder and gave it a shove. Now all six would-be assassins lay dead.

Tina pried the dead man's fingers from the dagger hilt and looked up at Rance. "He's wired. Bishop heard it all."

With Tina's dagger, Arturo sliced open the assassin's black pullover, exposing wires. "She's right. Now he knows it was a setup."

Yanking the device from the dead man's body, Rance crushed the mini-transmitter under his heel. "And that's all he'll get."

Tina picked up the fallen portrait of the knight and leaned it against the wall. "The top of the frame is only cracked, and the painting itself has not been damaged. It appears that Sir William was true to his word. He was looking out for me…"

"Oh come now," Arturo moaned, interrupting. "When this guy," he said, nudging a boot against the man with the broken neck, "hit the wall, the impact loosened the nail holding the portrait."

Tina's eyes flashed. "You believe what you want…I'll believe what I want. It was Sir William to the rescue." From the fire in her eyes, A.T. knew better than to pursue the discussion.

Mac was now in the room. She had been behind Al on the top of the stairs and missed much of the action. "We'll need you, Tina and Adriana to dispose of the bodies," Rance said, noting the wincing look on his wife's face, "And clean up as best you can. Sorry, honey—but A.T., Al and I have a date with the Bishop and his crew."

"Are we heading for their inn?" A.T. asked, rubbing his palms together. Rance nodded yes.

With hands on hips, Mac challenged her husband's orders. "Great! You guys have all the fun, and we girls get the dirty work." She pointed to the fallen leader of the dead assassins and shook her long hair from side to side. "And what do you recommend we do with them—wall 'em up in the dungeon?"

Rance displayed a wide smile. "Why didn't I think of that?"

"You can't be serious?" Adriana asked skeptically.

"Yes, I am. While you three clean up as best you can, we three will carry the bodies to the dungeon before we go after Bishop. Later you can drag them into the tunnel—then replace the stones, sealing the hole we crawled through. The chapel side of the tunnel is already sealed.

They won't be found until the next time someone excavates the tunnel." He shrugged his shoulders. "Besides, how could we explain this carnage to local authorities? We'd be tied up in red tape for weeks and our search would come to a screeching halt."

"It will be difficult enough explaining the blood on the hardwood floor and walls, and holes in the tin ceiling," Mac added. "You guys do what you have to—we'll do our part. Soap and water, and a good scrubbing can do wonders. Right ladies?" Tina and Adriana nodded in agreement.

"Mixing water with dirt scraped from the dungeon floor will quickly harden after we fill the mud around the cracks between the replaced stones," Tina suggested.

"If we toss dry dirt on the surface while it's still wet, it'll appear old and dusty: no one would ever know that an entrance ever existed," Adriana offered.

"Hey," Al said. "Sounds like you've done this before."

Adriana winked at Mac. "Why yes, my dear. And no one ever found the body of my first husband."

"*Dio Mio!*" A.T. shuttered. "She's one of us."

Lord Alvin L' Ami displayed a perplexed expression.

Chapter Ten

THREE TIRED AND FRUSTRATED FRIENDS returned to the castle house after six hours of an exhausting search for Bishop and his three henchmen. The drowsy-eyed innkeeper had explained that the four men had left without notice in the middle of the night. The sound of tires spitting gravel had pulled him and his wife from a sound sleep. All he could remember was that their car had taken the Edinburgh road over an hour and a half ago.

Rance explained to the wives sprawled on the couch and plush chairs that they had pushed the SUV at top speed in pursuit to the airport. No planes had taken off in the past four hours except a chartered plane that had left minutes earlier. "You just missed your friends," the attendant on duty informed them. "An' noo, I arenae obliged tae provide passenger names, number o' persons, oor destination. I'm sorry, gentlemen."

A.T.'s eyes searched the dimly lit drawing room. "Wow. You ladies did a marvelous clean-up job." He looked to the ceiling. "And how in the heck did you fix the bullet holes?"

"Gray duct tape matched the gray tin ceiling. We merely cut circles to plug the holes," Tina said proudly. "And as you can see, the portrait of my hero Sir William again hangs proudly on the wall."

"We simply straightened the frame: the ornate carvings hid any damage. Then duct-taped the back, and like magic, it looks new," Mac finished the explanation.

"Wonder what Sir William would have done with duct tape in his day?" A.T. pondered aloud, thought a minute, and added, "Probably used it to tape a sarcastic wife's mouth…" A size four and a half slipper sailed over his head. They were too tired to laugh but managed.

"Wait till you see the job we did in the dungeon," Adriana said with a yawn.

"If I ever come up missing," Al warned, "check the cellar in my estate first. I'll probably be behind one of the walls."

"Or a hole in the floor," Adriana added, then stretched and headed toward their bedroom. The other couples followed her lead. It had been a long and trying day.

"WELL, ONE THING ABOUT TODAY'S CHAPEL SEARCH," A.T. said, "we don't have to worry about Bishop and his goons listening or sneaking about."

Rance shook his head. "I've got a nagging feeling that we haven't seen the last of that bunch. The big guy didn't appear to me like someone who would give up easily. No. His greed is as large as his girth. We had better stay on our toes."

"And speaking of toes, Tina, did you ever find that slipper?" Al laughed, finishing his last cup of coffee and bite of egg.

"*Si*. I threatened not to sleep in the same bed with the Italian stud if he didn't retrieve it for me—but now he's all huffy over our nocturnal visitor."

She had everyone's attention. A.T. rolled his eyes. Tina read their collective minds. "Right. Sir William appeared this morning while the human battering ram snored like a drunken sailor."

"What did he have to say this time?" Mac asked.

"He thanked me for believing in him," she answered, sticking her tongue out at her husband. "And I thanked him for honoring his word to protect me. Then he smiled, nodded, and dissolved into thin air."

"Too bad he didn't tell you where to find the treasure," Arturo said.

"What? And take all the fun out of this morning's search," Rance said, dumping his plate in a sink full of soapy hot water.

One by one, the treasure hunters deposited their breakfast dishes and followed their leader over to the chapel. As before, they split up in pairs. The Testaccio team was assigned to the lower and smaller chapel: teams Rance and L' Ami gave the main chapel their attention.

Dozens of ornate columns, including the delicately carved apprentice marble column were inspected, not once, but several times by both teams. Wooden cabinets were opened, and bibles and vestments closely looked at: even the numerous stained-glass windows were scrutinized for possible clues. Ceiling carvings were examined, and small sculptures of angels and masks were checked to see if, after twisted, pulled, and shoved, a secret compartment would open.

Hours passed quickly, but the silence and sense of creating a sacrilege in a holy place weighed heavily on their consciences. Whenever Adriana passed in front of the main altar, she had the urge to kneel and ask forgiveness for trespassing in this house of God and history. Mac later confessed that she too felt a certain unease, as though she should be there to pray, not seek treasure.

Beneath their feet in the smaller chapel, the Testaccio team had worked their way from the stairway, past the knights' tombs and small altar, and now edged their way toward the corner void of any religious icons. It appeared that whoever designed and built Rosslyn Chapel did not complete the job. Or whatever had been there had been removed.

"You continue," A. T. said to Tina, "I'm going back to the castle house for the portable sonic-wave earth-penetrating detector and a large electric lamp." He motioned behind him with a nod. "Not to worry—Sir William here will protect you." He dashed off when she leaned down to take off her boot.

Stopping to tell the others where he was going, Arturo mentioned the bare corner floor and wall. "It doesn't make sense—all the marvels of art and history above and below—then nothing at the far end. I'm going to scope for a hidden tunnel or tomb."

"I don't know about you guys," Rance said, rubbing his stomach, "but all this searching is making me hungry—it's after three o'clock." He looked at Mac. "How about you ladies accompanying A.T. to the castle house and bringing back a stack of sandwiches and a couple bottles of wine? I'm going to have another peek under the altar."

Tina and A.T. had joined the others for a late but welcome lunch. Now she and Arturo stood before the bare wall. Tina aimed a huge spotlight, and A.T. aimed the ground-penetrating wand. As he worked the electronic equipment from one corner to the other, she moved the wide beam of light in sync with him. "Nothing," he mumbled in disgust. "I was certain we'd find something. It had all the earmarks."

Pointing the bright beam to the floor, she said, "Don't give up, big boy—let's give the floor the once-over."

"Whoa!" he shouted. Four feet from the left-hand wall, Arturo noted a light shadow. "Run up and holler for the others. I think we've found either a tunnel or tomb. And ask Al to bring some digging tools."

Arturo explained to Rance and the three women that the shadowed area was the only place along the wall or floor that showed up on the monitor, and that from the measurements, the depth to the target was only three feet below the surface and the depth of the tunnel or tomb, eight feet.

Out of breath, Al skidded to a halt on the dirt floor, two shovels and a pickax in hand. A.T. relieved his friend of a pick, waving him away. "My find, my dig. Back out of the way, everybody."

The last ten feet of flooring in the dark area of the lower chapel was hardened earth, but Arturo's strength was up to the task. Within minutes, he had loosened up an area of about one foot deep and four foot square. Tina passed him a bottle of water. Rance reached for A.T.'s pick, but he refused to hand it over. "You two," he gestured to Rance and Al, "grab yourselves a shovel and clear away what's there—then I'll continue."

Al rested on his shovel handle as A.T. came close to breaking through. "Bet you ten to one, it's an entrance to one of the tunnels we discovered the other day that leads from the chapel to the waterfall cavern."

A.T. wiped his brow with the back of his hand and nodded. "And I won't take that bet because I believe you're right—unless what appears to be a tunnel also feeds off into a sealed tomb of sorts."

"Rumors of yet to be discovered tombs of knights and treasure abound," Adriana assured them. "Trouble is, one never can be certain where rumor and truth meet until whatever it is—is uncovered."

Lord L' Ami glanced at his wife, then at his two longtime friends. "Did I tell you two that if I turn up missing—check the walls *and* floors at my villa?"

Not batting an eyelash, Adriana retaliated, "They'd be looking in all the wrong places, my dear husband. Brother's large restaurant kitchen has a huge pot where he has been known to cook a large goat…"

Al threw both hands in the air. "Who invited her along?" he moaned aloud. "Rance. You and your big mouth."

"Um!" Mac cleared her throat. "Enough! Let's get back to the game at hand. Adriana won that round. Now dig."

With a grumble under his breath, Al went at the loosened earth with a vengeance. Four more swings with the pickax and A.T. broke through. It took five minutes for the three men to clear away the opening of an eight-foot by eight-foot tunnel that faced the direction of the waterfall cavern. Al was right.

"My find. My dig. I'm the first in," A.T. boasted. "Someone hand me that electric lantern. Let's see what this baby looks like."

Arturo disappeared from sight. His voice sounded hollow. "Looks to be in fairly good shape. No sign of a cave-in. The walls feel solid enough. I'll be right up."

Rance offered his friend a hand, pulling him out of the tunnel entrance. "Mac, I left three coils of rope, halogen flashlights, and our ear pods next to the chapel entrance: would you please get 'em and bring 'em down. Mole man here," he nudged A.T., "and I will walk the tunnel, tied together at a ten-foot gap. If the tunnel should cave in, I'll be able to pull him free. The remaining lengths of rope will be tied to me. Sir Sean will hold the end of the rope and follow when the line tightens. If I yell, pull as hard as you can. That's why we need you to anchor us, Al. Take that *why me* look off your face: we've done this before. Remember the tomb in Lower Egypt? Same scenario. Except I hope the outcome is different than it was then. Al nodded, recalling the scary event.

Rance looked at Tina and Adriana, who felt left out. "You two ladies trail Al with flashlights and lend a hand if needed. I'll explain to Mac when she gets back that her job will be to monitor our on-the-air progress in case of an emergency. Someone has to stay above ground."

Adriana leaned down and whispered in Tina's ear. "Is he always so bossy and sure of himself?"

Tina nodded in the affirmative. "He's always been the leader of the band. And the players wouldn't have it any other way." She looked into Adriana's searching eyes. "You wouldn't believe what those three have been through together the past dozen or so years—and survived."

"I'm not sure I want to know," Adriana whispered back.

Everyone donned their ear pods. A.T. dropped into the tunnel, followed by Rance. They tied off loops of rope, waved and disappeared at a fast pace. Rance provided a running commentary as he led Arturo, aiming the powerful lantern beam. L' Ami jumped into the tunnel gripping the end of the rope. "I'll let you know when the three fixed coils tighten," he told Rance. "Then Adriana and Tina will follow me with their lights." Five minutes later, the line tightened. Al called to the two women, and they too disappeared, leaving Mac alone.

"Small roots are beginning to poke through the tunnel ceiling: we must be outside the chapel perimeter. Watch your heads. It's a good thing that the tunnel is as wide as it is—or A.T. wouldn't fit through."

The hard yank on the rope nearly pulled Rance off his feet. "Sorry, old buddy," A.T. laughed. "I forgot we were attached by an umbilical cord."

"You had better keep it tight," old buddy. "Don't know if I could convince your lovely wife how her husband got strangled by his umbilical cord."

"Remember, you two. We all can hear your every word," Mac warned. "You wouldn't stand a chance in court, A.T."

"Well, that's odd," Rance said in a puzzled tone. "And I'm not referring to A.T., this time."

"What have you got?" Al asked.

"The dirt floor just turned into a stone walkway. In fact, the ceiling and walls are constructed of stone."

Arturo turned and rushed to his side. "If my instinct is correct, I'd say we're in the area where the extended ruins of the castle are located overhead. This must be one of the downstairs rooms of the original castle—but from what we can see—it's picked clean. There's nothing but nasty spiders living here now."

Recalling how A.T. hated cleaning out the spider-infested hidden rooms under the Russian president's bedroom, Rance turned and grinned. "And here you are. Sans your trusty broom." The reply was a wicked glare.

"Wait for us, you two," Al said. "We can eyeball it before you move on."

They could hear Mac repeating, "Damn. Damn. Damn," in her frustration at missing out on the latest discovery.

After fifteen minutes of poking about, Rance caught Al's attention. "How about going back and getting the penetrating wand—and give this room a good going over. See what you can find if anything. A.T. and I will plod ahead. The tunnel seems to be secure. Then follow us."

"What's the condition of the tunnel now?" Mac asked, concerned for Rance and Arturo's safety.

"It's narrowing slightly, and roots are thicker—and it's curving to the left."

"Must be heading straight for the waterfall cavern," A.T. added, "and I believe I can hear a faint roar of the falls up ahead…"

Arturo's observation was cut short by Al's shout. "Rance! You guys have to come see what we found. There's something under what was once a stairway that would have led up to the floor above—if it were still there."

"Where's Al?" A.T. asked when they arrived.

"He'll be back with the pick and shovels any minute," Adriana said. "Look at the frozen monitor."

"Damn, Rance. Do you see what I see?" Arturo asked in amazement. "Doesn't that look like the outline of one of those Knights Templar crypts next to that small altar?"

Rance nodded slowly, as if perplexed by what he saw. "If it's merely another resting place of some brave knight—I'm not comfortable with disturbing the dead."

"What if it contained a clue to the treasure?" A.T. asked. "Besides, since when did you become so squeamish?"

Looking into Tina's deep brown eyes, Rance answered, "Maybe since Sir William let his presence be known."

Tina spoke directly to her husband's best friend. "I respect your concern, but I believe if Sir William was angry with our presence—he would have told me in no uncertain terms." She thought a moment and continued. "Perhaps he's here to point the way. Perchance he and the others buried in the chapel, like the Templar that bequeathed you his leather journal with the message, *Carpe Diem*—want you to find the treasure."

"Can't argue with that logic," Rance answered softly.

Before he could elaborate, Al burst in with the tools. "Good. You didn't start without me," he said, handing a shovel to each of the men. "My find. My dig. Right A.T.?"

"If you don't mind me offering a suggestion, husband," Adriana said with a forced smile. "We don't want to disturb these historical ruins—so I suggest that you use the pick to pry up each stone one at a time—and not shatter them with that weapon."

"I was going to do that," he said, winking at A.T.

L' Ami chipped away at the mortar around the edge of each section of stone flooring, and then, with assistance of the other two men, lifted them aside. Surprisingly, the earth beneath was somewhat moist, probably because of the close proximity of the river and falls. Rance and Arturo were busy digging when Mac interrupted. "It's getting real lonesome up here all by myself. I'm not having any fun at all."

Tina placed a hand on her husband's shoulder and gave it a little squeeze. "Mac. I'll change places with you. Okay? I'll be right up."

"You're a friend," Mac said with emotion. "Thanks."

"Okay. Can we get back to work now?" Al muttered to himself, loud enough to be heard.

Without a word, shovels attacked the earth with vigor. In no time, A.T.'s shovel hit a solid surface. The grave proved to be shallow. Adriana, on hands and knees, cleared away remaining pieces and chunks of dirt and mud. Below their feet was the face of a bearded knight wearing an egg-shaped helmet featuring a cross. His eyes were open.

"Whoever carved these prone statues was a master," Adriana said, in awe of the figure coldly staring up into her eyes. "He looks so real. Like he's been waiting for us all these many years."

"The Knights Templar were master masons," Rance reminded her.

Mac had arrived and peered over Adriana's shoulder. "He looks a lot like Rance when he's worn a fake beard."

"I believe you're right," Arturo said seriously, but with a grin. "Although this guy's a lot more handsome. Rance, were any of your relatives knights?"

Knowing his friend was making light of him, he answered, "No, but at times I've had to be as stone-hearted as this one." Deep down inside, he knew that what he had just admitted was true, especially when he recalled last year at the New Mexico Los Alamos Laboratory when he completely demolished a building full of renegade scientists developing an illegal bio-bomb that threatened to destroy America.

"Let's kill two birds with one stone," Rance suggested. "Al, why don't you continue digging—the monument is fairly shallow—and the ladies can help. A.T. and I will continue on to the falls cavern. If that's where this tunnel leads."

"Sure. As usual, you leave the dirty work to me," Al grumbled with a twinkle in his eye.

"And how about me?" Mac said staring at her husband. "I haven't had any real excitement since I was manhandled by that silent creature without a neck. And then A.T. took all my fun away by tossing him into the ravine before I had the opportunity to snap what little neck he had."

Adriana stomped her foot. "Don't complain, honey. All I get to do is crack heads with my trusty frying pan."

Breaking the sincerity of the moment, laughter filled the stone room for the first time in centuries. Rance and Arturo shook their heads without comment and disappeared into the tunnel. Convinced that the solid construction of the tunnel would make for a safe journey, Arturo looped the three-coil length over and around a shoulder as he followed his friend's lantern beam. Long thick tree roots had become an obstacle. Eventually, the tunnel narrowed as they approached the increasing sound of the waterfall.

Turning, Rance shouted over his shoulder. "By the looks of the hanging roots, there's been no foot traffic this way in ages. I imagine that at one time the passage would have been cleared." He stopped suddenly. Holding the lantern high, and added, "This looks like the end of the line. Better uncoil the rope: we're going to need it. The tunnel ends. Or has washed away."

Rance grabbed hold of the stoutest looking tree root and gave it a hard yank. "This one will do. Tie off an end. We'll rappel down to the cavern floor."

"Might I suggest that we go one at a time? I'm not comfortable with the root's ability to hold weight," A.T. said, grabbing hold of the root and applying all his weight.

Leaning over the edge, Rance's lantern beam lit the area below. "I agree, but if we fell, it's only about fifteen feet. Piece of cake."

"Well in that case, you go first. I've knotted the rope around two roots. Head out, Indiana."

Rance grabbed hold of the rope and tossed a deep frown at Arturo's Indiana Jones dig. He had always hated that comparison. His life was not fiction and far more dangerous. "Al. Ladies. We're at the end of the tunnel and using the rope to climb down into the cavern."

The reply came in tandem. "We know. Have you forgotten? We've heard every word—Indy." Followed by laughter.

Rance mumbled something into his mike and slid down the rope, stepping onto a huge boulder. Looking up he shouted, "Your turn, wise ass."

A.T. landed next to his friend, sporting a wide grin. "Now what?"

"When Mac and I were here—and before we entered the shaft to our left—I spotted a dark area at the back of the cavern. At the time, we were too far away to make out any detail." Shimming down the boulder, he headed toward the area in question. A.T. followed.

"From the smoothness of the rocks and boulders, the river must have flowed through here in the distant past and for many eons."

Speculating, Arturo added, "It could have been a branch of the river that flows above—becoming the waterfall that empties into the stream below. Perhaps man diverted its direction for a reason."

Rance's thought process was in high gear. "Suppose you are correct about diverting the river. Suppose the castle knights had a secret to hide, and they diverted the river in order to find a place to conceal that secret—with every intention to redirect the river to again flood this cavern—but for whatever the reason had little time or opportunity. What do you think?"

"You're a devious devil. But you could be right on. Maybe they were attacked by enemies before they could complete their effort…"

"You're making sense," Adriana voiced an opinion. "There were numerous times through the history of the castle where that could have happened. Just as you reasoned, Arturo."

"We're nearly to the area, Mac. It looks like another shaft. Much wider this time, but only four-feet deep. From its appearance, I'd say that at one time it was much deeper."

"Yeah," A.T. agreed. "From deep scratch marks on some of the surrounding boulders, I'd say that rocks and small boulders were removed, then shoved back in. If Rance's assumption is correct, something was buried at the bottom—and the debris dumped on top."

"But just like not having time to set in motion the river's flow, there wasn't time to complete filling in the shaft."

"Maybe the hole isn't very deep to begin with," Al offered. "It could be fairly shallow. It would have been a monumental effort to move that many rocks and small boulders when it wasn't necessary to hide something deep—especially if at some time in the future, they wanted to easily retrieve it."

"L' Ami, at times you're a genius," Rance answered. "Not too often, but once every ten years. And by the way, what does our knight look like?"

"Just as we expected. It's his last resting place. No treasure. We're filling in the grave as we speak."

"Have the ladies complete the job. Adriana's good at disguising a dig to look like nothing's been disturbed. You come meet us and bring a shovel along. Have Mac follow you. Once you're down, Mac will untie the rope and toss it to you. We'll need the rope to manufacture a bucket and begin to haul up the rocks—and your back muscles for the hauling. We're going to see what's down there." A.T. and Al moaned aloud.

Within the next hour the trio had fashioned a length of rope into a tight knit sling that would accommodate small and medium-sized rocks. Arturo entered the pit and selected the easiest to extract. Laying the bulky net over the rocky area, he managed to roll rock after rock into the makeshift rope bucket: then Rance and Al hauled them to the top and shoved them aside. From time to time, A.T. needed the assistance of one of his friends to maneuver oversized rocks into the sling, then the three of them struggled to drag the load over the lip of the shallow four-foot deep shaft. Muscles were strained—deep breaths were taken: two hours had passed.

"Rocks are softball size and smaller at the bottom," A.T. shouted. "Hand me the shovel."

"Do you need help?" Rance asked, shining his lantern to further illuminate the area.

"No. This is a one man job from here on out. As usual, you'd be in my way."

Arturo handpicked the softball sized rocks and stacked them on some of the remaining larger rocks. He used the shovel to scoop pebbles, tossing them high overhead, scattering his hostile friends. "Careful, Italian, or we'll roll one of these boulders on top of your dusty crown…"

"Leave my man alone," a threatening voice warned. Both Rance and Al had forgotten they were still wearing their featherweight ear pods.

"Damn. We can't go anywhere without being heard," Al lamented.

"Yeah. They're meant for two way communication—not mass media," Rance added with a shake of his head.

"Mac. Are you still by the tunnel's edge?" Rance asked.

"Yes. And Tina and Adriana are with me. When you guys are through, toss us the rope and we'll pull you up. Any luck in the pit?"

"No. We think the Italian bowling ball's a slacker. Al and I have come to the conclusion that marriage to Tina has weakened the old boy…"

"Rance. Keep that up and I'll have my husband put that shovel where the sun don't shine," Tina laughed.

"Cut the bull, all of you!" A.T. yelled from the bottom of the pit. "I need some help down here if everyone's through having fun picking on the only working man of the bunch. I think I've found something solid. Feels like a piece of metal. It's box shaped and square in dimensions."

Rance and Al nearly tripped over themselves scampering down. An outline was visible where Arturo had scraped away the soil from the edges. "Pry away the dirt around the object, and Al and I will try to lift it out," Rance said.

"What does it look like?" Adriana anxiously asked.

"Give us time," Rance snapped his answer. "We haven't pried it loose as yet." L' Ami raised one eyebrow and a shoulder.

Once A.T. had removed the earth from all sides, two handles were exposed. Rance reached for one: Al grabbed the other. They pulled slowly to relieve strain on the handles. "I've got it," Rance said, grasping both handles. "Al, get topside and I'll hand up it to you. A.T. you might give him a hand."

The ladies, excited and out of sight, jabbered away like a herd of magpies. Rance turned off his ear pod and tossed it aside, nodding to the others to do the same. "I'm sorry—but I can only take so much of this togetherness." Arturo and Al nodded a silent agreement.

When their mates went silent, the women knew immediately what had happened, and crossed their arms, flashing their eyes at each other, and fuming.

Rance took out a handkerchief and dusted off the metal box as best he could. Al tapped the side of the box with a finger. "There's a rusted clasp about to fall loose."

A.T. took the shovel and gave the loosened clasp a firm nudge: it came off cleanly. Rance, on hands and knees with both men looking over his shoulder, attempted to pry open the lid. It wouldn't budge. Reaching over his shoulder, he exposed an open palm. "Scalpel, nurse A.T."

Having read his mind, Arturo's knife was at the ready. Placing it on Rance's palm, he said, "I want that back when you're through, Doctor."

Using the point of the knife as a wedge, Rance went around three sides of the box, prying the lid open. Slowly, cracked leather hinges gave up their prize. Standing with the box cradled in his hand, he nodded for Al to lift the lid.

Al removed a folded sheepskin. A.T. held the lantern high. "There's something inside," L' Ami announced to his friends. Carefully unfolding the skin, he removed what appeared to be a single sheet of heavy parchment-like paper. "You know what this looks like?" he said, looking directly at Rance.

"Yes. It's a map similar to the one in the journal bequeathed to me by the last Templars, Bertrand, and Sebastian. And look at the words across the top. It says in Latin, 'Guardians Behold Our Keeping'."

"That's the same message printed across the top of the map in the journal in your cargo pant pocket," A.T. noted.

"Yes, and that map had me puzzled: it appeared to be only a section of a larger map."

Handing the box to Arturo, Rance removed the journal from his large thigh pocket and opened it to the page with the first map. Al held up his map and Rance placed his side-by-side. "Damned if they don't fit," he said in amazement.

Peering at the two maps, Arturo included his own observation. "They do look like parts of a whole map—but I can't make out any recognizable land mass." Glancing at Rance, he added, "We need the rest of the map to discover the treasure."

"And that's exactly what we're going to do. We're done here. We have two pieces of the puzzle. Next stop, Ethiopia. Specifically, Lalibela and their subterranean tunnels."

Unknown to the three adventurers, the last of Bishop's planted bugs, located in the cavern, was able to pick up their words over the roar of the rushing waterfall. When Bishop and his men had left the airport in their chartered jet, Paschal hid and had remained behind. It was his responsibility to monitor the last bug in case the group might return to the cavern. He was grinning ear-to-ear when making the call to report success. They knew where the three teams of treasure hunters were headed next.

Chapter Eleven

"WHEN ARE YOU WOMEN GOING to let up on your silent treatment?" Rance wanted to know. Once again placing the aircraft on autopilot, he turned to face Mac. "We'll soon be landing on that godforsaken strip of land we set down on when we were here last."

His frown deepened. Mac had sat in the copilot's seat most of the trip from Scotland and had not looked him in the eye or said a word. It was unnerving. "Look, Honey." He had said that before without success. "I'm sorry that we turned off the ear pods when we opened the box—but all the chatter was just too much. Not one of the three of us had females along on other missions. Not to mention our wives. It's all new. We're delighted to have you girls by our sides—but do give us time to adapt. We're trying. Give us some credit, will you?"

Throwing up his hands, he flipped off the autopilot and manually resumed control of the craft. Clamping his jaw tight, he scanned the horizon for landmarks. The low mountain range near the village was visible in the distance. Talking out of the right side of his mouth, he mumbled, "You had better take a seat with the others and tell them to buckle up: we'll be landing shortly."

Mac smiled and spoke for the first time. "I'll go back and alert the others—but I'll be by your side when you attempt your landing."

Still somewhat miffed, he asked, "What? Don't you think I can put her down without your help?"

"Oh, I have the utmost trust in your ability, my hotshot husband. It's not that. It's just that you need someone to keep an eye out for the wandering camels that you nearly turned into dog food on your last landing here." With a throaty laugh, she stood up, leaned over and kissed him on the top of his head, and left.

Shaking his head, Rance peered over his shoulder and moaned, "Women! Who in the hell can understand 'em? Not me."

As the wheels jarred their way over the bumpy terrain, both pilot and copilot remained alert for the herd of camels. Rance taxied the jet under the hanging branches of a close-knit group of trees whose long limbs made a perfect canopy to cache the plane. Shutting down the engines, he followed Mac to where his passengers were deep in conversation. Stopping just inside the cabin doorway, he stood with mouth agape. The other wives were chattering away with Arturo and Al. Wagging an angry finger at Mac, he growled, "You. You were pulling my chain all the time. What was that? Some kind of punishment?"

Everyone laughed at his discomfort. "Don't feel lonely, old friend," Al said. "These two," he nodded first to Adriana, then Tina, "gave us the same treatment. It was payback for leaving them out of the discovery of the box and map."

"It's a female thing," A.T. offered. "It's their form of warped humor."

Rance stood silent and without emotion. *Two can play at this game,* he thought, and brushed past Mac without a word. Opening the cabin entrance door and releasing the steps, he turned. "You women stay put. Unload and gather the gear by the tail of the plane. Be ready to move out when A.T. and I return from making arrangements with the village priest.

"Al, stay with them and keep a sharp eye and your weapon handy. Bandits have been known to roam these hills from time to time—and when we were descending—I thought I noted movement along the rim of that deep ravine to our left. It could have been an animal or wind blowing a leafy bush. Either way, it's safer to stay alert to the possibility of a band of bandits."

All three women first appeared shocked at Rance's stern tone, then stood stone still, glaring at the man who was spouting orders. Mac stared daggers. To her dismay and surprise, Rance placed his hands on his hips and stuck his tongue out at her, then bent over laughing. "You should see the looks on your faces. Turnabout is fair play, they say." By now, all three men were laughing at their wive's expense.

Mac stepped forward. "You are a rat. You know that." Rance mischievously shrugged his shoulders and nodded agreement.

Glaring at L' Ami, she turned on him. "What are you waiting for, Sean, an invitation? Get your butt in gear and haul out our gear. Didn't you hear what the boss of the chain gang said?"

Al's grinning expression changed to one of disbelief. "Damn!" he said, slapping his forehead. "She's worse than *him*." Now everyone was in stitches.

Before stepping out, Rance checked his 9mm Beretta. A.T. patted the pistol on his hip and motioned for Rance to move on. "Al, I wasn't kidding about those bandits." L' Ami acknowledged the warning with a hand movement.

Adriana tugged at Al's shirt sleeve. "Why do you always do as he orders without question? Both you guys do."

"My dear, you've only known us for a short period of time. A.T., Lord L' Ami, and Rance have worked as a team for a dozen years. We're joined at the hip. We know each others moves before one of us make a move. If not, we'd probably all be dead by now. Only one person can lead a team—and Rance, with his extraordinary talents and insight is the logical one. He's never let us down. Anyone one of us would give up their life for the other without hesitation. There's a bond of love between us three…" Looking at Adriana, he answered her inquisitive stare. Staring right back, he continued. "Don't look at me like that. You know what I mean—a manly kind of bonding love."

Mac and Tina couldn't hold it any longer and burst out laughing. Smacking his hands together, Al scowled and pointed to the luggage compartment. "Now that you females have had your way with me—get your tails in there and help me gather our gear outside."

Rance and A.T. had disappeared over a knoll just as Al and his helpers descended the stairway. Without alarming the women, L' Ami's trained eyes searched the surrounding brush and low-lying hills for signs of unwanted guests. Placing a hand inside his khaki vest, he slipped off the holster's safety strap, then picked up his duffle and case holding the ground-penetrating equipment. "Let's move everything over there," he said with a nod, "behind that large boulder. It'll be safer there."

"What's the difference?" Adriana asked.

Barely moving his lips, he whispered to the group. "So that when the shooting begins, the plane and gear won't be hit—and the boulder will provide cover."

"What...?" Adriana didn't have the opportunity to finish her question when her husband snapped an answer.

"Just do as I say! I'll answer your question when we're all safely out of range of bandits emerging from a cluster of thick bushes. I'm sorry to be so abrupt—but move it. Now!"

Mac and Tina had also spied the group of men approaching with rifles in hand and nudged Adriana forward. Both women were accustomed to danger: they obeyed without question. Adriana would learn. Al was the first to reach the large gray boulder and quickly pulled those in his keep behind him—then removed his weapon and leaned forward while releasing the safety.

L' Ami was an excellent shot, even with a pistol, but the men were still too far away—and there was an outside chance that they were friendly. A slim chance. Sighting in on the first man in line who he anticipated to be leader, he gently caressed the trigger. When the bandit chief raised his rifle to aim, Al squeezed off a shot. One down. Others fell to one knee to steady themselves to let loose a round. Shots rang out from their left. Two more were down. Rance and A.T. were running and firing in a zig zag pattern, heading for the remaining three bandits. As they turned to return fire, L' Ami took two out.

Tossing his rifle aside, the last bandit dashed for cover of the brush and toward the ravine. Rance motioned for Arturo to check on the downed men: he was going after the lone bandit. He raced up the side of the ravine. After reaching the top, he ran along the edge, soon catching up with and keeping pace with the man below him. Fifteen long paces ahead, he noted a wide gap in the lip. It was now or never. Rance made a swan dive for the bandit—and just as he was about to collide, he bent his knees. The sickening snap of his spine sounded like a broken twig. The last bandit was dead.

Grabbing the back of the man's filthy shirt, Rance dragged him up to the lip of the deep ravine, and with his boot shoved him into the abyss below. Returning to his friends, he gave orders to dispose of the bodies in the ravine. Noting the alarmed looks in the women's eyes, he explained. "These men took their chances when they chose to attack you four. If Al hadn't been able to hold them off—and A.T. and I had not returned—it would be your bodies at the bottom of that deep hole. Besides, we don't want to have to explain their deaths to the authorities. They don't take kindly to foreigners killing the locals—even if it was in self-defense. We could be tied up in red tape for months while we rot in their jail." Reluctantly nodding, they all began the grisly task of disposing of the bodies.

"Why did you and A.T. return when you did?" Mac asked.

Arturo answered. "We saw them just before we went out of sight and circled back, then..."

A.T. was cut short by Tina's throaty warning. "We've got more company—and they have guns, too."

Rance grinned when he saw the enthusiastic wave and welcoming smile of the multi-colored robed man leading a parade of villagers armed with ancient-looking rifles, pitchforks, and ax handles.

Returning the wave, Rance explained. "That's our good friend Father Gebra—he's head priest of this village, Lalibela. Mac, you remember, Father Gebra?"

Pleased to see a friendly face among the troop of armed men, Mac waved both hands at the village priest and returned a welcome shout.

"We heard gunfire," Gebra said with a broad smile, "and came to investigate." Turning to his men, he said something in the local Ethiopian tongue, and everyone cheered. "They are happy to attend you again, Mr. Rance. You and the lovely Mrs. Rance."

"The pleasure of visiting your village again is all ours, Father. May I present our associates, Mr. and Mrs. Testaccio—and Mr. and Mrs. L' Ami."

"You are all welcome," he said. "May I ask what occasion brings you back into our lives at this time? And the gunshots…"

"Just some pesky bandits that we ran off," was Rance's answer.

Ran them off into the ravine. Mac thought to herself.

Rance continued after frowning at his wife as if he could read her mind. "We're on an archaeological expedition—interested in the remnants of the Knights Templar. Your churches. Especially the church of St. George with its rooftop Templar cross."

Father Gebra chuckled: his black face was a myriad of deep wrinkles that distorted his features. "They all display the Templar cross. As you know, many years ago, they showed our people how to hew our abundance of red volcanic rock into useful structures. Churches, homes, and caves. Even the subterranean tunnels that you both visited."

"Yes, those subterranean tunnels are of special interest to our team. Will you give us permission to search them with our ground-penetrating equipment?" Al explained the function of the portable unit and the fact that it would not damage the area in any way.

"And Father, would you arrange guards for your aircraft under those trees?" Rance asked, pointing to his left.

Raising both hands, Father Gebra nodded, yes. "We will discuss your visit and needs over cups of Tella, our homemade brew, and a healthy Ethiopian meal of Ingera and Shiro Wat, a spicy stew. Lodging will be arranged as well." Turning, he ordered two men with rifles to stand guard by the plane, then motioned to his men to return home, waving his guests to follow.

ARTURO RUBBED HIS AMBLE GIRTH. "Love the spicy stew—and your home brew, Father Gebra…" He smacked aloud and made a kissing gesture with lips and fingertips.

"Before we leave, you must give the recipe for both to the little woman." He winced when Tina's boot toe collided with his shin. She agreed with the request but let him know she did not appreciate the *little woman* remark.

"Feel free to roam our simple village at your leisure, or rest." The priest offered. "But first, my attendants will show you to your accommodations that are now prepared for three couples. The small homes have been thoroughly cleaned and washed bedding made ready. We are a simple people—but pride ourselves on our God-given daily acts of cleanliness."

"I'm certain we all appreciate your efforts on our behalf and will enjoy your hospitality," Mac responded, nodding to the L' Ami's and Testaccio's.

"This evening," Gebra went on, "we will have a proper Lalibela welcoming celebration with food and music. Those remaining villagers not partaking in a religious ceremony elsewhere will join us in this festive occasion." Displaying a sheepish grin, he admitted, "We do not often have such a reason to celebrate." With a shrug of a shoulder, he finished. "Only when good friends come to visit."

"We're pleased to be called friends," Tina said, speaking for the newly arrived group. "I don't know how everyone else will spend time before the celebration—but I for one intend to visit St. George's Church. That's the one with the huge Templar cross on the roof?"

Rance proceeded to supply his friends with a history lesson. "Actually, the proper name of the Orthodox Christian church is *Bieta Giyorgis*..."

Gebra cut him short, and slowly bowed his head in agreement. "Doors are open through the day, every day. Be our guest."

Rance looked over at his friends, who were grinning. They were pleased that someone had finally silenced their learned but somewhat-of-a-showoff friend.

BISHOP'S MASSIVE BODY SUNK INTO THE SOFA of a less than desirable hotel in Ethiopia's capital city, Addis Ababa. Their chartered jet had landed at the Bole International Airport less than two hours earlier, in a city teaming with nearly three million people—eighty nationalities and eighty languages.

"And this was the best you could do?" the Bishop scowled at the embarrassed Paschal. "Damn it all," Bishop shouted as he squirmed in the shiny plastic-covered sofa. "Every time I take a breath, my ass squeaks like fingers over a blackboard."

Holding out both hands and wiggling his fingers, he demanded his three henchmen help him to his feet. "Help me—I can't move!"

Pointing to one of the beds, he growled, "And someone tear a blanket loose and drape it over this ancient plastic suction cup so I can again sit myself down."

Once comfortable, but still frowning at Paschal, who claimed ignorance when selecting the hotel at such short notice, Bishop proceeded to develop plans to head to Lalibela early in the morning. "Before sun up, we will pursue the treasure. Edmond, you have relatives here. Contact them and secure the necessary weaponry, and your other responsibility will be transportation." He glanced at Paschal and continued. "Something comfortable." Bishop's fleshy finger waved in anger at Paschal. "And you, if you can do anything right, find us the best route to Lalibela and stock supplies for our jaunt—including sufficient quantities of my favorite snacks and wine. Do you think that you can be trusted with this assignment?"

No longer intimidated and angry at being singled out, the little man matched the big man stare for stare, then backed down and timidly replied. "I will discover the most direct and the most comfortable route, but will not be made responsible for every stone, boulder, and mountain that may impede our journey—including a lake or two."

Silence hit the room. All eyes were on the huge man whose body overflowed into the length of the sofa. Suddenly he smacked both fleshy palms together and roared with laughter. The couch shook until it appeared that all four stubby legs would collapse. "I never knew that you had a sense of humor, old boy. Relax, Paschal. Relax. It'll be a long and tedious trip. Two cases of wine should be sufficient. Purchase whatever you three want for yourselves," he said, still shaking with laughter.

TINA SLOWLY OPENED THE ANCIENT CREAKING WOODEN DOOR. She was met with a strong whiff of pungent incense—followed by an eerie cast of ghostly shadows and beams of afternoon sunlight. Dust from the hard packed dirt floor appeared suspended within flickering lights and sun beams captured in space by candles placed around the church's main chapel. Thin slits high on the walls, allowing only slivers of light to enter, replaced wide stained glass windows that usually adorn western Christian churches.

Slipping through the door sideways, Tina, who thought she was alone in the darkened church, was startled by a lone figure wrapped from head to toe in a long black robe. The gentle repeated tap-tap of a six-foot long prayer staff was muffled by the packed dirt surface. Seeing the stranger enter, the tall bent figure nodded respectfully and slowly moved to the far dark corner of the church without missing a beat of his or her's thin prayer staff. Removing a chained crucifix from within her shirt, Tina kissed the cross and knelt to pray at the foot of a small and worn wooden altar.

"Do you wish to receive communion, Mrs. Testaccio?" whispered a voice from the left of the altar. Raising her head, Tina saw the kindly smile of Father Gebra. "Or do you believe that only a Roman Catholic priest can perform the miracle of transformation." Gebra placed both hands in a praying gesture and patiently waited for her reply.

Remaining kneeling while twisting her torso in his direction, Tina shook her head. "No, I believe that that decision is only up to our Lord. It's not for me to decide. Yes, I believe that you can perform the service: and yes, I do wish to receive our Lord in communion."

Standing, she turned her back to the priest and bowed her head. "Father, I do not believe I am a bad person—but in recent years I've seen and done things in service of my country that the average person would never experience."

Turning, tears streaked her cheeks. "Perhaps unforgivable things, Father Gebra."

Stepping forward, Father Gebra offered her a handkerchief, reached out and held both her hands, and asked in a gentle tone, "Do you believe in our Lord Jesus Christ—and that He can forgive you of your sins—if you repent and sincerely wish to be forgiven?"

Tina bowed her head and replied, "Yes I do, Father. I sincerely do."

Father Gebra asked her to kneel and placed both hands on her head and said, "My child, by the authority invested in me by God, I absolve you of your sins. Remain on your knees. I will return momentarily with bread and wine." Taking two steps, he turned, bent low and whispered, "This has been a very special day in my priestly life." Then he disappeared into the darkness of a doorway.

"WELL, YOU MUST HAVE HAD A FULFILLING DAY," A.T. said, when Tina entered the bedroom of their clean but modestly appointed red rock hut. He had taken a much needed rest while his wife spent the afternoon enjoying the sights of the ancient village of several thousand.

Sitting up and stretching after a long nap on top of the bedcovers, Arturo smiled a hello. "Your walk must have done you wonders: there's a certain glow that I can't put my finger on. Have you been testing the local brew?"

Tina laughed and shook her head. She had asked Father Gebra not to mention their meeting—and his response was that what had occurred was a matter of confidence. "No, my inquisitive husband: I am saving myself for tonight's festivities. And no, the glow's not a sign of pregnancy," she added, leaping into his arms. "I just feel refreshed."

Rhythmic sounds of drums and tambourines filled the air as groups of villagers began straggling down dirt roads and narrow streets toward the large gathering square. Fires were lit. Roasting pigs were set on hand-turned spits. And kegs of local Ethiopian brew were rolled out and placed on makeshift wooden tables with spigots inserted and wooden cups galore. Many carried their own homemade beer mugs.

Abandoning their typical khaki duds for the evening, the three couples wrapped themselves in traditional colorful hooded robes—which appeared to please the gathering of adults. Polite applause greeted the treasure hunters as they left their respective huts. Many locals had waited for their appearance outside their doors and lined the street leading to the celebration square.

"You'd think we were the bearers of gold and trinkets," Al commented in a whisper.

"Could be that they have very little to celebrate and will throw a party at the drop of a hat—or at the sight of strangers," A.T. surmised.

"I think it's wonderful," Adriana said. "It's just like being back in Tarego. We Spaniards like to party, too."

"You're telling me," Al said, staggering and holding his head as if cradling a throbbing hangover.

Always the stick-in-the-mud, Rance reminded them to go easy on the local firewater. "It's potent: and remember, we're up early in the morning to follow the guide Father Gebra has assigned to take us deep into the subterranean tunnels."

"Pay no attention to his majesty. I've heard that old line a hundred times—and he's always the last to leave," Arturo informed the ladies. "Why I recall the time he…"

"That's enough, big mouth," Rance interrupted.

"Oh, but I'd love to hear the rest of that story," Mac said, glancing first at A.T. then her husband. Leaning over close to A.T.'s ear, she whispered. "Maybe later when his majesty's occupied with a mouthful of roast pig." Displaying a wide grin, Arturo placed a finger to his lips and nodded. Rance flashed a scowl at both conspirators.

Rance was about to justify his warning when Tina stopped and pointed toward the square. "Look, Father Gebra's blessing the casks."

"He's most likely changing the foul-tasting water into wine and beer." A.T. said with an evil-sounding chuckle. He received an elbow in the ribs from his bride for what she believed to be a blasphemous joke.

Arturo stared at Mac. "She learned that from you, you know."

"Tell me about it," Rance agreed, rubbing his ribs, recalling Mac's well-aimed elbow.

Breaking from his friends and wife, Rance walked briskly toward the closest beer cask, turning only slightly to say, "Well, what are you waiting for, printed invitations?"

"OH ME," RANCE MOANED, STIRRING, ATTEMPTING TO OPEN HIS EYES. "What's all that racket," he asked in a groggy voice. Managing to raise his head six inches off the flat lumpy pillow, he spied Mac in the tiny kitchen off the bedroom. "Watch those pots and pans—please."

"I'm as quiet as I'm going to be, hot shot." She shook a frying pan at the prone leader of the pack. "You, who warned everyone last night. Sera, Father Gebra's guide, stopped by three times this morning. I told him that we'd call for him once his majesty is up, around, and coherent."

"And the others?"

"Not a peep."

"So they ignored my advice, too."

"Appears so. Though Tina and I waved at each other from our windows about a half hour ago."

"And why are you so chipper this morning? Makes me want to turn over and go back to sleep. You know if you think about it—we're in no big hurry to find the Templar treasure. If it actually exists." Rance placed the pillow over his head and moaned.

Mac walked into the small bedroom and gripping the corner of the covers, stripped the bed clean. "Up and at 'em, big boy. You cannot rationalize away your hangover. I read you like a book. Up. Wash up and for heaven's sake brush your teeth. It smells like a goat died in here."

Rance, now sitting up, pulled a sheet under his chin and gave her that *I'm so insulted* look. But she wasn't buying any of his *you hurt my feelings* gestures. "Then get dressed and see to your two friends and their wives while I make you a pot of strong coffee, eggs, and a rasher of bacon. We want to enter the tunnels before it gets dark." With that demand, she tossed a wet dish towel at him and spun away.

Sera, their ever patient guide, was forever stopping and waiting for his charge to catch up with him. All three men wore dark sunglasses, and Al L' Ami struggled mightily with the portable ground penetrating machine. Arturo was no help at all, Al complained. Following Mac's lead, Tina and Adriana had paced themselves last night—and were miffed with their husbands' obvious lack of constraint. It was also obvious that they felt little sympathy for their spouses' present aches and pains.

Al stopped long enough to beg a donkey from a vegetable market vendor, promising to bring him back before dark and to reimburse him for use of transportation for his electronic equipment. L' Ami's forced smile reflected relief when the farmer agreed.

The village square, where they met with Sera, was at street level. Below, the church rooftops were level with the surrounding streets and houses carved out of red volcanic rock. To make their way to the massive cavern that led to the steps into the underground tunnels, they had to descend into the alleys that connect eleven churches. Later, Sera would mention tunnels that also connected the churches. In the deep trenches and tangled maze of passages, they passed white-robed hermits carrying Bibles. Above, villagers going about their daily business stopped and waved at the group trudging below them in the narrow carved alleyways. Smiling, the three women returned the waves: the men barely raised a hand in acknowledgment.

It was noon when they entered the cave. All three men collapsed and sat on small dusty boulders. "You told us that this was going to be fun," A.T. teased.

"You're not having fun?" Rance said. Turning to Al he asked, "How about you, old buddy? Me, I'm having a blast." Tapping his forehead, he continued. "And a Simtex brick's going off in my head right now."

"What do you suppose they use to make that powerful brew," Al wondered. Sera said something under his breath.

"What did he say?" Arturo asked Tina.

"Couldn't tell for certain—but it sounded a lot like diesel fuel."

Everyone laughed. The men held their heads with both hands.

Motioning to a dark area fifty paces to the right, Sera waved for the group to follow him to the entrance and carved steps leading to the maze of tunnels below. Al removed his boxed equipment from the donkey's back and hobbled him close by. "You're handling that donkey like an expert, my husband," Adriana observed.

"That's because of all the experience he had last year with Wally," Rance said.

"Wally?"

Rance explained. "With Al watching my back, I went undercover as Herkimer Two Bundles to stop foreign arms dealers from stealing an illegal bio-gas weapon. He was disguised as an old prospector—and Wally was his donkey."

"He wasn't a donkey. He was a burro," Al corrected him.

"It takes one jackass to recognize another one," A.T. said, then went on. "Sera's waiting, guys."

Sera's lantern lit the way. Peering into the darkness and noting the worn curving steps, Al made a decision. "You guys are going to take turns with me carrying this contraption—and when we leave to come back to the village later today—it will remain down there until we've finished our investigation."

"Sounds like a plan to me," Rance said, "but we better remember where we leave it: there's a maze of tunnels below us."

"Why don't we girls use our electric lanterns to brighten the way? These stairs look dangerous," Adriana suggested. "One slip and it's a broken bone or neck." It was agreed, and miniature lanterns were removed from the men's backpacks. When the stairway lit up like a sports stadium, they could see the possible peril. A slippery clay-like wall veered to their left, but off the edge of the steps to the right, the wall dropped off straight to the bottom.

Sera, as patient as ever, stopped every ten steps to let the others catch up. Even though the carved steps grew in size and flattened out toward the bottom making for surer footing, they were slick with a damp slime. "Fourteen more step," Sera assured them. "Then choose tunnel to begin. Suggest go to left."

"Why is that, Sera?" Mac asked.

"That where many ancestor rest there. Most interesting. I visit often to thank for family."

"Is that the only tunnel where your ancestors have been laid to rest," Adriana asked.

"No, Mrs. L' Ami: many, many tunnel hold our people…" Sera paused a moment in thought, then continued. "…and others who came visit many year ago. Help build church. White men with red cross on chest." With a finger, he signed the cross over the front of his robe.

"Templars," Rance said with little emotion.

"Can you take us to where they rest, Sera?" Al asked, with little attempt to stifle his excitement.

It could have been Rance's imagination, but a dark shadow seemed to cross the guide's solemn features as he considered his answer. "I am not privileged to know that location—nor the final resting plot of King Lalibela."

"King Lalibela is buried down here?" Adriana asked in amazement.

Sera nodded. "Which tunnel, only Father Gebra know. Knowledge passed from abbot to abbot. No one else."

"If we cannot find the Templar tunnel on our own," Rance surmised, "perhaps Father Gebra will guide us." Sera remained silent.

"How are we to go about our search?" Mac asked, with a lost look on her face. "I can see tunnels leading out in every direction."

"Miles and miles of tunnels," Sera answered, with a shake of his head.

"If we were to split up—which is the most practical idea considering the extent of the search area—we'd get lost for sure," Tina said, staring at Rance for direction.

"Oh, he's got a plan," Al said with a wide grin. "It's called the twenty-four hour plan. Better known as—Plan S.H.I.T."

Arturo, trying his best to explain with a straight face, said, "Safely Hidden Ingested Tracking."

"Is that the best you can do," Tina said, taking aim with her elbow. A.T. moved out of range.

"Appears we have three doubting Thomases, Al. Open your bag of tricks."

L' Ami flipped a knob on the side of the container housing the ground penetrating unit and removed a plastic bag. Holding it out, and with a straight face said, "Ladies, here are your S.H.I.T. pills."

If looks could kill, they would have had to bury him on the spot.

"That's not funny, husband." Adriana did not appreciate the men's raunchy attempt at humor. From the looks on the other women's faces, she wasn't alone. Sera took a short stroll down the closest tunnel.

"Wait. Wait," Rance said. "Before you kill the messenger, hear my explanation. You've got this all wrong." He took the bag from Al and spilled the contents into his palm. What looked like a rainbow of jellybeans poured out.

"These are miniature tracking devices that we'll all swallow so we can track everyone's whereabouts in the tunnels on the electronic monitor."

He pointed to the exposed screen. "The color chosen will be noted by your names—and the color of the bleep will identify the person being tracked. He dry-swallowed the red bean. "When Al turns on the machine, watch the monitor screen." Rance nodded. A red blinking dot appeared. Walking around, he added, "See. That's me."

"But you swallowed it," Mac said with a disgusted expression.

Arturo laughed aloud. "That's where the S.H.I.T. comes into play…"

Al finished his friend's thought. "Within twenty-four hours it works its way through. You catch my drift?"

Tina's eyes were slits as she addressed the men. "If you ask me, gentlemen—you're shitting us. I know about the tiny devices but have never heard of them called *that*." Rance, Arturo, and Al shrugged their shoulders and presented three innocent-looking faces.

"Okay, that's settled," Rance said, changing the subject. The women were not falling for their brand of humor. Holding out his hand, he offered them the jellybean-looking devices. "Chose your color and record your name next to the color indicated on the board. A grease pencil is available.

"One other thing to remember," A.T. said with a serious expression. "After twenty-four hours, save the device: it's reusable." He had to run for his life, chased by three outraged females.

Chapter Twelve

"HIT ANOTHER ROCK, BUSH, RUT, OR RIVERBED and you'll walk the rest of the way," Bishop grumbled. Scrapes, dents, and a fine gray powder covered the once pristine and shiny black Mercedes. A swirling cloud of dust engulfed the vehicle as it sped, following a rudimental unpaved road. This part of Ethiopia was experiencing its third year of drought. Even the mighty Blue Nile waterfall to the left of the Mercedes had lost its splendor. No longer did the once loud roar and billowing mist capture the imagination of the viewer, now replaced by a gentle splash and thin gray fog.

Paschal had offered to drive, but Claude was punishing him for the poor choice of hotel in Addis Ababa. Now it was the Bishop who suffered—and he did not like it one bit. Somewhere after leaving the monastery they had stopped to rest and refresh themselves overnight, Edmond had managed to tear something loose from underneath their vehicle that had to do with the working apparatus of the air conditioner. Bishop wiped perspiration from about his face and glowered at the back of their driver's head.

Paschal was cramped in the back seat with the huge man, doing his best to stifle a grin. *That fat tub of lard*, he thought to himself. *It will do him good to sweat off two hundred pounds or more.*

Suddenly the car lurched violently to the left: Bishop's bulk slid on the slick leather seats, squashing the smaller man against the door behind the driver. Edmond had driven the left front wheel into a deep rut. Paschal screamed aloud. "Get him off me! I can't breathe!"

Bishop thrashed about, desperately trying to move, while Paschal remained pinned to the door and the side of the car. "Help me, you swines! Get me out before I suffocate!"

Edmond and Maurice threw their doors open and stepped into a thick cloud of dust engulfing the car. When Edmond came around to open Paschal's door to pull him out, he noticed that his shoulder was pinned in the corner of the back seat. "Maurice," he shouted, "pull on Bishop's arm to relieve the pressure while I pull on Paschal's arm."

Edmond pulled. Maurice pulled. Bishop huffed. Paschal was turning blue. Before passing out, a final thought raced through the little man's mind. *If I get out of this alive—I'll kill them all..."*

Paschal lay on his back in the dust. Edmond peered down at the lifeless body, motioning to Maurice. "He's not breathing. You'll have to give him mouth-to-mouth to bring him back."

"Like hell." Maurice scoffed and made a face. "It was your freakin' driving that did this, so you're responsible," he pointed at Paschal. "You give him mouth-to-mouth."

By now Bishop had managed to slide all the way out of the car and stood over the limp body. "You two useless idiots: lower me to my knees."

Both men were taken back that their boss would be willing to take on the unthinkable task of a mouth-to-mouth embrace. They were even more surprised when Bishop raised a mighty fist and brought it down on Paschal's chest with a loud thump. Paschal's body pitched upwards as though he were shocked by two electric paddles. The spastic movement was followed by a ghastly groan. Both hands grasped his chest as he brought his legs up into a fetal position. Taking a deep and painful breath, he whispered, "Did the damn car fall on me?"

"No. On the contrary, the boss man saved your life," Edmond explained

Blinking to focus his eyes, Paschal answered as best he could. "First he kills me, then saves my life? I was better off dead."

"And you will wish you were," Bishop growled, forcing his bulk into the back seat, "if you cause us any more delay."

Paschal pushed himself up to a kneeling position and burned Edmond with a stare. Brushing aside strands of stringy hair and dust from his face, he pointed first to the large man halfway in the car, then to the wheel stuck in the rut. "We won't be getting *that* out of the hole with your weight in the car." Paschal was well aware that any negative mention of Bishop's bulk was a no-no, but at this point he didn't give a damn. "And we'll need your magnificent strength to help us." He thought that a little flattery wouldn't hurt his chances of survival.

All three men stood outside the car and waited in silence as Bishop sat on his massive right cheek while rolling a deep frown. Reaching out with his left hand, he wiggled his fingers. "So, help me up. Or must I do everything around here?"

As three grunting and groaning men used a thick branch for leverage and Paschal revved the motor, rocking the car back and forth, a figure, naked except for a white wrap around his groin and carrying a brown bundle, ran through the brush unseen by Bishop and his men.

"IF ONLY I HAD HAD MY FRYING PAN," Adriana laughed, wagging a finger in Arturo's face.

"These gals are a lot faster than I realized," A.T. admitted, out of breath. "I had always allowed Tina to catch me and have her way…" Tina's elbow hit its intended target.

Sera stood back with a puzzled expression. This form of husband and wife humor was new to him and wasn't quite sure how to discern their playful banter. Rance noted the guide's frown and said, "Okay, boys and girls, Sera has a job to do so let's let him do it. Sera, lead the way to where your ancestors rest."

Five minute later, Sera raised a hand and pointed to his left. Three electric lanterns exposed the ghastly sight. There in a carved-out ledge five feet above the dirt floor were the skeletal remains of a number of deceased Lalibela residents. Strange religious carvings above the small burial cave identified the family plot. Similar burial caves lined the walls on either side for a hundred yards in this particular tunnel. There were miles to explore, Sera pointed out. Differing clans occupied their own tunnel: the priests had theirs in the deepest section of the maze. In some areas of the carved passageways, Rance, Mac, Al, and Adriana were forced to duck. In other areas where the domed tunnels were higher, they could walk erect. Walls were approximately six feet apart, except where there was a sharp curve. There was no evidence of cave-ins. Perhaps the keepers of the tunnels periodically removed any debris and patched collapsed walls and ceilings.

From time to time, they stopped to rest and allow Al the opportunity to scan solid walls and burial sites. Nothing unusual was found. "Bunched together, we're wasting manpower," Rance said. "We need to split up and each take a tunnel. Al and Sera will remain here and keep a close eye on our progress on the monitor. That unit also has the ability, within limited range, to map the tunnels and tell us which way to turn in order to stay within that range and how to walk the path of a maze. Everybody put on your ear pods and mikes that we used back in the Rosslyn grove tunnel. We can stay in touch. Al can direct us back if we get lost."

"What are we looking for?" Mac asked.

Rance pointed to a burial site. "I'm sure we'll find more of these throughout all the miles of tunnels." Sera nodded in agreement. "So let's give those a glance: no more. Pay attention to the symbols over the site. If you see anything written in Latin—or a symbol similar to those in the Rosslyn Chapel—give us a yell. Our best bet will be in the area where the Templars are interred. If we can discover it." He only offered the most basic advice for fear that Sera would sense they were more than interested archaeologists. Tomorrow they'll return without a guide.

TWO HOURS HAD PASSED AND EVERY FIFTEEN MINUTES each member of the team had reported either the same local burial sites or solid walls. Al glanced at his watch. "It's three o'clock. Let's turn back and take a different route towards me. I'll plot a course for each of you to follow."

"Good idea," Rance said. "Everyone okay with that?" Arturo and the three women agreed, knowing that the afternoon's venture into the depths of the subterranean tunnels was a bust. Interesting, but no brass ring.

"Shut the machine down, Al." Rance suggested, tapping the ground-penetrating metal container. "I'll help you lift it into that empty corner of the burial chamber. No sense on lugging it all the way back—then again in the morning."

"Thanks. Those batteries make it heavy and cumbersome," Al grunted as he lifted his side. "And my donkey friend thanks you, too."

Rance squeezed the guide's shoulder and said, "Thank you for your direction, Sera—but now that we've become familiar with the tunnels—your services will no longer be needed."

Sera appeared to be confused by Rance's surprise announcement. In an attempt to lessen the sting, Rance continued. "I will inform Father Gebra how helpful you were, my friend. And that it is no longer necessary for you to attend to us." Now they could openly discuss their focused search for the Templar section of the tunnels in the absence of Sera.

Placing hands together, Sera bowed and said, "Thank you, Mr. Rance." Looking up, he addressed the team. "It has been my humble pleasure to serve your needs. But I must warn you—there are areas within the system that I have as yet to visit. It is said that much danger lurks within…"

As they searched each others' faces for some kind of acknowledgment, Sera turned on his sandals and headed toward the stone steps to the surface. Silently, they followed their guide from the first burial site and up to the huge cavern where the donkey stood asleep with a contented look on his long face.

After a hardy traditional meal, limited refreshment and strong cups of kaffa in Rance and Mac's makeshift residence, Rance outlined the plan to continue their search for the five hundred-year-old Templar burial site. "It's logical that whatever we find that might eventually lead us to the treasure, whatever that may be, local burial sites are a waste of time. We must focus on finding where the Templars who build the churches are laid to rest. And a familiar inscription similar to those we've seen during our stay at Rosslyn Chaple and Chapel will be the key."

"Even Sera didn't know where the Templars are located," Adriana reminded him. "Only the abbot, Father Gebra, is aware."

"Let's cut our search time and come out and ask him," A.T. said, nodding to the others, looking for support.

Rance stood up and walked to the small open window, then turned. "That would solve our problem, wouldn't it?" Glancing out the window, then back to his friends, he went on. "I would like to hold that thought as a last resort."

Taking his seat on a wobbly wooden chair, he poured another round of coffee from an ancient pot. "It's better for everyone, including the good father, if he is kept from knowing the ultimate goal of our search.

It would result, I'm afraid, in more questions than we would be willing to answer. I only hope that Sera didn't hear too much of our conversation and put two-and-two together."

"Will we be splitting up again tomorrow as we did today?" Tina asked.

"No, I suggest that you and Mac go to the far side of the maze and then work your way to the end of that tunnel. Al will stay with the equipment and proceed as far as he can in the first tunnel, assisted by Adriana…"

Al interrupted Rance. "Back in the market square, I noticed a flat board the size of a half door. It had wheels on the bottom. They must use it to cart heavy vegetable boxes. I intend to borrow it to pull the GPU rather than attempting to carry the heavy SOB."

"Borrow it?" A.T. asked with a questioning tone.

"All I ask of you, my billiard ball friend, is to create a small diversion so I can easily borrow that which I need."

"Why, I have no idea of which you speak," Arturo answered with an innocent expression.

"If you two clowns will allow me to continue…" Rance was serious.

A.T. was not. "By all means, fearless leader."

Rance looked at his wife and said, "I'm getting too old for all of this nonsense."

"We all doubt that," was Mac's answer. "Carry on, dear."

"I'm not that dull-witted—yet," Rance said after taking a deep breath. "I know when I'm being put on, my dear. Anyway, where was I?"

"I don't know about you," L' Ami said, "but Adriana and I were with the GPU and heading south."

"Right. A.T. will take the next tunnel over, and I'll take the fourth one. Everyone keep in touch. Give us a shout if you find anything interesting. If you're still retaining your colored jellybean, fine—but if you need another—see Lord L' Ami."

"So they're not really reusable?" Adriana asked. When everyone laughed, her face became nearly as red as her long hair.

Al patted her hand and put an arm around her shoulder. "We'll discuss it in private, my beautiful Spanish frying pan-wheedling wife." Adriana was getting as proficient as Mac and Tina with her elbow, and Al flinched. Again, a round of laughter.

A soft knock on the door cut the laughter short.

"It is I, Father Gebra," came a soft voice from the outside.

Mac headed for the door. "Come in, Father," she offered, "and share our coffee."

"You are most kind, Mrs. Rance—but I've consumed sufficient cups of Kaffa for all of us this day. One more and I will never close my eyes this night."

"How may we help you, Father?" Rance asked, standing in his presence and offering his chair. "Is it about going into the tunnels without Sera?"

"No." Sera explained. "Just remain careful." Refusing the chair, he took a step back. "My reason for interrupting your evening will take but a moment. I wished to alert you to our new arrivals. They refused accommodations within the village and proposed to reside in a large, abandoned hut on the edge of town, one-half mile south. There are four men. One, a very big man dressed in a black hooded robe who informed me that he is a Bishop from a French monastery. The other brown-robed men are novice monks on a religious quest with their Bishop."

Everyone looked at Rance, followed by a group nod. Bishop and his henchmen had followed them and arrived in Lalibela.

"Thank you for telling us, Father. We look forward to meeting them," Rance said, forcing a smile.

"Oh, but no. I'm afraid they refused my invitation to enter the village—and mentioned that their order preferred to remain in solitude."

Rance placed a hand on Gebra's shoulder, turning him toward the door, saying, "Well if they change their minds, let us know. Thank you for the kindness of offering Sera's guidance, Father. He was most helpful." Rance snapped his fingers. "A question, Father. "Did the monks inquire about our jet?"

"I do not believe they would have noticed since they approached our village from the south-eastern route. The guards say all is well."

"You have a peaceful evening." Everyone said their good-byes as Gebra returned their waves.

Closing the door and turning to his team, Rance said, "My arse, they're monks."

"Monkeys is more like it," A.T. added.

"We'll have to be looking over our shoulders every moment now," Mac warned.

Rance motioned toward the door with his head. A.T. and Al read his mind and stood up from the table. "This time we'll be proactive. We'll take the encounter to them. During our initial walk around the village, I noticed the rambling hut Gebra was referring to."

Al nodded to A.T., "Give us both time to gather our goodies."

"Goodies?" Adriana wondered aloud.

"You know. Those shoot-'em -up toys," Tina answered.

Before Mac had the opportunity to say a word, Rance shook his head. "This one is for the boys." Turning to Al and Arturo who were about to leave, he continued. "I'll meet you both behind A.T.'s hut. If we stay in the shadows, we'll exit the village without being seen."

Five minutes later, the three long-time friends, bent over to avoid a visible profile, dashed from house to house and tree to tree. It wasn't long before a mud hut came into view, its silhouette darkened against the silvery moon. With Beretta in one hand, Rance flashed signals with the other, which included the showing of four fingers, then a tap on his watch. In four minutes, they would enter the hut. Al went to the left of the building, A.T. to the right. Rance proceeded cautiously through overgrown, thick bushes that brushed against what appeared to be a back entrance. With his back to the uneven red wall, he slid left to the edge of an open window—and peeked in. It was pitch black inside and quiet. Were they all asleep? It was a good bet that one, if not all, were loud snorers. One minute to go. Assuming that the old wooden door's hinges were rusted and would creak, Rance placed the pistol in his waist band and using both hands, hoisted himself onto the wide window sill. He heard sounds from both his left and right. Dropping quietly to the floor, he assumed the firing position. "Nothing here," Al whispered—followed by Arturo's echoed response.

"I found sleeping bags in the one large room and their luggage," Al reported.

"And there's a dust encrusted Mercedes parked under hanging branches of an ancient-looking tree around front," A.T. added.

"Well where in the hell...?" Rance never finished his thought. "The girls," he groaned. "Let's go."

Al and Rance were neck and neck, Arturo puffing a few steps behind, as they dashed the mile back to the village and to Rance and Mac's hut. Tossing open the door, Rance raised his hands and shouted, "No! It's me!"

Adriana stopped the swing of her frying pan just in time. "Next time knock," Mac warned. Each of the women was armed with a makeshift weapon. Tina held a butcher knife and Mac and old fashioned rolling pin.

"What's going on here?" A.T. asked.

"Not too long after you three left—we thought we heard someone try to open the front door that we had locked behind you," Tina explained.

"Then there was a rustling sound coming from the bedroom window shutters," Mac added.

"So why was the front door unlocked when I opened it?" Rance asked with a nod toward the door.

"Once armed, we were going to let in whoever it was, and clobber 'em," Adriana said, shaking her dangerous weapon overhead.

"Oh great," A.T. moaned, plopping down in a kitchen chair. "Four mad monks with assault rifles against a frying pan, a rusted butcher knife—and when these two," he motioned to his wife and Adriana, "were through with the bad guys—Mac was going to roll 'em to death."

Arturo rubbed his bald dome. "Tina, you know better than that," he scolded in a whisper.

Tina answered with controlled anger. "We were going to do with what we had. It was his idea," she pointed a finger at Rance's nose, "that we leave all our weapons hidden in the huts."

"And you didn't tell me where you stashed ours," Mac tagged on.

Rance knew when he was outnumbered. "My mistake. You're right, both of you."

"This isn't doing us any good," L' Ami reminded them. "We have Bishop and his three thugs out there in the dark gunning for us. I'm all for arming the ladies here in this hut—and we three go do a little monk hunting."

"That Bishop fellow's head would look good over our villa's main fireplace, right hon?" Tina flashed a determined grin.

"Agreed," Rance said. Turning, he faced Mac. "This time leave the door locked. Let them kick it down if they have to—then shred them with lead." He laughed. "That's another thing I always wanted to say."

Al looked at A.T. and motioned to the door. "We'll get the ladies a couple of automatic pistols and plenty of ammo. Rance, arm your bride. We go hunting in three minutes."

Rance and the others believed that the Frenchmen were after the Templar journal that they possessed and were willing to forfeit all their lives to obtain what Bishop thought would lead them to untold riches. Unknown to the team, Bishop was willing to wait until the treasure was discovered before closing his trap. In the mean time, he and his trio of cutthroats would enjoy making life miserable for the treasure seekers. Similar to keeping a fly alive yet pulling off its wings.

Chapter Thirteen

THE RAZOR SHARP KNIFE MADE A TWANGING SOUND as it solidly hit the target. Cheers exploded from the crowded market place as A.T. walked the fifty paces to retrieve his weapon. Besting the village men in the sport of knife-throwing was just the diversion L' Ami needed to sneak up behind the vegetable stand. On hands and knees, Al reached under the flap of the three-sided tent and slowly pulled the board on wheels out of sight. With the device secure under his left arm, he made his way to where the others were waiting, staying hidden behind the many tents. Out of sight and well within the deep alleyways heading toward the huge cavern, Al sounded a shrill whistle. Arturo bowed as he exited the square to the continued sounds of applause and disappeared below street level to join the others.

"It's a mystery as to where Bishop and his men disappeared to last night," Tina was saying when Arturo arrived.

"They vanished like a wisp of bad odor," A.T. added.

"You don't suppose that they're waiting in the subterranean tunnels for us to show ourselves?" Adriana asked with trepidation.

Rance stood by the opening to the stairway leading to the tunnels below. "I can't imagine how they would have known where we were, or for that matter, what we were searching for yesterday—unless someone within the village told them—and only two people knew for sure where we were."

"Don't forget the donkey," Al reminded them. "Any one of those Frenchmen could speak jackass."

"You won't get an argument from me," Rance said. "Either way, we need to be on alert in case they're waiting for us below. We all armed?" There were nods all around.

Everyone held an electric lantern to light the way. Halfway down, A.T. asked over his shoulder. "Lord L' Ami, how are you going to explain to that very large and muscular vegetable merchant that you swiped his cart?"

"Oh, when we're through with it, I'll bring it back with the story that I found it in the cavern with a few Ethiopian bills attached. That should do it."

When they reached the burial site where Al and Rance had placed the GPU container, they lifted it and set it on the cart. Al tried it out by pulling the rope handle. Luckily, the wheels did not sink into the hard packed dirt floor, and it moved with little effort. Al was all smiles. "Okay," he said. "Who needs a new jellybean?" Two hands attached to bodies with blushing faces were raised. He provided them with the same color that they had yesterday, enabling him to keep track by matching color to an individual.

Glancing over to Adriana he said, "These aren't reusable, either." For his effort, she made a noise with a wet tongue.

"Everyone recall the assignments discussed yesterday?" Rance asked. "Okay. But remember we may have some company down here. Stay alert. Make certain your ear pods are operative. And give us a shout if you suspect anything. Al can direct us to where you're located."

After high-fives all around, the team split up and headed for the assigned tunnels. Every fifteen minutes, they reported in. Thus far, nothing out of the ordinary was discovered. Neither solid walls nor the usual burial sites. None featuring Templar symbols. Every hundred feet or so, Al would scan walls on either side of his and Adriana's tunnel.

"Al, you got me on the screen?" Arturo asked. "I'm yellow. And no damn snide remarks."

"I can see you loud and clear," Al responded. "Got something?"

"Don't know for sure. There's an area here where the right-hand wall appears to have been dug out and patched. Probably just a cave-in that was fixed. But it deserves a look with the GPU. How long before you get here?"

L' Ami scanned the screen, adjusting a few knobs. "We've got one right-hand turn, one left, then another right, and then we'll be within spitting distance. Maybe ten minutes at the latest."

"Sounds good. I'll keep the drinks cool."

Rance cut in. "Give me a holler if you find anything, guys."

"There appears to be a box inside, approximately two feet wide by three feet in length," Al announced after scanning the patched area. "And only eight inches within the wall."

A.T. unstrapped a foldable shovel from his backpack and began to dig into the patched surface. Al notified Rance and the others of what the scan uncovered, and if anything of importance was found he'd let them know.

It wasn't long before Arturo called out, "It's a box, all right." Tossing his shovel aside, he reached in and pulled out a heavy-lidded container carved out of red volcano rock.

"That looks like a burial urn similar to those the Hebrews used in ancient times. They allowed bodies to decompose, then they interred the bones into what's called an ossuary." Brushing off excess dirt, Adriana continued her assessment. "There's a carved inscription on one side."

"What's it say?" Al blurted out.

Adriana gave him a look that said, without any doubt, *Hold your damn horses and give me a chance.* She stared at him until he shrugged both shoulders. "It's a man's name written in Hebrew."

"You can read Hebrew?" Al asked in a shy tone.

There was that look again. "Yes. It was one of several languages I mastered in Madrid where I studied archeology. Now, if you're finished asking questions, may I continue?" He nodded and looked to A.T. for support. None was forthcoming.

Giving the surface another cleaning, she said, "The bones belonged to Rabbi Yossi Tovya."

"A Jew buried on Ethiopian soil?" Rance's surprised response came loud and clear through their ear pods.

"Perhaps Father Gebra can explain," Adriana said. "Let's take it with us when we leave. If he can't provide a suitable explanation, the ossuary and contents needs to be sent to the Israel Antiquities Authority for a proper Jewish burial."

"Adriana," Rance responded, "place the ossuary on Al's cart. When we get topside, we'll take it to Gebra. He may have an explanation of the rabbi being buried in Lalibela—and may want him returned to his niche. If so, we'll seal him up tomorrow."

"Oh, but I'd love to take a peek inside," Adriana said with excitement.

"I'm certain you would. But for now, it's Gebra's call. Let's all get back to work," was Rance's final words.

Adriana placed her palm over her mike, turned to Al and A.T., and whispered. "Suppose the rabbi's bones are not inside—but rather something relating to the Templar treasure."

"I heard that," Rance said, whispering back. Adriana made a face as her two male companions laughed aloud. Both men pointed to their mikes. They were sensitive enough to pick up her words.

Before the ossuary controversy could continue, Mac cut in. "It appears that Tina and I are coming to the end of our tunnel…" Her last word hung in the air, followed by a muffled scream. Then a second scream and two loud words, "Oh shit!"

For a moment, there was mass confusion as everyone shouted at once. Arturo recognized Tina's screaming voice. His next shout was the strongest. "Tina! What happened? Are you okay? Speak to me!"

The next thirty seconds of silence felt like an hour. Then they heard the labored voice of Mac. "We...the ground fell out...from under us..." After that, Mac's words were garbled. What they heard next was the sound of rushing water and splashing.

"Mac!" Rance yelled, "what's happening?" Nothing.

"Al, can you spot them on the monitor?" Rance said, attempting to calm his voice.

"I don't understand it: both jellybeans are moving at a high rate of speed. Doesn't make any sense," Al said, frantically twisting dials.

Tapping a finger on the screen, L' Ami drew A.T.'s attention. "One turn to the right—pass three tunnels—then turn left."

Arturo was on the fly before Al finished his directions. "Rance, A.T.'s heading for the girls now. You're a little further away." Al provided tunnel coordinates, and Rance took off running.

Arriving moments after his friend, Rance noted that A.T. had already slipped off his backpack and was sitting on the edge of what appeared to be a sandy sinkhole leading down into a rushing stream. Quickly removing his boots, A.T. stood and tossed them to Rance. "I'm going in after them. Take care of my boots and pack." Before diving in, he tore off his ear pod and continued. "Find Father Gebra. He may know about the underground river and where it comes out above ground." Tilting his head and displaying a grin of confidence, he added, "I'll see you there with Tina and Mac." Gripping the ear pod in his teeth, Arturo dove headlong, disappearing into the swiftly moving river.

Staring into the blackened water, Rance pressed his ear plug tight. It was Mac's voice. "Tina's hurt. Large gash...on her...forehead.

Coming up…she hit her head…on a hanging rock." Sounds of splashing water filled the void. Then she got her second wind. "Hurt my shoulder…don't know how long…I can keep her head…above water. Water's cold. Strength is waning. Need help…"

"Mac, if you can hear me—Arturo's in the water right behind you. Hold on. Help is coming." No reply, so he went on providing words of confidence. "I'm leaving to talk to Gebra. He must know where the river empties somewhere around here. We'll meet you there. A.T. will find you." Turning, he picked up Arturo's gear and sprinted to where Al and Adriana were waiting, having heard the entire conversation.

TINA FLOATED ON HER BACK, THE CROOK OF MAC'S LEFT ARM snug under her chin, cradling her head above water. The fast moving river level was two feet below a jagged ceiling. Holding Tina while pushing off low hanging rocks with her right hand was a painful effort for Mac. Unexpectedly plunging into a sinkhole, she wrenched her right shoulder in a failed attempt to grab onto the lip of the hole. Luckily, their backpacks acted as a flotation device in the rushing waters. A steady trickle of blood streamed down Tina's forehead, over her cheek, and down her chin. With each dunking, it washed away, soon to reappear. A wide gash on the edge of her hairline tended to bleed profusely. It was impossible to see in the darkness. Mac with great difficulty held her free hand over her head to ward off anything protruding from above, all the while moving her legs back and forth to float as best they could.

Without warning, the swiftly moving current slowed. Sensing a pooling effect to her left, she kicked in that direction. *There must be a bank here somewhere. The current continued on. That could be the only reason for the lack of current here.* Tina had lost her ear pod and Mac had forgotten that her's remained, although askew, cocked to one side and tangled in her long hair. She could smell the damp earth within reach. Stretching her right arm, she touched a muddy bank. Sighing relief, she whispered, "Hang on Tina. I'll get us out of this yet."

As she struggled to find a handhold, she felt her strength begin to fail. Both their heads sunk beneath the water. Sputtering and spewing out a mouthful of rank water, she felt something brush her leg. *Oh damn! Could there be crocodiles in here?*

A loud splash whipped her head to the right. Frightened, she nearly lost Tina below the surface. "Let her go. I've got her. Grab hold of the bank and rest," came the most welcomed voice of Tina's husband.

"Rance said you were on the way: I had forgotten. If Tina has no objections, you're due for a big kiss."

Removing a waterproof flashlight from his cargo pocket, A.T. managed to find Mac's hand in the dark. "We'll discuss that with her later: right now, turn on the light while I keep Tina's head above water. We need to know what we're up against."

Mac was correct. The river entered a small cavern and calm water pooled next to a vegetation-free muddy bank. Flashing the light along the edge, she found a spot twelve feet to the right where the river's speed increased. "There's a large root poking through the side of the bank," she said, shining the light in Arturo's face.

"Well, I'll never see it, now that you've blinded me," he said with little humor. "Let's make our way there—but don't get caught in the current. Hand me the flashlight."

Carefully edging their way along the bank, Mac reached out, grabbed the root, and pulled herself close. "Slip off your backpack and toss it on the bank, then use the root to climb up," A.T. suggested. "I'll give you a boost with my free hand. Then take the light, balance it upright to light up the area. When you reach down to pull Tina up, I'll push."

Mac did as she was told, and after two loud grunts, A.T. managed to shove her over the top. Wiggling like a worm, she slowly pulled her entire body off the bank's edge. Flipping into a sitting position, she took several deep breaths and was startled to hear Tina groan. "It's okay," Arturo assured his wife. "I've got you. And we'll have you out of the water in no time." She mumbled something neither could understand, blinked, and made a weak attempt to smile.

A.T. removed Tina's pack and handed it up to Mac. He nodded to Mac and shouted, "Now!" Placing both hands on his wife's bottom, he lifted her overhead, assisted by the water's buoyancy. Mac grabbed Tina under her arms and slid her over the muddy surface of the bank. If A.T. hadn't immediately grasped the protruding root, the strong current would have swept him away. With Mac's help, he was over the edge and on a firm but slippery surface.

Tina was sitting up, cradling her head with both hands. A.T. gently removed her hands, "Let me take a look at that gash," he said with utmost concern. "Mac, you're fond of shining that flashlight in people's face. Shine it on Tina's wound."

"Here," Mac said, removing a wet but clean towel from her pack. "Wipe the mud off your hands."

They were both relieved to note that blood had started to congeal. A good sign. "You're going to have a nasty headache, but the wound's healing," he assured her, and used a clean corner of the towel to wipe away the trail of blood.

"Rance, did you hear all of this?" A.T. asked.

"Yes, loud and clear. I'm relieved to hear both Tina and Mac are okay. Never doubted you'd come to their rescue. I haven't heard a word from Mac since she alerted us about the sinkhole."

"She still wears her ear pod, but something malfunctioned. Where are you now?"

"Trying to locate Father Gebra."

Arturo took the flashlight and scanned the cavern. "Can't make out where we are at the moment—but I'll snoop around. Right now, we're at your mercy. If this is a dead-end," he glanced at Tina, "we may have to get back in the water and hope the current will take us to wherever Gebra says it surfaces at ground level."

Mac leaned close to A.T. "Darling, it's wonderful to hear your voice. I'm looking forward to being in your arms again."

"That's incentive enough for me to find you guys."

"And the L' Ami family will spring for the beers tonight," Al broke into the conversation.

"Bring a thick wallet," A.T. countered.

Tina stared at her husband: her head fell forward and slowly lifted. "I…thought for a while…that I'd never see you again." She caught Mac's eye. "…thought that Mac and I were goners and that we'd drown for sure."

"No more talk like that," Arturo said. "I'm going to see how far this bank extends along the underground river." Leaning over, he kissed the top of his wife's soaked head, picked up the flashlight and stepped away. Turning, he pointed to the girl's backpacks. "Mac, break out the other two flashlights and keep an eye on Tina. She's still woozy. Don't let her go to sleep. She may have a minor concussion."

RANCE RAN THROUGH THE TRENCHES AND FROM CHURCH TO CHURCH in an effort to find Father Gebra. Outside the doors of St. George's, he heard a soft chant and the rhythmic beat of hundreds of prayer sticks tapping the hard-packed earthen church floor. A service was in session. Torn between waiting until the service was over and interrupting, he chose the latter. The three were safe for the moment. But something needed to be done immediately.

He walked to the side door and quietly slipped into the darkened church, just behind the altar. Motioning to a deacon standing close by, Rance told him that it was a matter of life and death that he speak immediately to Father Gebra. Shaking his head, the deacon informed the foreigner that his request was impossible: the service had just begun and would last another two hours. Rance grabbed the man's wrist and applied pressure, assuring him that if Father Gebra weren't outside the door within the next five minutes, the service would end abruptly. Rolling a deep frown, the deacon slowly nodded, and shuffled toward the altar where Gebra was quietly addressing worshipers gathered with their long prayer sticks.

Gebra ended his sentence, glanced at Rance leaving the church, and whispered for the deacon to take over the worship service. He had faith in his friend Rance, and if he had made such a threat, something was indeed wrong and needed immediate attention.

"Yes, my son," Gebra said with a slight bow, "how may I be of service to you?"

Feeling a sting of guilt, Rance apologized for the necessary threat and explained what had occurred in the tunnel Mac and Tina entered. Shocked, Gebra said that he was well aware of the underwater river and the ever present danger of a possible sinkhole. "That is precisely why we had erected warning signs and a barricade to prevent anyone from stepping past the barrier."

"We saw no such sign or barricade," Rance said, slapping his forehead with a moist palm. *The Bishop. Now we know why they disappeared and what they were doing.*

Setting aside his revelation, he explained Mac, Tina, and Arturo's predicament. "All three are okay, except Tina suffered a gash on her head. They're camped on a ledge in a small cavern underground." He placed a firm hand on the holy man's arm and went on. "Do you know where the underground river exits? Or if there's a way to walk out of the cavern?"

"Yes. It surfaces into a deep ravine two miles west of the village." With both hands pressed to his cheeks, Gebra continued. "Oh my. I am afraid that no one, to my knowledge, has ever been in the underground river—so I will be of no assistance in that matter—but I can have someone lead you to the ravine."

"I'll take any help that I can, Father. And again, my apology for the disruption of your service."

"No need to apologize, my son," Gebra said in a soft whisper. "God is in no hurry. He has all the time in the world. And elsewhere…" At the door, he turned and explained, "Brother Sera will be right out to take you to where the river appears at the foot of the mountain."

Seeming to talk to himself, Rance asked, "Did you catch all that, A.T.?"

"Ten four, good buddy, as your American truckers say."

"Have you found a passage out of the cavern? Come back." Pausing a moment, Rance asked, "And where did an Italian pick up on trucker's lingo?"

"From watching Smoky and the Bandit movies, good buddy. And to answer your question, there was nothing to our right. I walked the bank and after about one hundred yards past the bend, it drops off into the river. Nothing above. No apparent caves. I'll check on the ladies and search to the left. Out."

"HOW ARE YOU TWO DOING?" A.T. asked, squeezing Tina's shoulder.

Mac flipped him a power bar with her left hand, then used it to cradle her right shoulder, saying, "Found these in my pack. Tina has a stash in her's as well. At least we won't starve for the next few days."

A.T. couldn't miss Mac's discomfort. "You hurt your shoulder?"

"I believe it'll be okay: it's just a pulled muscle, I think." Arturo nodded acknowledgment.

"We also have four bottles of water," Tina contributed.

"Come sta?" he asked tenderly.

"Vorrei birra." Tina answered with a shy grin.

"If you're thirsty for a beer, I guess you're feeling better." Before walking away into the darkness of the cavern, he raised an eyebrow at Mac. "Nothing stronger than a beer for the lady. And no peanuts. Got that?"

"Yes, Warden. Whatever you say. Just find a way out of here."

Arturo's wide beam illuminated the way along a treacherously slick ridge. Closer to the cavern wall, the firmer the footing. More sandy than muddy. Jagged rock and outcrop ledges were abundant. Shining the light along the wall, A.T. proceeded, choosing to walk the firmer footing. His beam reflected off a wall that ended his search. Water flowed beneath and from out of solid rock. He could go no further. They were trapped—and if they took to the water—they had no assurance that there was a way to the surface. If they were forced to dive underwater, could they hold their breath long enough to surface outside?

Backtracking, his beam flashed over a curious-looking rock formation he hadn't noticed before. It appeared manmade. Moving in for a closer look, he stood dumbfounded. Directing the beam up the side of the wall, he thought out loud, "I'll be damned. There are steps leading up into a partially hidden cave high above the wall, close to the ceiling. They were carved and camouflaged to be part of a natural rock formation, but through the years it looks like much of the veiled disguise of surrounding soil and smaller rocks has fallen away, exposing the steps."

Placing one foot on the bottom carved step, he thought of Tina and Mac waiting for his return. Before investigating the cave above, he would have to brief them on his find and his decision to explore another possible passage to the outside. Mac had to stay with Tina, who was in no shape to travel just yet. She needed to preserve her strength if they were forced to swim out.

"I HEARD YOU TALKING TO YOURSELF," Rance said as he ran west, following in Sera's footsteps. "When you get back to the ladies, check out Mac's shoulder. She's never been a complainer. She'll just suck up the pain and say nothing."

"Will do. Did Gebra know where the underground river exits?"

"Yes. That's the good news. The bad news is that he's not aware of a walkout exit within the cavern. To his knowledge, no one has ever been inside the cavern."

"Well, someone sure in the hell has—and they carved a stairway up to a small cave entrance. I'll provide you with a running ringside seat as I go. You'll be the second to know what I find."

"No, he won't," L' Ami interrupted him. "Adriana and I are hanging on your every word."

"Damn! I don't have any privacy."

"Pardon me," Rance said, "but we've just passed the house where the Bishop and his crew were bunked. The car's gone—and I suspect they are, too." Without stopping, Rance explained what Father Gebra had told him about the sign and barricade that should have been at the end of the tunnel where Mac and Tina were investigating.

"Now we know what that bunch was up to when we couldn't find 'em," Al speculated.

"Can't wait 'till I get my fingers wrapped around that bastard's fat neck," Arturo growled.

"You'll have to beat me to him," Rance chimed in.

"Wait!" Rance said. "Sera stopped and now is pointing to a surging flow of water spouting out from what appears to be a small hole in the foot of the mountain and emptying into a deep ravine." Shaking his head in dismay, he went on. "There's no head room. If I can visualize your circumstance, you'd have to dive and swim underwater until you're spit out of the tube—and there's no way of knowing how far that would be. You all could drown trying."

"I've already anticipated that scenario," A.T. said. "That would have to be our last resort—other than blowing the top off this damn cavern and the mountain above. Then, of course, we'd be buried for eternity in Ethiopia like the rabbi in the ossuary."

"If you could get me some help moving the GPU to the site of the water flow," Al said, "then maybe, just maybe, we could determine how far it is from the cavern to the exit." Considering his suggestion for a moment, he added, "That's assuming it can penetrate the side of the mountain that far in."

"You three do the best you can," Arturo said. "In the meantime I'll check on Mac's shoulder and Tina's head, then I'm heading up those steps and see where they take me."

"Better discover a way out of that cavern and mountain, A.T.: if a long swim underwater is your last resort—it's not a sure bet," Rance reminded him. "Good luck. We'll all be listening."

AFTER ATTENDING TO THE NEEDS OF THE WOUNDED WIVES, Arturo, with his flashlight beam leading the way, ascended the carved steps to the darkened cave at the top of the cavern's wall. The cave itself was well hidden by two natural outcroppings on either side of the opening. Without a powerful steady beam, unlike a burning torch, he would have missed it completely. And of course, time had worn away the attempt to camouflage the stairs. At any point in the past, anyone with a torch that had passed this way would not have seen the passageway or cave.

"Okay guys, the ladies are doing well, and I'm heading up the stairway. I'll be back on your favorite radio channel once I have something interesting to report—or if I run into a lion or big bad bear. Out."

Chapter Fourteen

"NO, I DON'T WANT YOU TO SABOTAGE THEIR AIRCRAFT, you skinny imbecile," Bishop said to Paschal with a wild wave of both arms, just missing his head. "You heard what our village contact said about the two women. Edmond's little joke of removing the sign and barricade could cost us a fortune. If those two die, and as a result the others leave for home without finding anything, we stand to lose everything we've worked for these last few weeks."

"Well, what do you want me to do? Polish their plane? Make their coffee?"

"You little slug, you're getting too mouthy for your own good." Bishop wagged a finger in Paschal's face. Edmond and Maurice grinned and made faces at their senior partner's misfortune.

"Tonight, after the two guards fall asleep, I want you to sneak over to the aircraft's nose gear wheel well and plant a homing device. We can't keep up with them in that infernal jinxed car we're burdened with—but we can learn where they go next—and be close behind in a day or two."

"And don't place it where the wheel, when it's up and locked, will knock it loose," Edmond said, offering his advice with a sly smile. Paschal showed him all five fingers of his right hand and pointed to the middle finger with his left.

Bishop's huge body stepped between the two men on the verge of a brawl. He grabbed both by the nape of their necks and shook them hard. "After this is over and we have the treasure, you can skin each other alive for all I care—but not before then." He shook them a second time for good measure. "Understand?" The men shot daggers at one another as they nodded in agreement.

Later that night, after the fire warming the change of guard turned from a bonfire to embers, Paschal slipped around the backside of Rance and Mac's jet, and with a small pen light insert the tracking device provided by Claude, the Bishop.

ARTURO TESTACCIO'S BEAM CLASHED WITH SHADOWS of the two rock outcroppings on either side of the cave, giving the impression of a winged creature guarding the opening. "This is damned spooky," A.T. whispered, as if some unseen entity would hear his words other than his friends wearing their ear pods.

"Are you in the cave yet?" Adriana asked.

"Don't push me, Mrs. L' Ami. I'm on the top step now, about to enter. All I have to do is untangle myself from the largest spider web I've ever seen."

"Our big Italian hero hates spiders," Rance interjected. "Isn't that right, old friend?"

All they heard was a loud and deep intake of breath and then silence. Moments passed. "A.T. You okay? Can you hear me? Say something, damn-it-all!" Rance barked into his mike.

The next sound they heard was an audible gulp and, "Holy Shit! It's Rosslyn Chapel all over again!"

Arturo opened his flashlight beam to wide-angle while the three listeners asked questions all at the same time. "Settle down, you guys. Give me a few minutes to absorb what my eyes are witnessing. It's unbelievable."

"What is?" Adriana asked.

"What I see before my very eyes…"

"Which is?" Rance asked, raising his voice.

"Naked dancing girls," A.T. answered. "Will you give me a damn minute, all of you. If what I'm seeing is not a mirage, I'm going to need help here."

"Tell us what you see," Rance asked again. This time his voice expressed frustration. "I have an idea for getting you three out without diving underwater. Given Tina's condition, she probably wouldn't have the chance for success that you and Mac might have. And, I'll be by your side in less than an hour."

"What's your plan?" both A.T. and Al asked simultaneously.

"You tell me what has you so flabbergasted—then I'll explain."

A.T. let out a deep breath. "Before me is an exact duplicate of the main floor of Rosslyn Chaple—except it's carved out of red rock."

No one said a word for a dozen heartbeats. "Okay. As hard as that is to swallow, we believe you," Rance insisted, then thought a moment and corrected A.T.'s assumption. "You're wrong. Considering the time frame, what you see is not a duplicate of Rosslyn Chapel—Rosslyn Chapel is a duplicate of what's in that cave."

Spinning on his heels, he provided them with elements of his *plan* as he jogged back toward the village and the subterranean tunnels. "Al, break out the longest coil of rope that you have—and I'll scare up the sturdiest sharp stake I can find, along with a large hammer and..."

"...to drive into the baldheaded Italian's heart? It's long overdue," Al laughed.

"I'll have the last laugh when you two see this, you Sean Connery fraud."

Rance ignored his two best friends and continued to explain. "We drive in the stake at an angle—making certain the surface is solid—and tie off the rope. L' Ami won't be with me. He and Adriana will guard the stake in case the Bishop and crew show their ugly faces. I'll enter the river holding onto the rope, taking a second coil to be on the safe side, then join Mac and Tina on the bank. Also break out the first aid kit, Adriana. I'll take that with me and tend to Tina's wound before joining Arturo in the cave."

"I see where you're going with this," A.T. said. "If we can't find a way out on foot, you and I pull ourselves back to the tunnel, using the rope as leverage against the strong current."

"Yes. You got it," Rance answered as he entered the village. "Mac holds onto the end of the rope until we're safe—then secures it around her and Tina's waist, and we pull them both to safety."

Rance spied Father Gebra and finished. "I'll be with Al and Adriana in less than a half-hour. See you soon."

"I'll light a few torches for your arrival."

"Why is it that I always miss out on all the fun?" Al complained.

"Someone has to watch the fort," was all Rance would say.

"THAT'S APPROPRIATE FOR THE OCCASION," L' Ami said with humor in his voice. After driving a healthy-sized sharpened post on an angle into the tunnel floor, Rance made a hangman's noose and slipped it over the end, then tightened the loop.

"We'll save it to slip around the Bishop's fat neck," Rance said.

"And it'll take all of us to lift him off the ground," Adriana added to Rance's thought.

Looping the second coil of rope over his head and under his arm, Rance motioned toward Adriana. "She's just as vicious with or without her fry pan."

"She's a redhead. What more needs to be said." From the look on his wife's face, Al knew he was in trouble. Again.

Rance stepped to the edge of the sinkhole. Turning his head, he said, "We'll keep in touch." Then, like A.T., he held his ear pod between his teeth and plunged into the swift, surging underground river.

Aware of the overhanging rocks, Rance was prepared and avoided the hazard. In no time, he heard Mac's voice and saw her beam of light. "Rance! Swim to your left! Follow my beam! Grab hold of that root!" Following directions, he scrambled up the slick river bank.

Adjusting his ear pod, he swept Mac up in his arms and smiled at Tina. After a long embrace and kiss, he asked, "How's that shoulder doing?"

"It's just a little sore," she answered, massaging her muscles. "Tina's much better but could use some doctoring."

Digging into a cargo pant pocket, he removed a small waterproof bag. "Mac, there's everything you'll need in this first aid kit to patch Tina up, including anti-infection ointment. Play nurse while I see what her husband stumbled into."

"Now you want me to play nurse when we have company," Mac chuckled, winking at Tina who had just received a hug and encouraging words from Rance.

Throwing them both a kiss, Rance headed for the carved steps that A.T. had described. "You still awake, old buddy?"

"Just watch those steps," A.T. came back. "They're fairly steep for an old timer like yourself."

"Well, I'll be damned!" was all Rance could think of saying as he stood dumbfounded, taking in the magnificently designed architecture of the massive room before him. A.T. had lit all the torches surrounding the perimeter, and others anchored in torch holders attached to a number of decorative columns. What he noticed immediately was the absence of the apprentice column, the delicately carved column in the Rosslyn Chapel named after the apprentice who was slain out of jealousy by one of the master carvers.

"Well? Damn it all," L' Ami shouted. "Was the Italian correct?"

"Yeah. One of the very few times," Rance answered, still rooted to one spot. "You two should see this. You have no idea what you're missing." Grinning at his friend, he continued. "But someone has to watch the fort." Both men tore off their ear pods. Al's response could have shattered glass.

Realizing how unfair it was that the others could not share in the wondrous sight, he made a decision. "Adriana. Go topside. Talk to Father Gebra in private. Ask him to supply four guards he can trust with weapons. Have him station two at the top of the stairs leading into the subterranean tunnels—and another two by our anchored post. Just tell him that you two are going to join us to rescue Mac and Tina: say nothing more. Got that?"

Adriana said something in Spanish so fast, no one understood what she had said. After pumping his arm and shouting, "Yes!" Al interrupted. "I believe that was Spanish for, 'You bet your sweet bippy, I do.' "

"Thought that you two would like the idea. But you'll have to get wet in the process."

"We're both drip dry. Be with you guys soon."

"Nice move," A.T. agreed. "I've had the opportunity to look around. You do the same while I round up the two injured ladies. Wait till they lay eyes on this incredible find." He remained silent for a few moments then said, before slipping away, "Imagine. A Templar chapel hidden under the feet of those living above. The Knights Templar who helped build the churches of Lalibela—built their own in secret."

Arturo's eyes widened. "You don't think that…"

Rance cut him short. "Let's not get our treasure before the donkey." Placing a finger on his ear pod, he gave further instructions. "Adriana. Also ask the good Father if he would be so kind as to rustle up enough food supplies to last us for two days…"

"That includes a keg of the local brew. It'll float," A.T. said, heading down the carved stairway. "Medicinal purpose," he added, "for the injured women. Good for the circulation and builds stamina, I'm told."

Out of breath from running, all Adriana could get out was, "…and splitting headaches."

Rance wandered around the Templar chapel waiting for A.T. and the women to arrive. He was amazed at the similarity of nearly every element of the hidden chapel to the one they had spent a number of days searching in Scotland. They had discovered the second piece of the map in a smaller chapel below the main one above. Here he'd observed only one level—below Lalibela.

Tina, feeling much better, was excited about the discovery her husband had made. Both women were enthusiastic about the opportunity to see it all for themselves. "It'll be grand to see Adriana and Al," Tina explained. "For a while there, I didn't think I'd see any one of you again."

A lone tear appeared and slowly worked its way alongside her nose as she looked tenderly at Mac. "You, dear friend, saved my life." Then a smile brightened her expression. "So, you have permission to kiss my husband—but only on his cheek." A much needed collective laugh ensued.

"Lay a hand on my wife and I'll break both your arms," Rance whispered into his mike.

"That tears it," Arturo said, pulling out his ear pod and threatening to toss it in the river. "There's no privacy whatsoever with these infernal contraptions."

"Just stick it back in your ear and lead the ladies to the chapel."

Adriana's news broke up the banter. "I'm on my way back with four village men and supplies—and I can't wait to see what you've found."

Leaving Mac and Tina to marvel at the interior structure of the Templar chapel, Rance and A.T. went to assist Al and Adriana out of the water and retrieve floating baskets of supplies. Reaching down to grasp Adriana's hand, A.T. frowned and asked, "Where's my keg of beer?"

"I drank it all before leaping into the river," Al answered for her. "Thought I'd float better," he laughed at his bewildered friend.

"Better grab hold of the second basket, A.T.—before it's swept away by the current—it's full of your favorite brew," Adriana warned.

Prepared to jump in after the basket full of beer, Al caught A.T.'s arm. "Here, take hold of this rope, it's attached to the floating brewery."

"You two can handle the supplies," Adriana said with anticipation. "I'm joining Mac and Tina. You said the stairway was to our left?" A.T. nodded yes. Following the beam of her flashlight, she carefully picked her way along the sandy pathway to the carved stairs.

"Wow!" was all Adriana could muster as she walked in a circle, staring at the carved flowers on the ceiling. "They were right. It looks just like Rosslyn Chapel—except for the missing apprentice column—and of course, the red volcano rock instead of marble."

"You studied archeology, Adriana," Mac said. "Do you suppose that both renditions of Rosslyn Chapel are in reality duplicates of an earlier, yet undiscovered structure?"

Adriana studied Mac's face before answering. "You have a very inquisitive mind and would make a great investigative archeologist. I had not thought of that. The answer is that it's possible. Perhaps we're looking at an exact duplicate of a room that existed in Solomon's Temple. The temple where it's rumored the Knights Templar uncovered their original wealth."

"I don't know about you guys, but before we begin a search for something that will lead us to the treasure," Rance said patting the cargo pant pocket with the Templar journal and piece of the second map wrapped in a waterproof pouch, "we should have something to eat."

"And to quench my thirst," Arturo added, opening the second basket.

"And let's stow our ear pods in our pockets," Rance suggested, "and give our ears a rest. We can all hear each other in here."

Everyone was too excited to relax and enjoy the food, so they wolfed down Father Gebra's offering, and went about the task of searching for hidden compartments. Rance split the team members up, each taking a section of the chapel. Being familiar with the chapel in Scotland, they moved about quickly, no longer in awe of the beauty created by master craftsmen. For hours, they pressed every carved face and pulled on any object that appeared to be a possible handle of some kind. With disappointing results.

L' Ami glanced at his watch. "Topside, it's after five o'clock and the treasure seekers union rules are to knock off work five sharp. I say we call it a long day and retire for refreshments."

"And I further suggest that we dust off the top of the small altar in the middle of the room and utilize it as a table," A.T. agreed. "Tina, pull my thermal blanket out of my backpack Rance retrieved for me and use it as a tablecloth, then I'll line the bar with the finest brew in Lalibela."

Adriana added to the lighter mood. "I'll get the dried meat, snacks and bread." She laughed, "We'll have a picnic."

"Somehow I don't believe that that's what our chapel builders had in mind," Rance offered, "but they're not here to object." Peering over both shoulders, he added, "I don't think."

While they ate, Rance gave his assessment of the afternoon's unfruitful search. "We've pushed, pulled, poked, and prodded every possible hiding place we could find—and with no positive result. We're missing something. I can sense it. But can't place my finger on what's on the edge of my mind."

The huge cave with its ornate chapel became silent except for sounds of chewing and occasional swallows of Lalibela's best. "I suggest that after our main meal we all hit the sack early and resume again first thing in the morning. Maybe one of us will have an epiphany by then."

Each couple, comforted in each others arms and wrapped in thermal blankets, enjoyed a rewarding and much needed deep sleep—except for one—who woke after an enlightening dream. Adriana stirred, careful not to wake her husband. She recalled the flames and the cries of agony of a man roasting alive. The date was October 13, 1307, she recalled. But there was something significant about the flames and the infamous date of the 13th. She lay wide awake until the others began to move about.

"Oh, my kingdom for a cup of coffee," Arturo moaned.

"Goat juice will have to do," Tina said as she poked him in the belly.

"Yeah," Al chimed in, "and my kingdom and wife for a shot of JD, oof!" Adriana had learned the old elbow move from Mac.

Rance stood and stretched sore muscles. "Mac, how's your shoulder this morning? A rock bed makes for a hard mattress."

She followed his lead and began her normal morning stretching exercises. Rotating her right arm, she answered, "It's a little stiff, that's all. Pain's gone."

L' Ami looked at his wife and made a face. "What's wrong, dear? You have a strange expression on your face. See a ghost like Tina did back in the Rosslyn Chaple?" He'd soon find out.

"Nothing I want to talk about until the night cobwebs clear," she said. "Let's have a little breakfast and get on with the day." Glancing in Rance's direction, she asked, "What's on the agenda for today's search?"

Raising both shoulders he shook his head and for once appeared not to have an answer. "I wish I knew—and I'm open to any and all suggestions. Anyone?" No one offer to respond. "Okay, Adriana's breakfast sounds like a plan."

"Breakfast?" A.T. shivered. "That stuff Gebra sent along as breakfast looks like gruel, smells like gruel. I'd rather have another beer."

"…if you hadn't finished off the last bottle yourself," Tina reminded him.

"Oh yeah," he admitted.

"Gruel's a staple," Rance said. "It's mashed grain mixed with goat milk. Very nutritious."

"That's not the way I hear it," A.T. countered. "They used to feed it to prisoners as a form of torture."

"Well, I'll have my eggs over easy, darling wife. Did you bring your frying pan with you?"

"If I did," Adriana chuckled, "you wouldn't still be standing, my dear husband."

Rance smacked his hands together. "I'm glad to see that we're still one happy treasure-seeking family. Might I suggest that we dump A.T.'s gruel in the river, each have a delicious breakfast power bar, then go about the task of the day? At this point, I have no plan except to continue what we were doing yesterday. Hopefully, we missed something."

Two hours into the search, L' Ami slapped the side of one of the huge pillars in frustration. "Damn it Rance, there's nothing here."

Rance walked over to his friend and leaned against the structure. "I hate to admit it, but you're probably right. I'm at a loss as to what to do next."

"I have an idea," Adriana said meekly.

When Rance said, "Let's hear it," she became somewhat intimidated by the others' attention as they gathered around. Straightening her posture and flipping her long red mane, she explained.

"It was last night's dream…"

Arturo looked at Tina, then Adriana. "It wasn't Sir Willy again, was it?" Then he backed away out of Tina's elbow range.

Giving A.T. a nasty stare, she continued. "It had to do with flames and the number thirteen." Becoming very uncomfortable, she shuffled her feet. Al placed a comforting hand on her shoulder which seemed to give her the courage to go on. "I saw de Molay being burned at the stake. At least in my dream. And if you'll remember, he died on the 13th day of October." Everyone nodded.

"I woke up with two impressions—flames and the number thirteen." She gestured to the torches along the perimeter of the circular room. "As I lay awake, I counted the number of torches. There are twenty-six in all. Thirteen, starting from the right to the center—and thirteen from the far left to the center."

Rance snapped his fingers. "Two rows ending in thirteen at the center entrance to the chapel room, and flames." Stepping close, he shook her by the shoulders. "Now that's a clue worth pursuing. Good job, Adriana.

"Al, you take the thirteenth torch holder on the left. The one to the right is mine. Twist it both ways and try pulling. Let's see what happens, if anything."

Both men did their best, but nothing happened. "Do it in tandem," Mac suggested.

Al looked at Rance and said, "Now." They twisted the flame holders to the left. Nothing. Then to the right. Same negative results.

"Pull straight out on the count of three," Rance said.

Everyone held their breath. Nothing. An expression of utter disappointment crossed six glum-looking faces. Then a low rumbling noise spun them on their heels. To their amazement, the small center altar began to sink into the floor. By the time they arrived at the spot, the top of the altar was five feet below the chapel floor.

Rance sank to his knees, illuminating the darkened pit with his bright beam. "It appears empty. The only thing visible is the altar. I'm going inside to check out the corners where my beam can't reach."

"Rance," Mac said. "What if the altar rises, leaving you trapped inside the pit?"

"I'll have to take that chance," he said and pointed to his two best friends, "and they'll have to find a way to get me out." Slipping over the edge, he completed his thought. "That's their problem. Not mine."

Mac searched the ceiling for help. A.T. placed an arm around her shoulders and said, "As long as I've known him, he's always been like that."

"I'll second that," came out of Al's mouth.

"Hey guys!" Rance shouted from below. "I've found a box made out of red rock. It's about three feet by four and a foot high. I'll place it on the altar. A.T., lean over, grab hold, and hand it up to Al."

When the box was removed, Rance managed to wiggle his way to the top of the altar, and then pulled himself up onto the floor. "That wasn't so bad," he said to Mac, who didn't appreciate his matter-of-fact attitude.

"Al, let's push those torch holders back in place to see if the altar will move to its normal position." They did, and it did.

A.T. picked the heavy box off the floor and placed it on the altar. After looking it over, he said, "Honey, there's a long knife in my pack. Would you please get it for me—there's a seal of some kind binding the lid to the box. I think I can break the seal with the point of the knife."

"I'm going to be disappointed if the bones of another wayward rabbi is inside," L' Ami said under his breath.

It took the better part of ten minutes to make a dent in the substance the Templars used to seal whatever was inside the mystery box carved out of volcano rock. Al took over when Arturo's hand cramped up. Then it was Rance's turn.

"It's finally coming off," Rance said with a wide grin. "There," he said, lifting the lid. Everyone strained their necks to peer inside.

"It's empty," Adriana groaned.

"No," Rance corrected her as he reached in and pulled out a dark folded piece of what felt like vellum. Laying it on the altar, he carefully opened it as everyone gasped in surprise. It was the third piece of the map with words written in Latin that said, *'Guardians Behold Our Keeping.'*

"What is this?" Mac moaned. "A Templar version of a Snipe Hunt?"

"Something like that," Rance answered, removing the original Templar Journal and the map they had found in the Rosslyn Chapel. He laid out the journal with the page opened to the first map: then unfolded the second map and matched it to the right hand side of the first. "This new map fits perfectly into the bottom left hand corner."

"We're missing the bottom right side to complete the map," L' Ami noted.

Rance agreed. Folding the maps to return them to his cargo pant pocket, he added, "And I've got an idea about that…"

Before he could finish, Adriana offered her opinion. "We'll find it on Oak Island."

Closing his eyes, Rance shook his head. "More experienced explorers and treasure hunters—including your husband—have searched that island and its money pit for hundreds of years without success. His head slowly moved from side to side. "No. I have a better idea. I think."

"I agree with Adriana," Al said. "There's something about that island and the mysterious stone's carving that I felt with my fingers while crawling on my hands and knees in the fog."

Rance's eyes were mere slits as he asked a question of his two best friends. "Those Templars, on the run from their enemies, were a sly and inventive bunch. Put yourself in their boots. If you wanted to hide a treasure—be it gold or ancient relics—where would you hide them?"

Raising a hand to halt the reply, he went on. "Recall, if you will, eight years ago when we were in the Iranian desert to rescue a diplomat's kidnapped daughter. A powerful warlord kept her captive in a small cave surrounded with thirty of his men—all well armed. We didn't attempt the rescue by eliminating the small army. There were too many to be successful. It was too risky. What did we do?"

Al and A.T. eyes met. A silent message passed between them. A.T. stated what they both recalled. "We caused a diversion."

L' Ami completed the recollection. "While you and baldy crept as near to the cave's entrance as possible without being seen, I circled around to the backside of the mountain and set a charge of explosives, then made a dash for the confiscated weapons carrier we had hidden away."

Arturo picked it up from there. "When the explosion rocked the mountain, all but two of the warlord's army went in pursuit of those who had set the charge. We subdued the guards, rescued the girl, and Al met us with the vehicle. The diversion worked like a charm."

"And that's what I believe the Oak Island Money Pit is. A masterful diversion perpetrated by clever Knights Templar..." Rance never had the opportunity to complete his thought. A loud rumbling met their ears, and the cave floor shook so violently it threw them all to their knees.

"Let's get the hell out of here! They planted a booby-trap!" Tina shouted as she stood, unsteady, then made a run for the entrance. Mac and Adriana followed on her heels. Chunks of the carved ceiling fell throughout the temple. Dodging the falling debris, Al tripped but managed to get up and follow Adriana to safety. Arturo turned to see Rance make a mad dash for the altar to retrieve the map box just as the main pillars began to crumble inward. For seconds, the red rock pillars fell against one another forming a broken tent-like structure above Rance's bent figure. More of the delicately carved temple tumbled down as billows of red dust filled the cavern. Arturo ran to help his friend who would, in a matter of moments, be crushed by the teetering pillars. Against all odds, A.T. placed his hands and shoulder on the lead pillar in an effort to prevent it from falling and block Rance's path out from under the collapsing structure.

As strong as A.T. was, he was no match for the weight of the falling column—but his effort was just enough to give Rance the fraction of a second needed to escape. Shoving Arturo from behind, they ran through the red dust storm caused by the collapsing booby-trapped Templar chapel. Leaping over broken chunks of carved rock and dodging falling pieces of art, they emerged onto the steps, coughing and covered in dust.

Chapter Fifteen

RANCE RELAXED WHEN THE JET LEVELED OFF at forty thousand feet and placed the craft on autopilot. They had serious planning to do if they were to uncover the spot where the Knights Templar would have sailed after implementing their clever and elaborate hoax on Oak Island. *Their* diversion. Entering the underground river and using the rope to pull themselves back to the subterranean tunnels had work as planned. Thanking Father Gebra and the villagers for their hospitality, they told two white lies. They expressed disappointment in having found nothing of interest in their quest—and no, they had not noticed a tremor felt throughout the area. It was the searcher's collective opinion that the collapse of the temple was due directly to a booby trap, triggered by the movement of the altar, set by the Templars to ambush and entomb those who had discovered the map in the box.

His five fellow treasure hunters were grouped around the small conference table, drinking coffee and examining the three sections of map. "Any ideas forming as to where our Knights would have set sail after planting their hoax?" Rance asked, taking a chair next to Mac. His question was answered by a smattering of murmurs and shaking heads.

"Well now," he said, snapping open a crisp new map of America's northeast coast, "let's see what we have here. Where could *we* have sailed to if *we* were on board a Templar ship loaded with treasure? Leaning forward, his finger stabbed Oak Island, a small dot off Nova Scotia. Using the same finger, he pointed out Prince Edward Island to the north, then a small unidentified island above that. And further northeast, Newfoundland and a cluster of islands. "Take your pick of islands—or Nova Scotia itself—or out across the Atlantic," he ended with a deep sense of frustration.

L' Ami placed his empty coffee cup over the bay where Oak Island was located, not far from the Halifax Airport. "Here's where I say we start. Digging around the Money Pit remains on hold until the boss man, Fred Nolan, returns. I've gotten acquainted with the small group of guards he maintains. By now, they're probably bored to death and lax on security." Filling his cup from a bottle of JD, he looked up at Rance and lifted it to his lips. "That's where I say we start, forget about where they would have sailed—at least for now. I've got a gut feeling about this."

Rance gave him a thumbs up. "Okay. Unless anyone has objections, let's go with your gut feeling." An agreement was unanimous.

Closing his eyes to recall a photo in a history book, Rance explained what he saw. "There was a stone discovered deep within the Money Pit with strange markings. Circles with a dot inside: squares with dots around the outer lines: a number of equal length crosses: and something that looks like a question mark."

"A Halifax professor believes that the translation says, 'Forty feet below two million pounds are buried,' " Adriana added to the story. "However, after studying the professor's interpretation, in my opinion the symbols are too modern-looking to be believable."

"You're right, Adriana," Rance approved. "That was my analysis as well. They look like symbols you'd find on the side of a spacecraft from outer space, rather than carved by a Knight from the fourteen century—master mason or not."

"A.T., hand me my bag behind your seat," Al asked. Slipping a note pad from a side pocket, he opened to a page with an ink diagram. "This is the sketch I made during my visit to Oak Island and the Money Pit a few weeks back. Note the placement of the drilled rocks and the triangle of stones. I've drawn lines between each major element. They make a large and perfect triangle—and then there's the smaller triangle of stones."

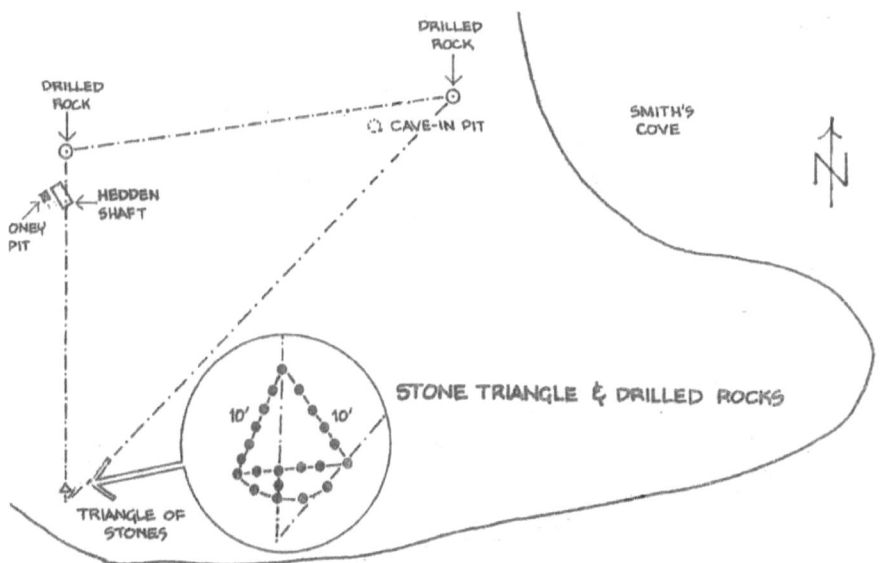

Rance rubbed his chin and remained silent. Arturo mumbled, "Look out everyone. Boss man's conjuring up a plan."

"Maybe we should all take a shot of Al's JD before my learned husband speaks his mind," Mac suggested with a wide grin.

"I could use one even if he doesn't say another word," Tina chimed in.

"You of no faith," Rance said without a hint of humor. "If I can continue," he waited for their answer. Silence. So he continued. "Think about this," he said, tapping Al's sketch. "That. Those rocks *are* a map."

BISHOP STOOD IN AN OUTSIDE COFFEE SHOP, rubbing his ample behind and scowling at Paschal, who had been on the receiving end of the big man's foul comments. As before, Edmond had managed to strike all the same rocks and potholes on their return trip to Addis Ababa, and Claude, the Bishop, took Paschal's name in vain with each jarring bump. All four were as dusty as the dented vehicle. Ever since the air conditioning ceased to operate, they were forced to lower the windows—which only increased Bishop's displeasure and attack on the helpless man. To Paschal's credit, he matched the boss, scowl for scowl.

"I don't like what's going on in that pea brain of yours, little man," Bishop warned. "It's a good thing that I cannot read that warped mind, or I'd slit your throat."

Changing the subject, he pointed at the electronic tracking monitor Maurice was holding on a tabletop. "Are they still out over the Atlantic?"

Paschal looked over Maurice's shoulder. "No. It appears that they've landed somewhere in Canada." Reaching over, he tapped several keys to align coordinates with an overhead satellite. "There. The aircraft is sitting on the tarmac at the Nova Scotia, Halifax Airport."

"Ah yes. Just as expected." Bishop smiled and wiped beads of sweat from his forehead with a well-worn silk handkerchief. "They are headed for Oak Island—site of the Money Pit excavation." He raised a single stubby fat finger and followed it with two more. "First. Rosslyn Chapel in Scotland. Then the subterranean tunnels in Lalibela. And now, the Money Pit of Nova Scotia. They must be on the trail of *our* treasure."

"The women: I wonder if they survived?" Paschal thought out loud.

"For them to fly directly from Ethiopia to Nova Scotia—it's a good guess that they survived their swim. If two of the wives had perished, they would not pursue the treasure so soon," Bishop speculated.

"...and," Paschal added, "they would be after our sorry asses. I'm sure they figured out by now who removed the warning signs and the barrier."

Bishop finally sat down: some of the pain in his rear had subsided. "If there's any indication that they've hit pay dirt, we'll get our chance soon enough. And be ready."

Downing his third cup of coffee, he whispered through his teeth, "Where in the hell is Edmond? He ought to be back from returning *your* rattle trap by now."

Poking a finger at Paschal's chest, he demanded to know, "Is the chartered craft preflight complete and fueled? I'm anxious to be on the move." He poked again. "Have you made reservations at a private home for the week on the island? One with four bedrooms, running water, electricity, and air conditioning: a house unlike the shack you secured for us in Lalibela." Paschal sipped from his cup and barely acknowledged the question. He was fuming deep down inside. *When this is over...*

RANCE LOUNGED ON THE KING-SIZED BED of the Oak Island Resort and Spa, his hands entwined behind his head. Mac assumed the same position. Both were lost in their own thoughts. Leaning over to kiss his wife's cheek, Rance said, "Somehow I don't feel like we'll find the fourth corner of the map here—but I have to give Al his due. His gut feelings have seldom been wrong. Though he's given up on his original cross theory."

Mac stretched and sat up with her back to the headboard. "When you piece the three sections together, you have an ancient map of the known world, at least the Atlantic Ocean portion with rough outlines of land masses on either side. If we could find a similar map, it might provide us with what the bottom quarter of the map would have looked like."

Rance sat bolt straight and slapped his thigh. "By damn! You may have solved the riddle."

"What do you mean?"

"If you recall, we pretty much agreed that the Knights Templar designed the Money Pit as a hoax—as a diversion. And remember what I said offhand when Al showed us his sketch of the stone placement?"

"You said that those rocks *are* the map: or something like that."

"I wasn't really serious when I said that: it just came out. Well, now that you stimulated my mind with your observation, I believe that I'm right."

"I'm delighted that I was of help—but right about what?"

"If we could find an ancient map of about the same vintage that would provide us with the bottom corner—then superimpose Al's sketch coordinates over the completed map—we might have the location of the treasure we've been searching for."

Mac grinned. "We make one hell of a team. Mr. and Mrs. Adam Rance, treasure hunters par excellence."

"Sounds nice, but aren't you forgetting Mr. and Mrs. L' Ami and Mr. and Mrs. Testaccio? We have to give them some credit."

"If you insist," she said, leaning over to embrace her husband.

AL WAS HARD AT WORK BUYING DRINKS FOR HIS long lost friends. Spotting two of the pit guards he had made friends with on his last visit, he invited them to his table and asked the bartender to bring a full bottle of Jack Daniel's, two more glasses, and a bucket of ice. It was necessary to learn the schedule the guards followed during the day and night shifts. Burt and Sam, his new drinking buddies, had just gotten off duty: the night crew was watching the site. L' Ami's wheels were turning. A thermos of drugged coffee to sedate them would do the trick. An early morning gift from their new friend would place them in a deep sleep long enough for the team to survey the area without interruption.

A slight nod by the man pouring from a bottle of Jack Daniel's acknowledged the arrival of five thirsty and hungry Oak Island visitors. Once L' Ami had all the information needed and his companions had staggered home, he would join his wife and friends for dinner.

When Al arrived at his friends' table, they were discussing Mac's suggestion in whispered tones. Adriana had taken up the subject with animated interest. "I've studied the three pieces of the map Rance has in his possession. It will be nearly impossible to use the coordinates derived from Al's Money Pit diagram."

"And why is that, my Spanish Butter Cup?" Al asked, picking up the dinner menu.

"Because, dear husband, maps during the period of time in which they were drawn, were very rough, at best. Landmass outlines of Europe and Africa were fairly accurate, though often distorted. Just familiarize yourself with the three pieces we have: you'll see what I mean. Outlines of the Americas were just that: nondescript land contours."

"Unfortunately, she's correct in her assessment," Rance agreed. "Unlike today's maps, those drawn five hundred years ago lacked the exact measurements and accuracy of continent placement that we presently enjoy."

"But you told me that..." Mac was about to question him on their bedroom discussion when he stepped on her words.

"Yes, as I had expressed to you, I believe we can use the three maps in our possession plus a piece of an ancient map to provide us with the missing bottom right corner—specifically the vicinity around the continent of Africa. With all four corners programmed into a computer, we can reconstruct the ancient continent placement and compare configurations to a modern day map of the lands, lesser oceans, and rivers on either side of the Atlantic Ocean."

"Then we can superimpose Al's sketch over the newly constructed map," Tina observed.

"You're right on target," Rance said. Mimicking Al, he picked up his menu and added, "Tomorrow, we'll split up the team. While the men give the site a good look-see—after the guards take their long nap—the ladies will search the various museums for copies of ancient maps and a facility where they can use a computer without being bothered by onlookers. Adriana will take lead on that portion of tomorrow's mission. She's the expert on the subject." Snapping the menu, he said, "Now let's eat."

Adriana beamed with pride. The other two women might have felt slighted but knowing full well that Rance had been hard on their Spanish sister in the past, they felt her assignment was deserved.

With an expression of utter puzzlement, Tina said, "Something's been bothering me ever since we set foot in the Templar chapel by that raging underground river. How in God's name did they cart those huge columns, altar, pulpit, and other carved objects down those steep stairs and through tunnels hardly wide and high enough for us to pass through?" She paused and went on. "They couldn't have floated them on the river: it flowed in the wrong direction."

Rance gave her a fatherly smile and turned to Adriana. "Would you like to answer her question?"

"Thank you, master," Adriana said, tongue-in-cheek. "Tina, they didn't transport what you witnessed: they carved the chapel out of the volcano rock as they did the churches above ground."

"Carved all that out of rock," Tina blew out a low whistle.

"Indeed. Very much the way the hidden temple of Petra was formed. In the Jordanian desert, through a narrow deep gorge, the original inhabitants carved a huge and magnificent temple out of the cliffs—with a multitude of rooms leading from the façade into the temple."

"Where did they put all the rocks and dirt they took out?" Mac asked. "They couldn't dump it all in the river."

"I believe I can answer that," Rance said. "A few nights back I took a quick tour of the cavern past where the stairway leading underground is located. In the back of the cavern, there are what appear to be discarded rocks of varying sizes. At first I thought they were from church construction—but now believe they came from the manmade cave temple—as Adriana correctly described."

Al, sitting to Rance's left, leaned over and changed the subject. "Tomorrow's diversion's taken care of. All I need is a visit to the hotel pharmacy to purchase a thermos, a bottle of sleeping pills, and fill the thermos with hot coffee in the morning. A courtesy morning cocktail is all Burt and Sam will need: then we can snoop to our heart's content."

During the meal, Arturo questioned the wisdom of giving Adriana the Templar Journal and the two recovered maps. Bishop and his henchmen could have them under surveillance. Rance assured him that the originals would remain in his keep. Using the hotel's printer, he had made color copies of all three maps. Besides, after considering Tina's expertise with weapons and Mac's martial arts talent, he had complete confidence in the ladies' ability to take care of themselves.

"I HOPE TO HELL you know where you're going," A.T. said with concern. The early morning fog hung close to the surface of the water as Al rowed his partners across the bay in a small, rented boat. The motor was off so as not to give away an approaching boat, alerting the guards.

"Just let me worry about that, baldy," L' Ami snapped. "I'm the one doing all the muscle work and growing blisters on my sensitive hands. Relax and rest that large Italian butt until we get there. I'm taking the long way into Smith's Cove. From there, it's a short walk to the Money Pit site. You two hang back out of sight while I greet my drinking buddies and safely put them to sleep. When I whistle, come ahead."

"Whistle? You mean like a bird call?" A.T. needled his friend. "Which bird? We don't want to react to the wrong bird."

"You two birds can the chatter," Rance intervened. "Sound travels on water and Al's drinking buddies may hear more than a bird call."

Twenty minutes later, out of breath, Al jumped to a rocky shore to tie off the boat and pull it close. Rance tossed him the thermos. It was a good thing that the fog had thinned considerably, because the terrain was rough between the shore and the site. Appearing from behind a lone tree, L' Ami shouted to the startled security guards. "Burt, Sam, it's me, Al! I've brought my good buddies some coffee!"

They first reached for their guns, but once recognizing their new friend, they relaxed and embraced the idea of hot coffee. The fog was both cool and wet. He and the coffee were a welcomed sight. Burt unscrewed the cup and poured steaming liquid into his cup. Al flipped a second cup to Sam. Burt did the honors. They drank heartily as the three discussed the weather, Jack Daniel's, and the boredom of their job. Al refused coffee, claiming that he had had his fill already, but suggested that they relax by a large tree stump. Fifteen minutes later, both guards were snoring up a storm. L' Ami whistled.

UTILIZING A COMPUTER at the Halifax main library, the three women grouped around the widescreen monitor. "We've gone through a dozen ancient maps of Europe including Africa—and you've seen," Adriana said in frustration, "they are all distortions of the actual contours of the land masses."

"The Templar maps are superior to the ones you've pulled up," Mac observed.

"And of course, the outline of the Americas in no way resembles our maps of today—they merely show a flat non-descript surface with hundreds of inlets," Tina added.

"One thing though, you have to applaud the mapmakers for their colorful renditions," Adriana said pointing to the screen, "of giant wide-mouthed serpents swallowing ships whole and…"

"…and puffy cheeked angels blowing the wind from all corners of the known world." Tina finished Adriana's thought.

Mac chuckled aloud. "In nearly every map, the continent of Africa had a different shape—a few were close to what we now know it to be—and others had shapes of every design, from a long narrow continent to one that wrapped around touching India. What imaginations."

Tina added her observations. "Imaginations? We've seen round maps, square maps—and even one map indicated a box-like earth."

"Well, it's been an interesting and informative hour and a half but hasn't brought us any closer to finding a bottom corner to match the two-thirds we have," Adriana said, her frustration mounting.

Mac asked, "Does this computer have the ability to download scanned objects—and then move them about on the same page?"

"According to the home page data, yes. What do you have in mind?" Adriana asked.

"Presently we have three separate portions of the map puzzle. I'm suggesting that you scan each in, fit them together, and save it. If we come across a map that's closer to the actual shape of Africa, you then insert it into the missing corner. From what we've seen so far, that's the best we can hope for."

"Right," Tina agreed. "At least we'd have one whole map to work with instead of three or four pieces."

"That way Rance can do his magic by overlaying Al's sketch coordinates over both the Templar map and a current one to see if they match—or contradict each other," Mac suggested.

Adriana's fingers flew on the computer keys.

"THEY'RE SLEEPING LIKE BABIES," A.T. said, noting the two guards slumped against the stump.

"They'll feel a little woozy when they open their eyes and realize what happened to them," Al said. "And it's a good thing that the girls checked us out of the hotel before heading for Halifax, because these guys are going to be mad as hell at me—and no doubt come looking to string me up."

"Once we're through here and drop the boat off at the dock, we'll hail a cab to take us directly to the Cambridge Suites Hotel in Halifax. Mac made the reservations this morning after our early breakfast."

Rance pointed to L' Ami's chest pocket. "Let's take a peek at your sketch. Then walk us through the site."

"To our north, not far from the bank leading down to the water, is the first drilled rock—a few steps from a useless caved-in pit. Walk almost due west for approximately four hundred feet and we'll come to the next drilled rock. A few feet due south and we'll run into the Money Pit and the Hedden Shaft. Continue south another three hundred feet and you'll see a most interesting gathering of drilled stones laid out in the shape of a triangle."

"You mentioned that a Mr. Nolan had a map in his possession indicating intersecting lines making a cross next to what you called the Headstone," Rance reminded him.

"Unfortunately, I have no knowledge of the map except to say that it's reported he has one. But I can direct you to the Headstone."

"Save that for later," Rance said. "Right now I'm interested in the formation of the triangle of drilled rocks. We'll leave the Templar's fake Money Pit to the treasure hunters."

Rance was on his knees crawling from one drilled rock to another when A.T. made an observation. "Stand up so you can appreciate the triangle and tell me what you see."

Doing as he was told, Rance stood and ran fingers through his hair. "Each side of the triangle is approximately ten-feet in length making a perfect pyramid with the same number of stones on each side."

"And at the base are four additional drilled rocks in the form of a quarter circle," A.T. finished the evaluation.

Rance's eyes narrowed when he said, "This is the most significant find so far. Point me in the direction of the Headstone."

An odd cone-shaped stone made of rough sandstone lay partially hidden by clumps of dried grass. Weather-worn markings were carved into the soft surface. "No wonder you used the Braille system, Al—the carvings are barely visible."

"Can you make anything out of them?" Arturo asked, kneeling down for a closer look.

While Rance ran his fingers over the raised surface, Al mentioned what he'd been told by Sam—to date, no one has been able to decipher the message of the Headstone. Shaking his head and walking a circle around the stone several times, he suddenly stopped and grinned. "What?" A.T. asked.

"Those sneaky sons-of-guns," he laughed. "They wrote their message in Latin—then buried the Headstone upside down. No wonder it's never been deciphered."

Glancing over at the sleeping beauties, he asked L' Ami, "How much longer do you figure they'll be out?"

Checking his watch, Al tilted his head. "Another two hours if we're lucky. What do you have in mind?"

"We need to break into that shed over there," Rance said, motioning with his head, "and borrow a couple of shovels. We're going to dig the dirt out from around the Headstone and see if we can read the Templar message—then replace the dirt and grass to hide our dig."

One half-hour later, they had a wide hole around the stone two feet deep. All three men were on their knees, brushing away loose dirt. "Okay," Rance said, "Let's see if we can read this thing."

Arturo and Al stood watching their friend with his head in the hole, inching his way around the rock. Out of patience, A.T. asked, "Well?"

Without moving his head, Rance raised a finger, signaling to stay calm. Moments later, he sat back on his haunches, looked up, and dusted his hands off. "You won't believe this…"

"Try us," L' Ami said, irritated by Rance's delay.

Standing and grabbing a shovel, he said, "Let's get the dirt and grass back in place before those guys wake up, and I'll tell you what they wrote."

A.T. grumbled. "You know, you always do that to us. I'm not shoveling anything until you tell us what the message said."

Rance, as usual, enjoyed the moment, then answered, sporting a wide grin. "It says, 'Guardians Behold Our Keeping.' "

Chapter Sixteen

"ONE THING WE KNOW FOR CERTAIN," Rance said, referring to a blow-up of L' Ami's sketch of the Money Pit site pinned on the wall of his and Mac's suite, "is that the Templars were fascinated by pyramids." Walking to the wall, he ran his finger over the dotted lines from the first drilled rock closest to the water's edge—then to the second by the Money Pit—to the triangle of stones. "A large pyramid and a smaller more defined one."

"And they're keen on burying things upside down," A.T. reminded him.

"Don't forget—diversions," Al said, heading for the mini-bar. "Anyone for a refill?"

For the better part of the next five minutes, the three friends sipped their drinks and silently pondered the sketch and the possibilities associated with the three elements, pyramids, upside down burials, and diversions. Arturo Testaccio's wide grin broke the spell.

He glanced first to Rance, then to L' Ami. "I know just what you're thinking, my Italian friend," Al said, reading his mind, grin, and mischievous twinkle.

"That makes three of us, but I'm not going to be the first to utter a word." Rance threw them a sheepish smile and continued. "Mac might have our room bugged." They all doubled up in hysterics.

"Well, I'll be the brave one," Al said wiping his eyes. "We were all thinking that this is the first time in many a moon that it has seemed like the good old days—just the three of us dodging bullets and beating up on the bad guys."

"Yeah," A.T. said. "And tearing apart another of Rance's plans that might get us all killed."

"And most often...came close," L' Ami added under his breath. Heading for the bar again, he turned and raised an empty glass of JD. "Here's to the good old days. Days that I wouldn't trade for anything in this world." Rance and A.T. returned his gesture with gusto.

"Do you two remember the time...?" Arturo's offering was cut short by the jiggle of the door knob and a plastic key-card slipping into the electronic door lock. "It's the women," he whispered and closed his mouth.

When the door opened and three bubbling females entered, it was L' Ami who blurted out, "We were just saying how much we missed you gals." Rance and A.T. looked at each other wide-eyed, then shot their rat-friend a nasty *how could you* look.

Adriana was all smiles: they had accomplished their assignment, and she was anxious to report their success. After a hug and a kiss from her husband, and noticing the large reproduction of Al's sketch, she picked up a handful of push pins and headed for the wall. Unrolling the large rolled up sheet in her hand, she tacked it next to the other. "There's our ancient map of the world," she boasted.

"As close as she could get it—under the circumstances," Tina added.

"You should have seen what Adriana had to work with: renditions of old maps didn't even come close to being accurate," Mac said.

Rance stepped up to the large map that included the recently discovered section from the Templar Journal, plus the bottom right-hand corner lifted from the computer. Surprisingly, it was a good fit. It would have to do.

Standing facing Adriana's map with hands on hips, Rance considered the possibilities. How could they use the Templar maps and Al's sketch to pinpoint the treasure, whatever it was? He nodded his head.

"We have our work cut out for us. Adriana, you, Tina and Mac did a fine job. Thanks."

"Don't applaud, Husband. Pour us a drink," Mac suggested with a grin.

They lounged in Mac and Rance's suite in an atmosphere of satisfaction, enjoying their drinks. Next they would have to confront the difficult job of rationalizing and fusing Al's sketch with the Templar composite map. After an early dinner, they would attack the map's puzzle with refreshed minds.

"THE BARTENDER REMEMBERS the three couples," Paschal reported to Bishop, who occupied most of the plush curved booth in the bar of the hotel where the six treasure hunters had stayed. "He also said that since they had totaled up their tab and paid the bill—he's pretty certain they had checked out this morning."

"You should have let me take them out when we had the chance, Boss," Maurice moaned. Edmond grunted and nodded in agreement.

"You're both idiots," Bishop said through his teeth, then downing a half glass of red wine, he signaled for another. "Paschal, tell the bartender to bring me a full bottle this time, and while you're at it, get these two some brains."

Paschal stormed off, tired of always being the go-fer. Returning to the booth, he felt a tug on his shirtsleeve. Angrily yanking it away, he looked into the eyes of a man whose hair was white as snow, his eyes a clouded blue and his skin as tan and leathery as an old work glove. "The name's Sam, it is, and this here baldheaded gent with the pancake flat nose is my partner, Burt…"

Tossing them a nasty expression, Paschal prepared to step away before Sam finished his introduction. "…we're guards at the Money Pit, we are."

"You are, are you? And why would that interest me?" he asked, knowing full well that he wanted to hear more. "What interest is that of mine?"

Sam grinned and nodded to Burt. "We couldn't help but overhear you gents discussin' a group that was stayin' here and left first thing this mornin'. Burt and I would be wantin' to know where the three gents ran off to. The dirty bastards drugged our mornin' coffee, they did. Could have gotten us fired, they coulda'. The early mornin' dew made the sod real soft—and they were footprints all around the site. They were after somethin' but nothin', as far as we could see, was disturbed."

Paschal clapped Sam on the shoulder and turned to get the bartender's attention. Raising two fingers and pointing to Sam and Burt, he motioned to serve them whatever they were drinking, and then pointed to himself, indicating to put the drinks on his tab. "You boys have earned yourselves drinks on me—and if we run into the three gents that drugged your coffee—we'll give 'em your regards." He showed them a closed fist. They grinned with satisfaction.

"Those two old clowns," Paschal motioned with his head, "I was talking with are Money Pit guards. Seems that our friends drugged their coffee earlier this morning so that they could snoop around without being bird-dogged."

"Did they say where our friends were headed next?" Bishop asked.

"All they know is that they've checked out."

"Edmond, open your laptop: see if their plane's still at that small airstrip," Bishop ordered.

They leaned forward, stretching their necks to view the screen with its blinking red tracking dot. "Still there, Boss. Our friends are still in the area."

Bishop was silent, stroking his numerous chins. "They're most likely using their real names: there's no reason not to," he surmised.

"Hack into the reservations listing in all major hotels in Halifax—and see if the names of Rance, Testaccio, or L' Ami surface."

Eight minutes later, Edmond's eyes lit up. "Here they are, Boss. They're all staying at the Cambridge Suites Hotel in Halifax. They're scheduled for check-out tomorrow."

"Excellent," Boss said, rubbing pudgy palms together. "That can only mean one of two things: they found what they were looking for—or they failed."

Pointing at the laptop, he continued. "Check with the airport and see if they've filed a flight plan: then check on available aircraft for hire."

Edmond looked up from his computer. "You want a jet plane, right?"

"No, idiot," he answered with a look of utter frustration. "We want a WW I biplane to race after a Lear Jet." Slamming his palm on the table and spilling everyone's drink, he sneered, "When this is over, I don't want to see hide nor hair of the three of you. I'm sitting with two idiots and another who can't even rent a decent car."

Bishop apologized to the bartender for the mess and clean-up and handed him a wad of bills for his trouble. "We're in luck," Edmond reported with a whisper. "Not two minutes ago, a flight plan was called into airport operations. They're heading for Spain."

Bishop's lips parted, then turned up into a wide grin. "They must have something, or they wouldn't be heading home. None of them are quitters. It's time to strike."

Considering his plan, he added, "And in case we fail—Edmond, charter the fastest jet available and have the pilot file a flight plan into the Seville Airport. It's a short drive to Tarego and their castle from there."

"This time, Edmond rents the car and *I* drive," Paschal said with conviction. Without wasting another breath, he asked, "Explain: 'It's time to strike.' "

"We kidnap one of the wives and use her in a trade for whatever it is they discovered that will point us to the treasure."

"WE NOW KNOW THE TEMPLARS UTILIZED three elements when concocting their last *'Guardians Behold Our Keeping'* message," Rance said, standing with his back to the suite wall. "One, a large and small pyramid: two, deception—The Money Pit: three, they buried the message carved on the rock, upside down."

"…and that takes us where?" Arturo asked.

"It takes Al up front to help me—because you're too short to reach the pushpins holding up the sketch and map," Rance answered with a raised brow and a smirk.

In response, A.T. brushed the back of his fingers off the end of his chin in typical Italian fashion. His gesture brought a suite-full of good-natured laughs.

Tying a loop of stretchy string with a square knot, Rance placed a pushpin in Oak Island on the map and hung the circle of white string over the pin. Next he tossed a pin to Al and had him stick it in the Rosslyn Chapel location in Scotland—while he stuck another in Lalibela.

"Take a corner of the string and loop it over your pin," Rance said, "and I'll stretch my end over the Lalibela pin. There. We have a perfect pyramid connecting the three locations that we had searched."

"…which proves?" A.T. asked humorless.

"We're not through yet, short-stuff."

Taking a piece of hotel stationery, Rance folded the top of an eight-and-a-half by eleven sheet of paper, so all sides were the same length.

He had a square. "Are you making me a party hat?" A.T. asked with a twinkle in his eye.

Ignoring his sarcastic friend, Rance folded the right and left sides, making a peak at the top. He had made a triangle, a perfect pyramid. Turning the small pyramid upside down, he fitted the small base up against the large string pyramid base. "Looks like an inverted iceberg: the exposed part is larger than the piece below the sea," A.T. remarked.

Again he was ignored. Rance appeared puzzled. "Something's not right," he muttered. "The peak of the small pyramid is pointing to the Atlantic Ocean between Spain and Africa."

"Perhaps it marks the spot where a Templar ship sunk in stormy weather," Adriana offered an observation.

"I hope not," her husband moaned. "I don't relish going deep-sea diving in *those* waters. Davy Jones can keep his Templar treasure."

Mac, suddenly animated, leapt to her feet and nudged her husband aside. Poking a finger on the lower right-hand portion of the map, she said with enthusiasm, "You're forgetting one of the Templar's three elements: deception."

"How's that?" Rance asked.

"It's simple," was Mac's matter-of-fact reply. "Your large string pyramid's base is in line with the north and south compass symbol visible on the computer generated map—and the compass symbol that exists on the three-pieced Templar map is slightly different."

Using a finger, Mac tapped the north-south compass on the upper right-hand corner of an original Templar map. "See here, the arrow is not straight up and down as in the bottom corner of the computer portion of the map—it's slightly tilted to the west." Looking him in the eye, she poked his chest. "That's the Templar deception. Angle your string pyramid base to match the compass arrow and see where the small pyramid's tip points."

Tina and Adriana softly applauded their treasure-seeking sister's deductive powers. Following her direction, Rance and Al realigned the string pyramid's base. Once done, Rance did the same with the upside down pyramid. Gathering around the map on the wall, they gasped aloud. Tina was the first to speak. "It's…it's pointing to the exact location where your…de Molay Castle…is perched on the cliff overlooking the Atlantic Ocean."

PHYSICALLY AND MENTALLY EXHAUSTED, yet outwardly excited, the couples retired to their own suites. Rance had made a call to have the jet serviced and filed a flight plan for home. Mac excused herself, informing her husband that she needed a new shower cap and was going downstairs to the gift shop to make the purchase. She'd be right back, she said, kissing him on the cheek.

With her attention focused on the digital elevator numbers, Mac had failed to notice two men slipping up behind her. Edmond, the skinny one, grabbed her arms and pinned them back as her shower cap flew in the air. Her reaction was immediate. By instinct, the third-stage black belt, Rance-trained martial arts expert spun around. Although Edmond had her by a few pounds, Mac was four inches taller and had a strength advantage. She now faced the man with no neck that had attacked her in the Rosslyn Chaple. When Maurice took a step forward, Mac, using his partner as leverage, kicked out and up. The tip of her boot caught him just under the chin, smacking his Adam's apple. Maurice grasped his throat with both hands. His eyes bulged as he gasped for breath.

Planting both feet firmly on the carpeted hallway, Mac used her weight and height to push hard, propelling her and her assailant backward into the ceramic tiled wall. Edmond's head whacked hard against the unforgiving surface: his hands released their grip and Mac pulled loose. Keeping an eye on the short stocky would-be attacker sucking oxygen, she watched the other slowly slide down the wall and into a slumped position. Turning her full attention to no-neck, Mac took one step toward the elevator doors and spun on one foot. One long leg circled the air and with a whipping action, struck no-neck on the left side of his square jaw releasing a string of spittle and blood. She had broken his jaw. Maurice, though full of anger, knew he was in no condition now to pursue the bitch. He glanced quickly at Edmond, unconscious on the floor, and decided the best thing to do was to disappear. It appeared as though he wanted to say something, but words failed him, so he turned and ran for the exit doors.

Mac leaned over and retrieved her shower cap bag, nudged Edmond with her toe, and pushed the UP button again. As she stepped in, a uniformed hotel employee stepped out. She nodded to Edmond and said, "You better call hotel services to take out the trash."

When Mac unlocked the room door, Rance looked up from reading the Templar Journal and opened one hand as if to say, *"Well, what took you so long?"* He waited for an answer.

"Short version," she smiled. "I was momentarily occupied by two old friends." Closing the journal, Rance was all ears. "One was a skinny mousey-like fellow—the other was built like a Mack truck with no neck."

Now Rance was on his feet and strolling toward the door. She had just described two of Bishop's henchmen. Reaching for the knob, he looked over his shoulder and asked, "Explain occupied."

Mac slipped between her husband and the door. "You're a little late, my dear." She said, placing both hands on his chest. "The last time I saw no-neck, he was hightailing it for the exit trying to catch his breath—and the mousey one was slumped against the elevator wall." Pulling him away and toward the mini-bar, she added, "But I would think he's long gone by now."

Refusing to move another foot, Rance rooted himself to the floor. "They attacked you?"

Reaching into the cooler, she handed him a Canadian brewed beer and removed one for herself. "Well, I wouldn't call it a full-fledged assault. It was more of a moment's tussle."

They moved over to the bed and sat down. Mac described with animation her various moves and the effect they had on the two would-be kidnappers. At least, from their brief comments, she assumed they were in an attack mode.

Rance's eyes hardened as his mind absorbed Mac's words and sorted out the possible implications. "I had better warn both Al and A.T. about this," he said. "The girls could be in danger. My guess is that they intended to use you as a hostage—and then offer to swap you for whatever they think we had found. There's no way they could have known about the journal and maps." Placing a finger to the side of his nose, he continued. "But…but they somehow traced us from Ethiopia to Oak Island and here."

He thought for a moment, and his puzzled look turned into a forced smile. "It would have been easy to check all the hotels in Halifax to see where we were lodging. But how in the hell did they know we were flying across the Atlantic to Canada? Our flight plan was bogus."

Rance picked up the phone to call the others. His first call was to L' Ami. After relating Mac's experience, he asked Al if he still had the handheld bug finder with him. The answer was in the affirmative. "Good. Meet me in the lobby with the electronic gadget in five minutes: but before you do, call Arturo, tell him what happened to Mac, and have both Tina and Adriana accompany him to our suite. There's adequate sleeping room here. He's to guard the women while you and I go to the airport."

Hanging up, Rance went over to his bag, removed his Beretta, and strapped it to a calf holster. "What are you going to do at the airport?" Mac asked.

"We're going to de-bug our aircraft. While we were in the underground tunnels, they must have attached a tracking bug somewhere in the plane. We didn't leave footprints from there to here. The only way to know where we were headed was to track us electronically. The aircraft has a bug problem that Al will exterminate."

BISHOP WAS IN A RAGE. PASCHAL WAS ALL SMILES. Edmond held a washcloth filled with ice to the back of his head, and Maurice sat in the corner of the room making gurgling sounds while massaging his throat. "One weak woman took you both out!" Bishop shouted, flinging a half-full wine bottle across the room, missing Paschal by inches.

Leaping up, Paschal charged the fat man who took up the better part of a couch, then stopped midway. An old style German Lugar was pointed at his chest. Gaining courage, he walked slowly toward his boss and stopped three feet away. "You and your gun no longer have a hold on me. I can't and won't speak for these two," he said with a firm voice and nodded in their direction. "I'm prepared to die, so I won't take your shit anymore. Once we get the treasure and I take my share, you'll never see me again." Turning his back on the Bishop, he walked toward the door with the intention of going to his room. Stopping with his palm on the knob, he finished his act of defiance. "Shoot me now if you've a mind to—otherwise stow the weapon in the folds of your fat."

Bishop's face was blood red. His finger tightened on the trigger as he held his breath, then thought better of squeezing it. He was too close now and needed the man who had just, for the first time, displayed an ounce or more of courage. They knew where the treasure hunting team was headed next. The flight plan had them arriving at Rance's de Molay Spanish Castle later tomorrow. And Boss and his trio of thugs would be close by. But this time with reinforcements. For a hefty price, a contact in Madrid would supply a handful of Spanish mercenaries. Bishop smiled at the thought. The new hirelings would do all the dirty work, be paid in cash, and he would reap the benefits. As agreed, half for him, and the other half would be split three ways. Staring at the closed door, his eyes were mere slits. *And I had better keep a close watch on Paschal. He's becoming an independent bastard and could become a problem before this is over.*

Chapter Seventeen

L'AMI WAS INSIDE THE PLANE WITH HIS MAGIC WAND searching for additional tracking devices like the one discovered last night: the ladies were busying themselves stowing food and drinks for the Atlantic flight to the castle landing strip. Before leaving the hotel, Mac had phoned Mr. and Mrs. Benito alerting them that they would be home later that afternoon and to prepare two guest rooms. Adriana had phoned her brother, Tome, and explained that although she would be staying at the castle with her husband, she would stop by their restaurant as soon as possible. Tome was delighted and invited them all to dinner that night, or if they would rather rest, they were welcome the following evening.

It was barely sunup: Rance and A.T. had circled the plane five times performing a preflight check and nosing around every possible orifice and hiding place for a bug or explosive device. Rance made an okay sign with a finger and thumb and motioned Arturo toward the small folding stairway. Grabbing the ropes attached to the two caulks wedged in front of the main wheels, he flung them aside and followed his friend into the plane. "Who's going to be my copilot for the first leg of this forty-two thousand foot-high journey across the great pond? I need someone to keep me awake," Rance said, taking a cup of coffee from his wife's hand. "Don't everyone speak up at once."

"Your lovely wife already made that decision, Captain sir," A.T. spoke up. "And after she demolished those two bozos last night, no one was going to give her an argument."

Following her husband into the cockpit, Mac playfully smacked Arturo on the back of his baldhead and said, "And don't you forget it."

Tina laughed aloud and said, "Mac, I could have used you on our honeymoon. This old bald Italian is hard to handle at times."

Before ducking in the cockpit, Mac turned and said, "I'm certain he's no tougher to handle than my prince charming that suffers from the John Wayne syndrome...' "

"What's that?" Adriana wanted to know.

"That's when he says, 'Yes, dear,' to all my questions or requests, then goes on and does what he wants to."

"Does that sound familiar?" Tina sang out. Adriana was vigorously nodding up and down in agreement.

L' Ami shouted to the captain. "Get this bird in the air! The gals are ganging up on us back here."

Taking her seat and strapping herself in, Mac glanced over at Rance with a mischievous grin. "You three are like cloned peas in a pod."

Without pausing in his checklist, he answered, "That's what makes us so successful, my dear. We move and think as one. Without that ability, we would no longer exist."

Taking his eyes off the laminated checklist, he finished his thought. "It's the presence of you ladies that could cause a miscue—and that could lead to mission failure," he said with a deadpan look.

Any other woman who had heard those words from the man she loved would have hit the ceiling, but Mac understood what he meant. Any distraction in his past world of black ops missions could have caused a major failure. And maybe one or all of the three men's lives. She remained quiet.

Silence in the cockpit was deafening, and Rance sensed that his words were the cause. Laying a hand on his wife's thigh, he apologized. "Sorry. I spoke out of turn. At one time, what I said would have been true—but we're not on our own now—and A.T., Al, and myself, are delighted to have our wives by our sides. We wouldn't want it any other way."

Mac displayed an approving smile and said, "I knew what you meant, but the apology was genuine and accepted." Patting the throttles, she continued. "Like L' Ami said, 'Get this bird in the air.' "

Rance contacted the tower, cranked up the jets, and followed the air controller's runway direction. Four minutes later, the treasure hunters were airborne and climbing to their cruising altitude over the Atlantic Ocean. Leveling out, Rance relaxed and glanced over at Mac whose eyes, up until thick clouds obstructed the view, were watching whitecaps far below.

"What are you thinking?" Rance asked.

"For one, I was thinking that T.P. will look like a full grown German shepherd by now."

Laughing, Rance challenged her observation. "We haven't been gone that long, my dear. It only seems that way."

She cocked her head and nodded once, then paused. "My other thought had a deeper meaning." Turning away, she watched the clouds thin out, then thicken.

"Well?" Rance said in a soft whisper. He had all day and neither one would be going anywhere for the time being.

Pursing her lips before answering, she sighed and said, "After we find the Templar treasure…or not…what next? Danger and adventure is in your blood—and now it's in mine." Motioning back toward the cockpit door with her head, she added, "The same thing goes for our friends."

"A year ago, we all vowed never to take on another government assignment and to retire. That's why we moved into the Spanish castle and both Arturo and Al to their Italian villas. Remember?"

"Yeah," she replied as if to scoff at the thought. "And as a result, I was personally attacked in Rosslyn Chaple—and we were both trapped in a pit. Then we were all set upon by a band of mercenaries in the castle. Not to mention your altercation with Bishop and his men in Tome's restaurant—and later outside de Molay Castle. Oh…and how could I forget falling in a sinkhole and nearly drowning in the underground river in Ethiopia, then nearly being crushed when the Templar cavern collapsed?" By her expression, she expected an answer.

"You left out a few details and especially your recent encounter with two of the Bishop's men in the Halifax hotel lobby," Rance reminded her. Throwing up both hands, he asked with a straight face, "But who's counting?"

"That's just the point," Mac answered with a gesturing finger poking his shoulder. "You once said that you drew danger like dead meat draws flies. And nothing has changed during your pretend retirement."

Mac leaned to her left and kissed his cheek. "And I wouldn't have it any other way. I'm hooked."

"You know, I didn't foresee any of this," he said with an apologetic tone. "We all set out on a nice relaxing treasure hunt. Nothing more. Then the deadly flies began to circle."

Mac was about to respond, but Arturo opened the door and interrupted the conversation. "Set this bucket of bolts on autopilot and come join in the merriment. We're about to have a light snack and a few brews. All except the pilot. But not to worry, my friend—I'll drink your share."

Unbuckling, Mac squeezed Rance's upper arm. "If he's a good boy, mommy will allow him one beer." This brought a frown to Rance's forehead and a wide grin from his Italian friend.

"We need to discuss the plan to search de Molay Castle and grounds for the treasure—if the map and our speculations are correct," L' Ami noted.

"If so, it was right under our very noses all along," Mac said.

"More like under your feet," Al corrected her. Addressing Rance, he went on. "Before we left the hotel, I phoned a source in Madrid to access two more ground-penetrating units like the one we have—and three deep-penetrating metal detectors. Chances are they may beat us to the castle: if not, they'll arrive first thing in the morning."

"Well," Tina said, holding up one foot. "I'm happy for you, Al, but right now all I can think of is getting my feet out of these boots and my khaki pants, shirt and jacket. We've been in and out of various Indiana Jones design outfits ever since leaving most all our normal clothes back at de Molay Castle. I want to feel like a female again."

"Indiana Jones wore a leather jacket and hat," A.T. reminded her. "You're thinking about the actor Richard Chamberlain as the adventurer, Allan Quartermain, in *King Solomon's Mines*."

"Don't forget *Allan Quartermain and the Lost City of Gold*," Rance said, poking his jacket. "Quartermain wore the khaki outfit."

"Quartermain!" A.T. shouted. "After our stay in hot and dusty Lalibela—and until I stepped in the Canadian hotel shower—I was feeling and smelling like a quarter horse."

"You won't get any argument from any of us," L' Ami laughed.

"And who's kidding who: you'd never wear an Indiana Jones hat," A.T. said to Rance. "It'd mess up your hair."

Rance placed a palm atop Arturo's bald head and hit it with his other hand. "And you have nothing to cover up except liver spots."

"…I'll have you know that I don't have…"

Before A.T. had time to complain about his friend's cheap shot, Al broke in. "I'm thinking," he looked over at Adriana, "of getting an old-fashion crew cut and trimming my beard into a mustache and goatee. What do you think, guys?"

"Great idea," Rance agreed, "and I might join you with the mustache and goatee." Clearing his throat and glancing sideways at Mac, he finished his thought. "If Mac agrees."

Wrinkling her nose, she said, "We'll see what it looks like."

"I agree with Tina," Adriana said. "I want to feel fresh and frilly again for my husband."

"Mac tells me that you've been in touch with your brother, Tome," Rance said. "And that he's invited us to dine with him either tonight or tomorrow night. If you have no objections, could we change those plans by one evening? We've got much to do tomorrow when the new electronic equipment arrives from Madrid—and the Bishop and his crew remain a threat—even though we rid ourselves of their tracking devices. Tomorrow's Wednesday. How about Friday night? Give him a call: schedule our dinner at his restaurant for Friday and alert him to keep an eye out for the Bishop or any of his men. He knows what they look like. Ask him to call us right away if he does: and also if he notes any strangers lurking about the village."

Picking up the men's favorite phrase, she answered, "That sounds like a plan to me." Everyone had a good laugh, washed down with swallows of Canadian beer.

Later in the cockpit when Rance was again on manual control, Mac again brought up the subject of their life-after-adventure, so-called retirement. "You know," she began, "we had only been in retirement for a week before we began this quest. We've never really had the opportunity to experience an actual retirement life."

"What do you call the time we spent in retirement in our New Mexico mountain lodge?" After Rance said it, he was sorry he had.

Mac looked at him like she couldn't believe what she had just heard. "First of all, I spent many of those days in disguise as an old man's spinster daughter—you as Herkimer Two Bundles—in cahoots with an American Indian clan—and flying around the world with an Arab weapons dealer. Not to mention the secret tunnel to the facility where an illegal bio-bomb was being developed—and you blowing it to smithereens along with the rogue scientists. Then there were the two aberrations: the long-dead Indian shaman and a giant blue rabbit. And don't forget…"

Rance stopped her. "All right. All right. I got your message." She was right, he had no argument. They hadn't gone into retirement: not in the true sense of the word.

Changing the subject, Rance said, "I heard Adriana explaining to you about the new foundation that one of her relatives in Madrid was forming: it's a group of philanthropists pooling finances to promote the restoration of Spanish castle ruins. You're a castle owner—and you're wealthy. Why not join them? Adriana could introduce you to the group. Give it some thought. I'll support you in whatever you decide to do."

Now it was Mac who remained silent. Since that conversation with Adriana, she had given it considerable thought and was encouraged by her husband's proposal. Yes, she could become interested and involved with a project like that. But what about her ever-restless husband?

RANCE WAS ATTACKED THE MOMENT HE STEPPED off the Lear's stairway. Staggered by the weight of his assailant, Rance managed to wrap his arms in a bear hug as they both tumbled to the ground—and rolled about on the airstrip's well manicured grass. A deep growl welcomed him along with T.P.'s wet tongue. Straining to stretch his head away from the shepherd's moist kisses, Rance responded with a loud, "Ugh!" This triggered laughter from his wife, friends, and Mr. and Mrs. Benito who were part of the welcoming party of three. This included the rambunctious German shepherd.

Shoving the dog away, Rance, still on his back, looked up at Arturo and said, "Don't laugh, friend. He's named after you, his Uncle Trash Pile."

Mr. Benito clapped his hands in celebration and informed his employers and their friends to follow his wife. She had set out an antipasti tray and liquid refreshments on the front lawn. He would see to getting their luggage and equipment into the castle, making a point to tell Lord L' Ami that earlier in the day a large wooden box from a company in Madrid had arrived at the castle addressed to him. Pointing to the airstrip, he expressed his surprise when a strange plane landed on the private strip and unloaded a box.

Everyone looked in L' Ami's direction. "Hey, what can I say: I've got connections." Heading up the hill toward the castle, he held out his hand for Adriana to follow and suggested, "Let's see what Mrs. Benito has for us: I hope it includes a bottle or two of Jack Daniel's."

A long table covered in a red and white tablecloth greeted them, along with six comfortable chairs. Samplings of meat, bread, cheese and crackers with a spicy red dip was the main offering—with a selection of red and white wine, a cooler of beer, and a bottle of JD. Due to the diminishing sunlight, Mr. Benito had turned on the outside spotlights to illuminate his wife's display. When Mrs. Benito exited the large carved front doors carrying a tray of plump red grapes, the weary treasure hunters applauded her efforts. She curtsied slightly and blushed. Rubbing his hands together, Rance said, "Mrs. Benito, you're a real treasure. Now, let's eat."

Surprisingly, after one large swallow of whiskey and with a mouthful of cracker and cheese, Al stood and motioned for Mr. Benito to follow him to the wooden box resting on the castle's tile entrance way.

"Find a crowbar and open the box: and save the material for repacking. I'll take care of the equipment and bring it inside."

"What was that all about?" Arturo asked. "That was the first time I've ever seen you take just one swallow of anything."

Al greeted his Italian agitator with the typical back-of-the-hand off the end-of-the-chin salute that A.T. was so fond of dispensing in similar situations. "Ah ha!" Arturo laughed, "I knew I'd make an Italian out of you yet, Frenchman."

"If you can control your outbursts for a moment, husband," Tina complained. "Reach over and hand me that bottle of Sangria."

"When these three get on a roll, there's no stopping them," Mac offered with a shake of her head.

Rance held a hand over his heart and replied with a tear in his voice, "We're so misunderstood."

"*Caballo abono*," Adriana hissed with squinting eyes. "You're all full of *caballo abono*."

"Did my sweet darling wife just call us what I think she did?" Al asked, trying hard not to laugh.

"That she did. That she did," Rance confirmed. "She said that we're all full of horse shit." Pausing for a moment, he placed a finger aside his nose and continued. "And we all know that she's right." Another round of laughter erupted. Even Mr. Benito, who was hard at work on the box, couldn't help but overhear and chuckled to himself. Ever since Adriana had arrived from Madrid to live with her brother Tome, her fierce independence had become legendary in the village.

Earlier merriment subsided in favor of stuffing hungry stomachs and attention to draining wine and beer bottles. Leaning back in his chair, Rance patted his middle. "Well, I believe we've done all the damage we can to Mrs. Benito's table. I suggest we all retire to our rooms: freshen up, take a short rest, and meet in the library at nine o'clock to discuss our morning search. Al, A.T. and I will give you a hand with the GPU's and metal detectors. They'll be safe just inside the foyer—and handy for use tomorrow."

Leaning forward and motioning the others do the same, Rance glanced back at the nearly dismantled wooden box and whispered, "Tomorrow I'm giving Mr. Benito a special assignment, complete with binoculars. He'll set up surveillance on the east turret and keep a watchful eye in the direction of Tarego. We can't afford to be bushwhacked by the Bishop or his men."

"Tome agreed to Friday night's dinner," Adriana said, "and assured me that he'll spread the word to notify him immediately if anyone notes an unfamiliar face in town."

"Sounds like a plan," Rance said, grinning at Adriana. Standing, he reached over to help Mac to her feet. "Come on, ma: castle ghosts await our return."

Recalling Sir. William of Rosslyn Chaple, Tina warned, "Let's not mention ghosts."

Chapter Eighteen

EARLY MORNING CHATTER ECHOED OFF THE CASTLE walls as six fully re-energized and enthusiastic treasure hunters retired to the library with steaming cups of coffee. Mrs. Benito's breakfast of eggs, slices of ham, toasted thick-bread, and slices of fruit had all but disappeared from the kitchen table. Appetites were in abundance, but easily satisfied. Mr. Benito was conspicuously absent. He had taken his role seriously and had camped on the stone turret before morning light. His wife promised to supply him with fresh coffee, as well as lunch. He had a mini-walkie-talkie with which to contact his wife for coffee, food, and to alert her to notify Mr. Rance if he spotted movement from the east.

 Castle de Molay's library was similar, yet much larger, than the one in Rosslyn Chaple: the walls were covered in oiled dark wood panels and the well-worn wooden flooring was blanketed in a huge, equally worn Persian rug. Thread-bare tapestries and numerous cracked oil paintings of knights on and off horses graced the walls: an ancient Templar shield guarded the space above a decorative fireplace. Three seven-foot plush sofas placed in the shape of a horseshoe faced the blackened stone fireplace. In the center sat a round wooden and hammered metal coffee table. An oversized black wrought iron chandelier with numerous stalactite spikes hung from above making those lounging on the sofas extremely uncomfortable.

 Rance and Mac sat on the middle sofa: the other two teams sat on either side, sipping coffee and listening to Rance outline the daily assignments. "As discussed last night, Al and I will take one of the GPU's underground to the late Templar's quarters." Finishing a last drop of coffee, he nodded at Arturo and Tina. "See if you can rig up something like Al did to drag his unit around in the Lalibela tunnels—and see what you can find above ground between the castle and the ocean cliffs. Check the old wooden shed behind the barn and horse corral. Mr. Benito might have something with wheels stashed away."

Holding up the decanter, Rance went about filling everyone's empty coffee cups. "We'll leave the third GPU as a backup in case one malfunctions."

He knew Mac and Adriana were anxiously waiting for their assignments, and he was deliberately taking his time. "Mrs. Rance and Mrs. L' Ami can assist Mrs. Benito in the kitchen and…"

Mac's sharp elbow to his ribs forced a sucking sound. "You're not very funny, Mr. Adam Rance," she said with meaning.

"You had better talk fast before I get my frying pan," Adriana warned.

"Get it anyway—just in case we don't like what he says," Mac suggested.

Rance surrendered. "You two design a grid pattern in front of the castle—and use those sophisticated metal detectors to sweep the area—including the horse enclosure and in and around that old wooden shack at the edge of the tree line." He knew he should have stopped right there but couldn't help himself. "That should keep you two out of trouble…*Oof*"

Mac grinned as Adriana smiled her approval. "I wish you wouldn't do that," Rance said, rubbing his ribs. Now everyone was grinning. The morning was off to a good start, and without further discussion, the teams set out on their assignments.

L' Ami hoisted the GPU in his arms and Rance carried the wand and cables. It was a struggle balancing the awkward unit down the trapdoor steps, but with Rance's hand steadying his bobbing and weaving friend, they finally made it to Sebastian and Bertrand's sparse living quarters beneath the castle. No one had entered the dusty room since Tome retrieved the body of the last Templar. Rance lit the two oil lanterns that through the years had blackened the dirt ceiling. Two cots, two chairs, and a table were all the brothers needed, and of course, a simple wooden crucifix was nailed onto the hard-packed dirt wall. In fact, it appeared that the room was carved out of a mixture of hard red clay and dirt.

L' Ami eased the GPU to the floor and glanced around. "I'd say that your two Templar friends were more prisoners than free men."

Rance slowly moved his head from side to side. "Yes, but it was a self-imposed, simple lifestyle. They themselves were not important in the scheme of things—as they saw it. The treasure's safety was paramount."

"Do you think we'll find gold coins or religious artifacts—or both?" Al asked.

"Your guess is as good as mine, my friend. Let's start with the wall that faces the castle. You monitor the screen and I'll wave the wand. Then we'll make our way to the far west wall."

Rance picked up a lantern, faced the wall, and held it high, revealing what appeared to be wooden shelving fixtures that had escaped their notice in the darkness. "That could be where they stored their supplies. It's a constant cool temperature in this room, and dried meat would have survived as well as other foods."

"I'd be more concerned with my brain going bad before the food. How could they live like this, years on end?" Al asked.

"We're forgetting that de Molay Castle was owned by the Templars—and even during the many years it fell in disrepair—those men who dedicated their lives to guarding the treasure's whereabouts would have had full run of the castle. Including bathroom and cooking facilities. Sebastian and Bertrand may have lived that way until I purchased the place and forced them into hiding below the trapdoor. And I suspect that it all depends on your priorities, dedication, and discipline. Religious fervor can accomplish wonders—if used positively."

"Yeah," L' Ami replied, making a face, "but all too often it's used to negative ends. Both in the past and even today."

"Well, we can't solve that problem. Let's get to work."

Arturo and Tina had indeed found a set of wheels in the old wooden barn. They were attached to a gardener's cart. The GPU rested on the cart. A.T. pushed it, and at times pulled it, to the ocean side of the castle. "I've got a hunch," he announced to his wife. "If the ship bringing supplies to the keepers of the treasure tied up below the cliffs— and wished not to be detected—there might well be a tunnel from the ocean to the castle."

"Sometimes you astound me with your insight, my love. Not often," she kidded, "only upon occasion."

Ignoring her dig, A.T. pulled as Tina waved the wand over the ground. It took over an hour to reach the cliff, and A.T. was tired of pulling the cart whose wheels often sank into the soft sod. He only made time when crossing the hardened landing strip. Sitting at the edge of the cliff to rest, Tina made an observation. Using her finger as a pointer, she drew A.T.'s attention to the formation of the rocks below. "The water's so clear you can see where the rocks below the surface jut out for some distance from the cliffs. No ship could drop anchor in those areas."

"They could drop anchor and stack supplies in a row boat and come ashore," Arturo countered.

"That's one way," she agreed, "but follow my finger. See there? That's the only place along the cliff edge void of submerged rocks. And if that's where the Templar supply ship slipped through a natural channel—that's where one would find a tunnel entrance."

She stood up, placed her hands on her narrow hips and displayed a smile of satisfaction. "And that means we're off the line of a tunnel, if there is one, by a good twenty yards."

A.T. peered over the edge at the perilous jagged rocks coated with slippery green moss. "Well, it's back to the GPU and the cart, because I'll be damned if I'm climbing down those rocks to find an entrance—if there is one."

The third search team of Mac and Adriana agreed they would scan the surface of the area around the shack next to the horse corral before the arduous task of designing a grid on the castle's front lawn. After forty-five minutes of finding and digging up handfuls of nails, an old, rusted horseshoe, a badly dented coffeepot, and a variety of metal items they couldn't identify, they decided to search the ground within the rickety wooden shack.

This effort proved to be as fruitless as scanning the area around the building. Heading for the two large barn doors, Adriana stopped and looked over her shoulder. "Let's see if we can pull that broken-down wagon away from where it lies in ruin and see what might be beneath."

One sturdy yank and the large wagon fell away in pieces. Rusted metal wheels stood their ground as the sides and flatbed turned to sawdust and splinters. Tossing aside the wheels, they set about removing what was left of solid pieces of wood. Much to their surprise, once the ground that once lay beneath the wagon was exposed, they discovered an old water well rimmed with finely-fitted stones.

"I bet this is the original well the Templars dug and used when they were building the castle," Adriana speculated.

Mac picked up a stone and dropped it in the well. No splash. Just a dry thud. "Seems as though the well is dry."

From the identical facial expressions, it appeared that both women shared the same thought. "You don't suppose..." Mac whispered.

"There's only one way to find out," Adriana answered. "And that means that one of us must go down…"

THIS IS THE UGLIST AND MEANEST BUNCH YET Bishop thought to himself as he sat before the mercenaries sent by his Madrid contact. From the pained looks on the faces of Paschal, Edmond, and even Maurice, they too were impressed, if not openly fearful. Straggles of men entered his hotel suite in groups of twos and threes until the last man slammed the door with authority. He was obviously their leader, a large barrel-chested man of about six foot five with a shaved thick head and a dark handlebar mustache. When he spoke, or rather growled, he would absentmindedly flick his one golden earring. Large black eyes tended to burn like hot coals as he intently absorbed the Bishop's instructions. Like a few of the others, he wore polished combat boots, camouflage pants, and a sleeveless denim jacket with a black tee-shirt beneath. Like his other well-muscled team members, his arms were like hardened tree stumps. "You call me Pitt," he addressed the fat man paying the bill for their services. "No one else's name makes a difference. They all report to me, and I alone report to you." Bishop acknowledged Pitt's demand with a symbolic nod.

"Yes, I do believe that we understand each other, Mr. Pitt," Bishop said, shifting his weight in a large, oversized leather chair. "I also believe that you were initially briefed on your assignment by our mutual acquaintance in Madrid. Is that not so?" Pitt raised the corner of his thick lips as a way of acknowledging his current benefactor, then rubbed a large bump on his man-sized nose.

"You need not know the reason for your mission—only that not a single person in de Molay Castle survives your attack—when I say the time is right. You and your team will be paid handsomely, having received half of the settled amount of cash up front. Are we still in agreement, Mr. Pitt?"

Pitt turned to his men and grinned, patting his right cargo pant pocket. Turning back to Bishop, his black orbs focused on the three men sitting next to their boss, and with an obvious look of distain said, "We will do what your people cannot. Hell," he laughed, "we'd do our own sainted mothers for this kind of money." The faces of Paschal, Maurice, and Edmond soured as Pitt's group joined their leader's boisterous laughter.

"I'll take your insufferable boast as a yes, Mr. Pitt." Pitt's scowl faded as he considered the fat man's words. Not fully understanding the insult, he grinned in agreement.

"Excellent. I will need a few more days to prepare my plan. As we speak, another paid associate visits the village a few miles from the castle and will notify me when the time to strike is appropriate. It is but a short drive to the castle from here. Until then, enjoy yourselves at the local Seville establishments. Do nothing until you hear from me. And for all our sakes, keep your men under tight reign."

"DAMMIT RANCE, THIS THING GETS HEAVIER BY THE MINUTE," L' Ami complained. "We've penetrated three of the four walls without a single bleep for our efforts."

"Forgive me," Rance replied with a mischievous grin. "I keep forgetting that you're the oldest of our little treasure-seeking band. Here, I'll change places with you. Give me the unit: you handle the wand."

Walking toward the west wall and the wooden storage structure, Al mumbled under his breath. "Next time you're hanging half-in and half-out of an elevator shaft door, I'll let the bloody descending elevator make Mac a widow."

"What did you say?"

"I said that they could have used a window in here," Al lied, although he was certain that Rance had heard him.

The wooden braces and shelving took up much of the entire wall space and had to be moved. Much to their delight, they discovered that the shelving was constructed in three sections and easily moved. Once back six feet from the wall, the men began the tedious task of moving from the left hand corner to the right. Rance held the heavy unit against his chest while Al ran the wand over the wall from top to bottom. A loud beep startled Rance, who nearly dropped the device. "Something's here," L' Ami said excitedly. "Put the unit down." He didn't have to ask twice.

This wall's texture was different from the other three: they were smooth, and this one had remained rough, resembling a recently plowed field. Rance ran his hand over the lumpy surface. Picking up the wand, he determined the left and right-hand edges of what he suspected to be a tunnel entrance. Dropping the wand, his fingers searched each lump of hard clay to his left. Nodding his head, first to Al, then to the right-hand side of the invisible entrance, he said, "Grab hold of those clumps and when I say, three, pull."

They tugged together. Only a slight movement. "That's strange," Al said. "The way it moved—is strange. Didn't you notice it?" Rance shook his head.

"Let's try again. This time, note the direction of the movement. I believe we opened a crack at the bottom."

They pulled. Rance dropped to his knees and inserted both hands in a gap at the base of the wall. "You're right, Al. Get down here and help me pull up. I believe the door's on a swivel and opens from the bottom up. Clay lumps are plastered on a thick wooden door to make it appear part of a solid wall."

As they lifted the heavy door over their heads, a swinging piece of wood narrowly missed connecting with L' Ami's head. One end was attached to a hinge adhered to the door's inside surface. When it stopped swinging, it hung vertical to the floor. Recognizing its intent, the men eased up on their lift and allowed the door to settle in an open position, held up by the prop. "Just like my grandpa's trapdoor—only this one is a trapwall—if there is such a word," Al observed.

Just when they were feeling proud of themselves, a shout emanating from inside the tunnel snapped their heads around. "Hi guys," A.T. said, welcoming his friends.

"What in the hell?" was all Rance could think of saying.

"How in the hell?" was all Al managed to utter.

Poking a thumb over his shoulder, Arturo explained. "Tina and I discovered that there was a tunnel from the cliffs to the castle. We could see from the cliffs where a ship could safely set anchor, so there had to be a tunnel entrance below the cliffs. I wasn't about to climb down, not on those slippery rocks. Tina, smart girl, had the foresight to bring along a length of rope. With Tina and the heavy GPU as my anchor, I gathered the courage to rappel down the cliffs and in time found the tunnel entrance." He held out his arms, and said, "And here I am."

"And here I am!" Tina shouted down from the top of the trapdoor stairs.

Before Rance and L' Ami had a chance to react, another shout from above spun them around. "I need your help!"

Recognizing Mac's voice, Rance dashed up the trapdoor steps, picking the smaller woman up and setting her aside. "Sorry, Tina," he apologized, then faced his wife. "What's wrong?" he asked, thinking the worst.

"Adriana and I uncovered an old abandoned well in that rundown shack at the edge of the woods: and with a length of rope I found looped over a corral post, I lowered her into the well…"

Out of breath from running up the stairs, Al blurted out, "My wife's down in a well? Is she okay?"

"There's no danger," she assured the concerned husband. "I braced myself by sitting down with my feet wedged against the low rock wall circling the well—and gently lowered Adriana to the bottom. But when I attempted to pull her back up, I realized that I lacked the strength. Then it happened…"

"What happened?" L' Ami wanted to know.

"I only managed to pull her up about two feet when the rope broke. There's no telling how long that rope hung on that post." Looking at Al, she quickly continued. "She's okay. No problem there."

"But you need a sturdy rope and some muscle," Arturo said, holding up the coil of rope Tina had tossed down after he had descended the cliffs. "I have both the rope and the muscle." He glanced at L' Ami. "You'll want to lend a hand, hubby. Let's get your gal out of the well." Pointing a finger at Rance's chest he went on. "And you…make yourself useful by informing Mrs. Benito to expect six hungry treasure hunters for lunch."

PLEASED THAT THE MORNING SESSION was partially successful, the conversation was upbeat over sandwiches and a pitcher of fruit-filled sangria. "I was perfectly fine," Adriana assured everyone, explaining her recent experience, "until Mac left, and it was as silent as an empty tomb down there. In fact, the next ten minutes felt like ten hours, and I'm not bashful to say that panic was setting in until I heard A.T.'s booming voice assuring me that he'd soon have me out—if he could get a little cooperation from my husband, who was dragging his heels." Al shook his fist at his Italian friend.

Rance tapped his glass with a knife. "We'll leave the well for now. Later Mac and Adriana can scan the shack floor. We now know how the supplies were delivered to the castle, and we're fairly certain that the room below the trapdoor was used primarily as a storage area until my purchase of the castle forced Bertrand and Sebastian to vacate the upstairs quarters."

In a failed attempt to start an argument, A.T. muttered, "You should be ashamed of yourself. Those nice old fellows…"

"Two glasses of sangria and the Italian bowling ball gets diarrhea of the mouth," Rance struck back.

"If I can get back to the job at hand?" he said, looking for permission from the target of his remark. Arturo mouthed, *Yes you may*.

"It makes sense to turn all our attention to the storage room below. I have a hunch that whatever treasure there is, the guardians would not want it to be too far from their immediate grasp."

"That does make sense when you consider, if the castle were ever attacked by land, the quickest escape route to the sea and a ship would be the tunnel," Adriana said, agreeing with Rance's theory.

"We left our GPU in the storage room: A.T., why don't you carry yours down there and join us. Mac and Adriana, round up shovels and picks in case they're needed." Glancing at his watch he finished by saying, "We'll all meet downstairs in half an hour."

Chapter Nineteen

"WE'LL START IN THE FAR LEFT-HAND CORNER and work our way along the floor toward the tunnel," Tina said, carrying the wand and cord, leaving her strong husband to lug the heavy unit.

Mac blew out the lamps that had filled the room with the odor of burning oil and soot, and Adriana replaced them with a number of electric lanterns that turned the semi-dark room into bright daylight.

Rance and Al scanned the floor opposite A.T. and Tina's area. After a full hour of hard work and perspiration, Mac served ice cold water to the four workers. Noticing Adriana's puzzled expression, Rance asked a simple question. "What?"

She looked up at him and hesitated, then explained. "Considering that we agree the Templars would have cached their valuable treasure in a convenient place for a fast getaway—what if we apply that same logic to where in this room they would have buried it? Whatever *it* is."

"Too bad that Sebastian's Templar Journal didn't mention what was hidden away," L' Ami said with a deep thoughtful sigh.

Rance's features changed as he stepped away from his wife and friends. Mac immediately recognized the expression and was suddenly concerned. It was the look he wore before leaving on a mission and attempting to disguise eminent danger. Al and A.T. exchanged glances: they too were familiar with the look.

Removing the journal from his cargo pant pocket, Rance held it up, opened it, and flipped through the fragile pages. Stone faced, he provided the hungry-for-information treasure hunters a brief explanation. "As you are all aware, much of the journal is written in a number of languages I'm familiar with—including Greek, Aramaic—and of course the predominant language is Latin."

As though suddenly weakened, he sat in one of the two wooden straight back chairs to continue. "I have never lied to any of you. You know that." This time he looked first to Arturo, then Al, both adding their assent without hesitation.

Tapping a finger on the open journal on the table, he began again. "Mostly, the journal tells of the illegal roundup of the Knights Templar—at the request of the pope and a king—throughout Europe and wherever they could be found. Then it details the burning alive of their Grand Master, de Molay, and the escape of a dozen or more Templar ships to ports in sympathy with the knights.

"There, the tale becomes a bit confusing, because the author or authors split their story into several different ancient languages—and not all words have identical meaning. Using my own imagination, interspersed with their writing, I have assembled a possible scenario.

"Their first concern was for the safety of what these guardian knights possessed in their keeping."

An anxious Arturo asked, "Which was?"

Holding up one hand, he answered, "I'll get to that in due time. Secondly, they had to devise a diversion—something that would send their trackers, then and in the future, on a wild goose chase."

"Like the Money Pit," Tina said.

"Exactly. Along with others. And third, it was essential that what they had in their possession was not scattered about in various lands. They needed one secret place to hide it all, in case the time came when they felt it necessary to expose what was in their keeping. And lastly, the treasure for which they offered up their lives must never be out of sight of the Knights Templar."

"Bertrand and Sebastian were the last Templars," Mac said. "And now they're both gone—and you were presented the journal on Sebastian's death bed—or so Tome explained."

Rance's chin touched his chest and his shoulders slumped forward for a moment, then he straightened in the chair. "Yes. Brother Sebastian did me no favor: the burden has been a heavy one. But let me continue. It's apparent that the journal map and the ones we found were meant for surviving Templars to interpret one day, the day when it was time for the treasure to be presented to the world. That day never came. And now we are the only ones who are privileged to know their secret, a secret held for hundreds of years.

"Now to answer A.T.'s question. I'm not really certain. Authors of this journal were not specific. We know that they were a wealthy order, but how much of their money was confiscated by the church, we'll never know. It's assumed that since many knights survived, even to a year ago, and they needed funds to continue, they must have escaped with pockets bulging.

"Money was only important to survive and as a tool to protect the real treasure assigned to their keeping—ancient religious holy relics."

"You're referring to the Holy Grail and the like?" Adriana could only whisper.

"Authors of the Templar Journal were not specific in listing each of the holy relics: they only referred to the accumulation of relics in their keep."

Standing, Rance closed the journal and tucked it in his pant pocket. "So you see, I have kept the lack of treasure information from you because I couldn't provide you with any encouragement or promise of gold, jewels—or anything of monetary value. Merely an interesting and intriguing adventure hunt with a touch of danger thrown in."

"Hell," Arturo said, "we're used to the danger—and who here needs the money?"

L' Ami gestured to his wife. "You never finished your theory of where in this room they would have buried...the stuff."

Adriana walked to the area between the stairs and the tunnel entrance and stomped her boot. "Here."

"Why not there," Rance said with a pleased expression. "Makes as much sense as any. Let's begin our assault. Mac, hand me your shovel."

Arturo picked up a two-sided pickax and lifted it over his head, bent on delivering a powerful blow. Rance quickly held up a hand and shouted, "Whoa! If there is a door to the treasure below, you'll splinter age-old wood. Gently, gently."

L' Ami inched a shovel's blade into the hard packed surface, placed a foot on the edge, and pushed. The dirt resisted his effort. He attempted to dig further with the same failing result. "Hell, this is like trying to break the surface of concrete."

"I wouldn't imagine the depth of earth would be too thick," Adriana offered. "If it were, they could not have gotten to it quickly, and it would be too heavy to lift."

"She's got a point there," Tina chimed in.

"Okay guys," A.T. said, wiping beads of perspiration from his shiny dome. "I'll gently," he looked sideways at Rance, "break up the surface as best I can. You two, use the tips of your shovels to scoop away the clay."

Both pickax and shovel did only minor damage to the hardened flooring. There were grumblings of: *'Damn but I bet it's already dark outside.': 'My back's killing me.': 'There better be at least a gold coin down there.': 'I could sure use a drink or two.'*

Three backbreaking hours later the sound of metal scraping on wood opened everyone's eyes. Picking up a pair of leather work gloves from the table, Rance dropped to his knees and began scooping clumps of clay off what they now believed to be the door to the Templars' cherished keep. Al helped by using the side of his shovel to remove the larger pieces.

"Mac, I remember seeing a broom against a corner in the room above..." Before Rance had the opportunity to finish, she disappeared up the stairs and quickly returned.

Rance brushed the pitted wooden door clean. In the center of the edge facing south lay a large metal ring. "That door's at least eight foot by eight foot—and depending how thick it is—one man could never raise the damn thing." Glancing at Adriana he asked, "How'd you know?"

Adriana pointed overhead. "That's the reason why I believed the door was below my foot. See that metal bar, two feet down from the ceiling, and extending from east wall to west wall? To raise the door, they would have tossed a chain over the bar and secured the end to the door's ring—then pulled—in effect, raising the door."

"Sister," Tina asked in awe of Adriana's on-target observations, "how old did you say you are? You sure know a lot about this." A bright smile was the fiery-haired Spaniard's only answer.

Arturo picked up the coil of rope he'd used to rappel down the cliffs and haul Adriana out of the well. He tossed it over the bar: Al tied the end around the door's lift ring. "On the count of three," Rance shouted, and the three friends pulled down on the rope. The ring lifted. Other than a loud creak, there was no movement.

"Let's give it another go," A.T. said with a grunt. "This time, you two put your backs into it!" All three voiced a grunt. The ring lifted, and the door screeched in protest.

Releasing the rope the three blew out breaths of frustration. Rubbing sore palms, Al thought aloud, "Those Templar guys were stronger than us lesser mortals."

"Or maybe they had more men on the other end of the chain," Mac offered an opinion.

"It's a good thing that the two old men who were the last keepers were not forced to expose the relics to the world—had that taken place in recent years," Adriana added.

"Pick up the rope, husbands," Tina ordered. "We fragile women will join you."

"Okay!" Rance shouted. "Again on three!" This time the ring lifted and with a ripping surrender, tore loose from the rotted wood. The entire crew fell on their backsides with a bevy of 'Ooofs!'

They sat there in a cloud of dust, their eyes wide with disbelief, then laughed until tears welled and streamed down their streaked cheeks. "Now I know it's time for drinks!" Arturo shouted out. There'd be no argument with that suggestion.

Before calling it a day, Rance stood looking down on the stubborn door. "It appears it isn't willing to give up its treasure easily. Tomorrow's another day—and another engineering feat to ponder. Let's get cleaned up: we'll rest for a bit and meet for one of Mrs. Benito's tasty dinners in two hours. But first we dust off, then it's drinks all around."

Adriana placed a foot on the steps to the room above when she turned and asked, "Rance, may I borrow your Land Rover for a brief time? I've talked to my brother Tome on the phone but would like to assure him that I'm all in one piece. I'll be back and meet all of you in time for dinner."

"Be my guest," was his answer. "And take T.P. with you. Ask Tome to keep him out of trouble." She mouthed thanks and kissed her husband, whispering that she'd be back in their room within the hour, and not to start without her. It was only the second time that Rance and A.T. had witnessed their friend blush.

"GATHER OUR RAGTAG TROOPS, PASCHAL," the man called Bishop ordered with a smile of greedy satisfaction, then returned his cell phone to his pocket. "Pitt and his men are about to earn their blood money. Our spy just informed me that the Templar treasure was discovered an hour ago in a room below the castle. In the morning, we set out for de Molay Castle and our long awaited prize."

Paschal, Maurice and Edmond turned over every rock and tavern in Seville until they found Pitt with a sultry black-haired barmaid on his lap and six empty beer bottles on the table. Tossing her off his lap, he roared with delight after Paschal whispered in his ear. "Fear not, little man: the Pitt crew will be at Bishop's side the first thing in the mornin', bushy-eyed and ready to spread mayhem," he roared with wicked laughter.

Slapping the woman on her behind, he ordered another brew and squinted at the Bishop's man. "I'd offer you a drink," he continued laughing, "but I'm afraid you'd get hurt." Turning his back on Paschal, his attention focused on the long-haired barmaid.

Paschal stared hard at the bully's broad back: his hand grasped the handle of his pistol in his pocket. Greed won over hatred for now.

A HAPPY GROUP OF TREASURE HUNTERS was a day away from discovering the secret of what the long-celebrated and anticipated Knights Templar had hidden deep below the castle. Spirits ran high as glasses of sangria and tankards of the local Spanish beer were consumed. Rance noticed Mrs. Benito off to the side, wringing her hands and looking quite concerned. Waving her over, he asked if she was all right. "Sir," she said with a weak voice, "my husband has been on top of the castle all day without relief—if I could only…"

"Poor man," Mac said, overhearing her disturbing report. "Please have him come down, by all means, Mrs. Benito—and we apologize for our thoughtlessness. Right Rance?"

Her message was clear. And she was right. "Tell your husband that we would be honored for him to join us in a drink once he's down. His diligence must be rewarded." Mrs. Benito looked surprised at the offer and backed out of the room, running through the castle and up three flights of stone steps to alert her husband. Her walkie-talkie batteries had died in the late afternoon, or she could have saved herself the stressful arthritic trip.

Mr. Benito, with hands clasped at his waist, shyly approached the noisy table. "There he is!" shouted A.T., standing and pulling an empty chair between his and Tina's. Placing an arm over the silent man's shoulder, he led him to his chair, and poured a pitcher of beer in a clean empty tankard. "Drink up. You deserve applause for sticking to your duty."

Everyone raised their drinks in his honor. The center of attention swallowed hard, bowed his head in recognition, and downed his drink in one long swallow. Anxious to leave, he was about to get out of his chair when A.T. placed one hand on his arm and with the other, poured him another drink. "You're not getting away that easily," A.T. told him. "You deserve to drink and eat dinner with us tonight. You're an important part of our team, Mr. Benito." The tired old man raised his shoulders and let them fall. His wife would be angry that he was consuming so much beer. What could he do but enjoy the forced attention? After all, he would explain to her later, Mr. Rance was their boss.

Immediately after dinner, Mr. Benito excused himself, and with a steady hand, A.T. deposited the bewildered and slightly tipsy husband to a fiercely scowling wife.

Relaxing with Cuban cigars, the three men sat in the library sofas discussing and planning how they would attempt to open the seemingly immovable door to the treasure it had kept hidden for hundreds of years. The ladies lounged in plush velvet wingback chairs by an open

French door balcony facing the picturesque ocean view. "How was your brother, Adriana? You didn't spend much time at the restaurant." Mac asked.

"He wasn't there. It was his day to play mayor, but I did stop by and spent twenty minutes in his office. He's as jolly as ever and pleased to note that I still own all my original parts—so he said. His outer office was crowded with many citizens with problems to solve and out-of-town Spaniards on official business. I only had time to cover the highlights of the last month. He's looking forward to entertaining us at dinner tomorrow evening—and said to be sure to tell you all hello."

Their conversation was cut short by Rance's waving cigar and shout, "Girls! We've got a plan. Come join us."

"We'll put out our cigars," A.T. laughed. "Rance forced them on us, I swear." L' Ami agreed, followed by a look of innocence.

When everyone was comfortable on the three sofas, Rance began. "Tomorrow, Mr. Benito will take his perch on the turret above. This time he'll wear one of our ear pods to be in constant communication with each of us."

"Assuming he's in good enough shape after what we did to the poor man tonight," A.T. said. "You should have seen the look on his wife's face. That alone would have sobered me up."

Rance continued. "Mac, you and Adriana take your metal detectors and resume searching the area around the well. Tina will accompany A.T., Al, and me into the room below. We need someone to assist with the equipment and fetch additional tools, if necessary."

"How do you intend to raise the door with the ring missing?" Adriana asked.

"In one of our upstairs tool storage rooms, I remember seeing a number of long steel rods. On the front and sides of the door, we'll dig away the clay, creating three small holes: then we insert the rods and use them as leverage to pry up the door. Once the door is partially open, we'll insert blocks of wood to hold it ajar. Next we insert the Land Rover's wheel jack in the front opening and jack the door up enough for one of us to slip through. And remember, we all wear our ear pods to stay in touch."

"Sounds like a plan to me," Adriana joked, stifling a smile. She was beginning to enjoy the surprised looks on Rance's face.

MORNINGS HAD SEEMED TO COME FASTER than usual the past few days, with all the excellent foods Mrs. Benito served and abundance of liquid refreshments. Late to bed and early to rise had become standard operation. Everyone was so anxious to attack the mulish wooden door that Mrs. Benito looked sincerely hurt when the hunters passed up breakfast and settled for coffee and Danish. Mac and Adriana were outwardly jealous of the others, having been assigned away from the real action, and they made Rance promise to keep them up to date on attempts to enter what they now assumed to be a room full of some kind of valuable ancient relics. He promised, tapping his ear pod to assure them both.

When the last drop of coffee followed the last crumb of Danish, Mac and Adriana headed out across the castle lawn to the wooden shack at the edge of the woods. Rance found the long iron poles he needed and met the others in the dirt room below the castle's floor. Arturo and L' Ami were already at work chipping clay from either side of the door: Tina was on her hands and knees working on the hard-packed edge at the front of the door.

Mac and Adriana took time to remove most of the splintered wood from the decaying wagon and stacked the rusted wheels and metal axle rods in a pile on the inside of the ocean-side wall. Now they had room to maneuver their detectors around the well in an eight-foot circle. Nine nails and a coat button were all they had dug up after fifteen minutes of searching. Suddenly Mac's back straightened. Wide-eyed, she looked at Adriana and tapped her ear pod and placed a finger to her lips. It was a frantic message from Mr. Benito, high above on the castle turret.

"Everyone!" he shouted. "There's movement from the woods behind the old work shack—and from the thicket of trees on the south side of the castle. Nothing from the road from Tarego on the east side." He paused, then shouted again. "I count two men edging their way around the shack..."

Rance broke in. "Mac, you copy that?"

Without thinking, she nodded yes, then with a hand movement directed Adriana to flatten herself against the ocean-side wall, but remained silent, afraid to alert the men outside. Adriana picked up one of the long iron wheel rods. Mac nodded and moved to the other side of the swayback doorframe. Both women took long shallow breaths and waited in silence for their would-be attackers to make their move. When a shadow appeared on the dirt floor, Mac raised her hands in the ready-position. She would try a martial arts move that normally worked on those who were unprepared to be attacked. First came the visible end of a sawed-off shotgun: luckily, it was angled upward. Mac grabbed the surprised man's grimy jacket lapels and yanked hard. Falling backwards, she placed a foot into his midsection and easily tossed him over her head. Instinct caused the gunman to fire harmlessly into the sagging roof. As splinters of wood and roofing floated from above, the assassin plunged headlong into the well, landing with a neck-snapping crunch.

Equally surprised by his comrade's brief shout and shotgun blast, the second man's hurried entry into the shack was short lived. Adriana bent the rusted wagon wheel rod over the back of his thick neck. He never had the opportunity to squeeze the automatic weapon's trigger.

Adriana looked down at the man at her feet and shrugged her shoulders and grinned. "I didn't bring my frying pan but this," she shook the bent rod over her head, "did nicely."

"Now we have a sawed-off shotgun and a compact Uzi," Mac said. "Give me a hand dumping your guy down the well along with mine. Both their necks are broken, they won't be going anywhere any time soon."

Rance had tried repeatedly to get a response from his wife and was in a panic after hearing the gun blast. Now he was shouting. "Calm down, my love," she finally answered. "Adriana and I have this end under control. Better watch yourselves—we just saw a group of unwelcome guests entering the castle with guns drawn. Keep your ear pod in place so we can hear what's going on. And sorry I didn't answer you earlier, but I couldn't chance alerting our two that we were in the shack—then things became somewhat busy until…"

She cut herself off and listened intently to what was happening to the others. A booming voice demanded that everyone stay on their knees and place their hands on top of their heads. Then Mac jumped when she heard the sound of intermittent machine gun fire and angry shouts. The booming voice could be heard over the chaos. "Get him! Don't let that bastard escape! And you two take care of the old man and the woman upstairs. No one lives. That's our orders."

Rooted helplessly to the spot, the two women felt the chill of their greatest fear creep over them. Were their husbands and friends alive? Perhaps they had been shot while still on their knees. Wrestling with her emotions, Mac glanced at Adriana, placing a finger to her lips and turning off her ear pod. Pointing to the castle, she explained. "We have to be careful that one of those attackers does not insert an ear pod and find out about us. It's our only chance to save the others if they're alive. Right now, we have to help Mr. and Mrs. Benito. Once they're safe, we'll turn on our earpods and hope for the best." Without another word, the two women sprinted across the lawn, dashed up the castle's stone steps and turned right, heading for the stairs that would take them several flights up.

Rance and his crew were busy digging and chipping away at the clay around the ancient wooden door when they heard Mr. Benito's nervous call alerting them to possible danger. They stopped what they were doing and remained still, listening to the shouts and gunshot emanating from the old shack. Those precious few minutes caused them to be caught by surprise. At the sound of hurried footsteps storming into the underground room, Arturo, working on the far side of the door, leapt to his feet and made a desperate dash for the tunnel among heated shouts and a spray of bullets. In a matter of a minute, he was in the dark, searching for the light at the end of the tunnel. It was a miracle that the shower of bullets hadn't sliced him in half. Thankfully, he had only suffered a minor wound to his right thigh. He launched his body off the edge of the tunnel and into the foaming ocean below. Once his outstretched hands broke water, he made a tuck like a speed swimmer: kicking his feet underwater, he propelled himself back toward the cliffs. Amid a scattering of bullets penetrating the angry water's surface, A.T. hid under an outcropping until he felt safe enough to peek out.

Livid that one of the enemy had possibly escaped, even though the three men who had pursued A.T. assured their leader that there was no way the man could have survived the hail of bullets, Pitt demanded that they return and search for the man's body. Grumbling, they re-entered the tunnel. Enraged, Pitt lashed out at the person closest to him. Rance moved at the right moment but was caught by the rifle butt under the chin. Had he not been alert, his chin would have been sliced open. Playing the part, Rance lay on his side as though unconscious. Pitt, using a polished brogan, kicked him in the ribs with such force, it lifted him off the ground. Tina winced. Rance remained silent.

MAC AND ADRIANA TIPTOED up the winding stone stairs, heading for the source of shouts and angry demands. Pitt's two men had dragged Mr. Benito down from the turret to where they had his wife standing and trembling in a small library lined with ancient weapons and faded banners. Outside the half-open door, Mac signaled Adriana that it was necessary they silently eliminate the two men taking pleasure in frightening the old people, so as not to alert the others. Mac slid a sword from a wooden mount on the wall outside the library, and her partner did the same, but chose a spiked mace at the end of a chain and wooden handle.

Their backs were to the women and both the Benitos were on their knees: the back of their heads faced the cruel bullies. Loud threats and cries of Mrs. Benito hid the shuffled footsteps. Mac waited until Adriana swung her weapon before lunging with all her strength. The man on the left gasped and straightened up on his toes as the thick blade entered his back and exited his chest. His weapon fell to the floor. The other man was caught flush on the right temple: the force of the heavy spiked ball buried itself into his crushed skull, killing him instantly. Blood sprayed across Mac's upper body. Looking at Mac with a horrified expression, Adriana dropped the mace and covered her mouth with her hand. Momentarily, she thought she had hit Mac as well.

"I'm okay," Mac assured her. Glancing down at her khaki jacket smeared with blood, she added, "But my dry-cleaner is going to hate this."

Relieved but somewhat annoyed, Adriana replied, "You and your husband have the same morbid sense of humor."

Mr. Benito, still on his knees, cradled his hysterical wife with one arm and pointed to the doorway with the other. "The attackers have your husbands downstairs. They got to them sooner than expected, I'm afraid."

Mac faced the doorway, ordered everyone to remain silent, and clicked on her ear pod. She listened with eyes squeezed tight, hoping for the best. Then she turned it off. "One man is talking—and the best I can tell—one of our group escaped."

From the look on Adriana's face, Mac read her thoughts. "No, I couldn't tell from what was said. I don't know who it was. There was a shout and a thud. One of them must have been struck—and I heard Tina make a whimpering sound. No, she wasn't the one hit: it was one of the two men left."

Turning to the Benitos, she asked. "Will you two be okay here?"

"Madam Rance, we owe you two our lives. Yes, my wife will stay here, and I will accompany you to save the others."

Mac raised a hand and shook her head. "Mr. Benito, you performed well—and now it's your job to protect your wife. Take both of their weapons in case you need them." She poked one of the dead men with her boot and said, "They won't need them anymore."

Waving Adriana on, they stepped quickly into the hallway. Glancing over her shoulder, Mac whispered, "Woman, you're downright dangerous with anything metal in your hand. Poor, poor, Al." They both laughed and then became dead serious.

Chapter Twenty

SHOUTS CONTINUED TO ECHO from the tunnel. L' Ami and Tina were sitting back on their haunches, hands atop their heads. Rance remained on the ground, blood trickling down his chin. Pitt was not aware that he had already lost four of his nine men. Three were in the tunnel and on the cliffs searching for A.T.'s body. That left only Pitt and one other to guard the woman and two men: one lay unconscious on the dirt floor. There was time before the men came drifting back through the tunnel. Rance moaned and held his ribs. He didn't have to fake pain: he hurt like hell.

He looked over at Al and without the giant of a man noticing, winked. Tina noticed the signal as well. Pitt gave Rance a glancing blow with his brogan. "Get up punk. Grab that pickax and busy yourself tearing up that door." His order from the Bishop was to kill everyone within the castle and leave. But curiosity had gotten the best of him. While there, he'd see for himself what treasure lay below their feet.

L' Ami and Tina watched their friend struggle to his feet, and as if in fear, shrink away from the larger man. With eyes cast to his feet, Rance moved slowly to where the tool rested against the wall. Grabbing the handle, instead of picking it up, he dragged it behind him, seemingly too weak to lift it to his shoulder. Losing patience, Pitt took a step closer and gave him a powerful shove. Rance tripped over his own feet and dropped the pickax. "Pick it up and do some damage to that damned door or I'll use it on you, puny man," Pitt ordered.

Doing as ordered, Rance lifted the tool and stepped on the sturdy old relic protector. Instead of standing on the dirt floor to attack the wood, he stood on the door and placed his back to the wall, facing the powerfully built man with the gun and his tough-looking associate.

Lifting the pickax over his head, Rance's eyes flashed between Al and Tina: and then with all his might, he buried one end of the two-sided pickax deep into the thick wooden door with a thud, the other end of the pick leaning toward his antagonist.

As hard as he tried, Rance couldn't dislodge the pick from the door's hold. "You weak piece of worthless shit!" Pitt bellowed. Pull it out or…"

Before he could finish his insult, the smaller man ran like a scared rabbit to the far end of the room. Pitt's man raised his weapon but was waved off. "I'll take care of this," Pitt said, flexing his massive arm muscles.

Rance walked slowly toward Pitt, who was egging him on with wiggling fingers. He had plans of crushing the weakling's head between his palms. L' Ami, recognizing the hard-look in his long time friend's eyes, nodded slightly to Tina, and was prepared to act. Pitt stuck out his chin and invited Rance to take his best shot. The smaller of the two men drew back a fist and just before he brought it forward, lashed out with lightening speed. An upward thrust of his foot caught the unsuspecting giant between his legs. Turning and taking a number of steps, Rance spun around and took a flying leap in the air, striking Pitt in the middle of his barrel chest just as he straightened up from his agonizing pain.

Rance's blow, as hard as it was, wasn't enough to fell the man, but enough to stagger him backwards. That's when both Al and Tina made their strike. From her knees, she dove at the back of Pitt's legs, toppling him over. Losing balance, Pitt's weight propelled him backwards: the upright free end of the stationary pick penetrated his back just below his shoulder blade. Screaming in pain, Pitt struggled to free himself, but before he could move, Rance jumped into the air and came down on the man's chest with both feet, driving the pointed pick through

Pitt's quivering body. A bloody point protruded through a black tee shirt: his eyes widened in disbelief, then tree-trunk arms fell silent by his sides. Pitt's man froze at the sight, and before he could raise his weapon, Al brought the working end of a shovel across the back of his head.

"That takes care of them: now for the three in the tunnel," Rance said as if it was all in a day's work. "I'll shout for them to return. Al and I will stand on either side of the tunnel with shovels. Tina, when they're within a foot of the entrance, turn off the electric lanterns. Count to five and turn them back on. The moment the lights go out—we swing." Looking at Al, he asked, "Got that?" L' Ami grinned and held up his weapon.

Rance cupped his hands and in a deep voice mimicking Pitt's, he shouted, "You assholes, get back in here on the double!"

Waiting, they could hear the scurrying of footsteps in the dark, then as the men entered the illumination from the room, Rance and Al raised their shovels. Suddenly it was dark. Two loud reverberating sounds of metal whacking skulls resounded. The lone standing gunman blinked his eyes just as Rance swung his shovel, knocking the pole holding the heavy tunnel door loose: it came down with all its weight, driving the last of Pitt's men six feet into the tunnel. When they lifted the hinged door and fixed the pole, they saw the man on his back: his nose was flattened—as were all his facial features.

"Oh, you guys have all the fun," Arturo complained, standing over the body of the leader of the nine assassins. "Look who I ran into upstairs." Mac and Adriana had followed A.T. into the room.

"How in the hell did you get out of the tunnel...?" Rance was about to ask A.T., when he saw his wife caked with blood from head to toe. "Mac!" he shouted, as he ran to her side. Holding her at arm's length, his eyes searched in vain for wounds.

"I'm fine. I'll explain later," she assured him. "But look at you: your chin is bleeding, and you'll need a dozen stitches."

He touched his chin and looked at his bloody finger tip. "A little scar will only add character to my manly appearance."

"He's too much," Adriana said, squeezing her husband to her chest. A.T. and Tina were in a welcome embrace, stifling a fit of humor at her reaction to Rance's playful observation.

Rance suddenly turned to the stairs leading to the floor above. "The Benitos. That bastard sent two men up to kill them. We had better…"

Mac grabbed his sleeve. "Adriana and I've already taken care of the two assassins. Both Mr. and Mrs. Benito are safe. There are two dead men in the well outside—two more upstairs—and five down here. Mr. Benito had counted nine in all—and all accounted for."

"What are we going to do with the trash?" Tina asked, gesturing to the bodies.

"I'll take the Rover back to the village and have my brother gather men to come and dispose of the bodies," Adriana said. "I'd phone, but according to Tome, the entire village's phone system will be out of service for the entire day." Rance nodded approval.

"I'll go with her," L' Ami suggested.

"Al, we've got much to do yet. Tearing up the rest of the door is one thing and moving the bodies outside is another. We'll need all hands to finish the job. Adriana can summon her brother's help."

"You're right," Al agreed. "But I'll walk her to the vehicle and be back momentarily."

"I thought you didn't want to destroy the door," A.T. reminded him.

"I've got a better idea, if what I suspect waits for us below our feet. Grab the big fellow's other arm and we'll pry him loose." After a moment's struggle, Pitt's body slipped loose of the pick with a sucking sound. Tina shivered.

Rance wiggled the handle of the pick until it came free. "I'll get started here. When Al returns, you two haul the asses of our dead friends outside on the lawn. And don't forget the two upstairs and the ones in the well. Stack them neatly for the mayor.

"Tina, you were directly instrumental in defeating the big guy. Thanks. Why don't you find Mr. Benito and ask him to come see me—and Mac, I suggest you take a shower and change into something less... colorful."

Spitting on both hands and rubbing them together, Rance set about splintering and tearing up the ancient wooden door while A.T. and Al went about removing the bodies. Mr. Benito stood at the foot of the steps until Rance noticed his presence. Resting the pick against the wall, Rance held out a hand and thanked the old man for alerting them of the present danger. He had saved their lives. During their brief discussion, Rance gave the man specific instructions. Mr. Benito understood, nodded, and left.

Bodies were stacked on the castle lawn like a wood pile. L' Ami and Arturo took turns with Rance picking apart the door that refused to give up its keep without a tough fight. When they had managed to poke two holes in the door, Rance held up his hand. "Let's do it the easy way." Both A.T. and Al laughed at the thought. Easy, like hell.

Taking the end of the rope, Rance looped it in and around the two openings, tied it off, then threw the other end over the overhead bar. "All right, gentlemen, let's yank it open."

They pulled and pulled, even leapt up to place all their combined weight on the rope. All they received for their effort was a loud creak and the groan of straining wood. "Let's burn the confounded thing," A.T. said in frustration. "The stubborn son-of-a-bitch won't give an inch."

"Must be made of Italian wood," L' Ami said sarcastically.

"Let me at that thing again," Rance said, untying the rope from the two holes. Using the pick, he attacked the wood between the holes with a vengeance. Bit by bit the wood gave way. Chunks flew in the air as the two holes became one large man-sized hole. Tossing the tool to the side, he knelt down to peer into the darkness below. "Hand me a flashlight, A.T."

"Well?" L' Ami asked.

"It's a medium-sized room carved out of clay like this room…" He paused. "Wait: there are shapes in the far corner that appear to be stacked boxes of varying sizes."

"Rance! Rance!" Mac shouted from the room above. "They've got Adriana—and it looks like they're threatening to kill her."

Before he had an opportunity to respond, L' Ami dashed upstairs. As he approached Mac, she silently pointed out the two open castle doors. Al could see the outline of three people standing about five hundred yards from the steps. One man held a white flag: the other stood behind his wife. He couldn't see them that well, but he assumed from the man's position behind Adriana, that he was holding a gun to her head. In a panic, he thought of dashing out onto the lawn, when a loud shout, "No!" stopped him cold.

Rance, standing next to his wife, motioned Al to their side. "I know what's going through your mind, old friend. But running out there will do no good: we need a plan first."

"Well I plan on ripping their hearts out," came Al's quick reply.

Placing a hand on his friend's shoulder, Rance assured him. "Have a little faith in me. She'll be fine: believe me. Find a broom pole and attach a pillowcase to the end and calmly walk out. Stop about twenty feet before encountering them. Begin a dialogue: stall 'em, and when you do, begin edging yourself to their left—providing me a clear shot." Motioning up with his finger, he ended by saying, "Sarah and I will be above on the turret. She and I will handle it from there. Take your time walking out. Give me time to set up." Giving his friend a squeeze on the shoulder, he ran up the curving stone staircase that Sebastian had helped to build.

Mac looked puzzled and turned to L' Ami. "Who's Sarah?"

"Rance has two sniper rifles. Mary is a single action used for one-shot, one-kill. It's most reliable at long-distance—especially in the hands of someone like your husband—when one shot is all he needs." Al quickly glanced toward the door. "In this case, where he anticipates needing more than one-shot, he'll defer to Sarah—an automatic."

"But Sarah is less reliable?" she asked.

"They're only five hundred yards away. At that distance, it wouldn't make any difference to Rance. I trust him with Adriana's life." Pointing upstairs, he continued. "Get me a pillow case: I'll find a broomstick in the kitchen pantry. I have to get out there before they become antsy."

THE BISHOP AND PASCHAL HAD WATCHED A.T. and L' Ami stack the bodies of their nine mercenaries on the lawn. Now, from their hiding place in the shadows inside the old shack, Bishop watched Maurice, Edmond, and the Spanish girl through his binoculars. "Pitt and his men were no match for three men and three women—but this will achieve our end. We'll trade one of the wives for the treasure."

Paschal asked for the binoculars and trained them on his associates and the redhead. Then he swung toward the open castle doors. "Here comes the husband waving a white flag." Bishop rubbed his palms together. Now they were getting somewhere.

L' Ami walked slowly, one long step after the other. It felt like he was walking in slow-motion and could sense Rance high above and to his rear. It wasn't the first time that he had placed his faith in his friend.

This time, his wife's life depended upon Rance's expertise, sharp eye, and steady hand.

The past president's Shadow Master nestled the stock to his cheek, inhaling the familiar odor of fresh machine oil. Only one adjustment was necessary. For once, there was very little wind off the ocean: humidity was no problem, and at that distance, gravity meant little. After sighting the targets in the crosshairs, he made a slight adjustment on the BDC dial, adjusting for ballistic drop compensation for battlefield variables. Sarah was loaded with 7.62 millimeter ballistic rounds, with one resting in the chamber. His finger caressed the trigger. L' Ami was halfway there.

Rance's mind flashed back to the time he had saved General Rubin Brock's bacon, years before he became Chairman of the Joint Chiefs. Rubin was pinned down behind an exposed rock, communicating with a group of special ops Marines. Brock thought he was a dead man, when out of nowhere, an Arab came galloping over a sand dune on horseback, standing up in the stirrups firing a rifle. Ducking his head, Brock was surprised when four Arabs tumbled from the rocks above and behind him. Four shots and four heads burst like watermelons. Then the shooter disappeared in the dust. It wasn't until years later, when a man called Rance Colby sat in the dark of the general's den holding a pistol, explaining that the man on horseback was the stranger holding the weapon, and asking for a return favor to find and eliminate a group of international assassins.

Al stopped approximately twenty feet from Bishop's men and lowered his makeshift white flag. "Have they hurt you?" Al asked. His voice was calm and controlled, but the look in his eyes was full of anger.

Edmond answered for Adriana. Pulling the obviously frightened woman close, he placed the pistol alongside her head. "We haven't hurt a single red strand of hair," he said with a wicked grin. "Yet."

While Al asked them what they wanted, he slowly edged his way to his right. Their left. Maurice, noticing his movement, raised his rifle from the holding position by his waist and pointed it at Al's stomach. "We'll trade the woman's life for the treasure. Simple trade," Edmond answered.

Rance blew out a breath of relief when he noted that the barrel of the weapon was not aimed at Adriana's head, but rather alongside her left temple. Good. L' Ami was stalling for time. Fine crosshairs zeroed in on the hand holding the pistol. It all happened so fast. Edmond's gun hand was shattered, and any reflex destroyed. A second later, the next bullet turned his head into a red mist. In the third click of a clock, Maurice's head flew back: a slug had entered his throat and severed his neck vertebra. He also had a hole in his chest. L' Ami had removed his khaki jacket and his 45 was tucked in the small of his back. He had fired at Maurice in tandem with the man on the castle roof.

Al rushed forward and gently held his wife upright. Her legs felt like jelly. Hanging on for dear life and with her head buried in the crook of his neck, she managed to ask, "How…who made that…unbelievable…shot?"

BINOCULARS SLIPPED FROM THE BISHOP'S HAND. "How could that be?" Words escaped from a mouth agape in wonder. "They're both dead. Our precious relics will never be mine," he uttered in disbelief.

"Relics?" Paschal asked with a look of distain. "Don't you mean gold, jewels…?"

"No, you tiny man. Ancient holy relics that belong to the church," he finally admitted. "What do we want with gold? Holy relics are priceless."

Paschal stepped away and faced the huge figure dressed proudly in a black suit and white clerical collar. "You really are a Bishop, aren't you? And you've been shitting us all along. You knew there was no gold, just your damned relics. Baudouin, Maurice, and Edmond died for no good reason. You fat bastard!"

With courage born out of anger and utter frustration, Paschal shoved Bishop with both hands. Stumbling backward and losing his balance, Paschal shoved several more times. Claude, the man known as Bishop, hadn't noticed the short wall surrounding the well, and without looking stepped over the wall to escape the little man's onrush. Before he could stop his momentum, the fat man slid into the well up to his waste. He was wedged solid.

Paschal stood over his former boss and laughed. "You'll be stuck there until you lose some fat." Leaning forward, Paschal focused his eyes on a small gold pin in Bishop's lapel. It was a circle with a crucifix inside. "You're a member of Opus Dei—aren't you? That's why you'd sacrifice us for your precious holy relics."

Irate, Paschal stomped away, muttering to himself. Picking up a discarded piece of sturdy four-by-four that Mr. Bonito had left behind from his woodworking chores, he turned to face the helpless man wedged in the well. "Don't worry fat man—you won't feel the pain of dying from thirst or hunger. You won't feel any pain at all."

The Bishop's eyes widened, and he gasped aloud just before his skull was shattered by the piece of wood. A smile crossed Paschal's features as he flipped aside his weapon and ran from the old wooden shack and disappeared into the woods.

Chapter Twenty-One

RANCE AND THE OTHERS GATHERED on the castle's entry steps waiting to greet Adriana and Al. When the two stepped off the lawn, Adriana released her grip on her husband's hand and fled up the stairs, straight to the startled sniper. Flinging her arms around his neck, he staggered back, his arms limp by his sides. First glancing in panic at Mac, then Al, his expression was of complete surprise, pleading, *what do I do now?* Both spouses nodded their approval. In the spirit of the appreciation Adriana displayed with her bear grip, Rance reluctantly hugged her back. "L' Ami, don't just stand there," he said with a roll of his eyes. "Pry your wife off this tired old man's bones. There's more work to do before we dine tonight at Tome's restaurant."

A.T. and Al went about adding two more corpses to the wood pile and the women accompanied Rance to the battered and scarred door that had sealed the Templar treasure for centuries. As Rance attempted to widen the hole, Brother Sebastian's last words rumbled through his thoughts: *Carpe Diem...Seize the Day.*

He had already made up his mind how to proceed next, and Mr. Benito was a key player in that plan. But where was the old man? Rance only hoped that the others would understand. No. He was certain that they would agree with his decision. Speaking of Mr. Benito. "Mr. Rance, Sir, there's another dead body," came the anxious voice from above.

"Damn!" was Rance's quick reply. "We'll soon have a cord of bodies."

Only the old man's legs appeared on the wooden steps. "The fat man is stuck in the well—and his head is...squished."

"Ask Mr. Testaccio and Mr. L' Ami to help you free the Bishop's body and add him to the pile. Wait. Before you go. Where are the ready-mix cement and the portable mixer I requested?"

"The mixer is in the shed: that's how I discovered the body in the well—and the leftover ready-mix from the castle's restoration is in the upstairs back storeroom." Mr. Benito ducked his head to look at his boss. "I'll need help dragging the mixer from the shed, but it won't fit down the stairs, I'm afraid."

"Make use of the two strong gentlemen outside. They can help lug the bags of ready-mix down here. Bring all that you have. And talk to Mr. Testaccio about the problem with the portable mixer."

Bending over, Rance tore loose the last piece of thick wood: he now had a jagged hole large enough to slip into. Inserting his legs, he turned his body to drop to the floor below. Mac handed him a flashlight and he disappeared from sight. Flexing his knees as his feet touched the dirt floor, he stood straight and flashed the bright beam in the direction of where he had earlier spied the boxes. Mac and the other women stood silently, stealing glances at each other and the dark hole. They could hear movement from below, but no ecstatic shouts of discovery.

Scraping noises from behind spun they around. It was the men with armfuls of ready-mix cement. Tossing four heavy bags in a corner, they dusted themselves off and asked what Rance had found. "He's been down there for ten minutes and hasn't said a word," Tina explained.

"Well, that's our boy," A.T. said with a shrug of a shoulder. "When he's ready to talk, he will—but knowing him like I do—he won't say a word until he's damn good and ready. In the meantime, we'll finish stacking the cement. There's a hell of a lot to stack. Then we'll get the mixer down here. I've got an idea, and I'll need that rope again."

By the time they saw a hand emerge from the hole, then another, then a grunt, and Rance's body pop up, the stack of cement was over six foot high. The first words out of his mouth were, "Where's the cement mixer?"

"First things first," Mac said, annoyed at her husband's secrecy. "What did you find down in that hole? We've been through enough the last month or so: we deserve to be told."

"Yes, you all have. I'm fully aware. But give me time to gather my thoughts—and I'll explain everything...I only hope that you'll understand."

Tina broke in, "A.T. and the others are using the rope to lower the mixer over the cliff down to the tunnel entrance. Then they'll pull it through the tunnel."

Adriana added, "And we're all very confused. What are you going to do with all that cement and the mixer...?" Both her eyes and mouth opened wide when the reason hit her. "You're going to seal the treasure entrance for all time. Aren't you?"

Perplexed at the thought, three pair of eyes searched Rance's expression for an answer. He still hadn't formulated an acceptable reply.

"Here's the cement mixer!" A.T. shouted from within the tunnel. Al and Mr. Benito were tugging on the rope with Arturo. "This blasted thing is heavy," he added, red-faced.

Rance turned to Mr. Benito. "We'll need a hose attached to a faucet above, with a shutoff valve down here so we can mix the cement."

"What in God's name do you intend to do?" A.T. asked.

"God has nothing to do with it," Tina answered for their friend. She looked Rance straight in the eye and continued. "Or does it?"

"He's going to seal up the treasure below!" Adriana burst out.

Now all eyes were on Rance waiting for an explanation. A look of pure guilt dulled his features. He had placed their lives in danger in Scotland, Ethiopia, Canada, and again in Spain. They had once discussed the possibility that there was no real treasure, in the true sense of the word, but only Templar relics. And now he knew that his first inkling was correct.

Rising to his full height and filling his lungs with a deep breath, he announced, "It is as expected. No gold or jewels. Only old wooden boxes hiding the guardians' secret keeping—holy relics that thousands of people sacrificed their lives for these many centuries."

Arturo glanced quickly at those in the dirt-filled room, and then to his friend of many years. "So? We all suspected as much. As mentioned earlier—what would we do with more money? We're all filthy rich already. It was one hell of an adventure—and we've all survived. What more would any one of us want? And I speak for all of us, right gang?"

Rance's heart lifted with relief at their positive assurances. "Okay then. A.T., that door needs to be completely demolished if we're going to fill the hole with cement. The boxes below are well out of the way and will not be touched by the flow of cement."

"Whoa, hold on there old horse," L' Ami said, physically holding everyone back with extended arms. "First. What did you find in that dark hole that we're sealing forever? Inquiring minds want to know."

Rance looked over at the stairs to the room upstairs. Mr. Benito hadn't returned with the hose. "It goes without saying: you're all sworn to secrecy. If not," he grinned, "I'd have to kill you all."

"Get on with it," Mac demanded.

Nodding to the hole, he explained. "There are eight old wooden boxes of various sizes, no doubt sealed by the Templars because each box bore the Templar emblem. A long thin box had *Lancea Longini* etched on the side."

Adriana couldn't help herself. "That's Latin for Lance of Longinus—meaning that the lance said to have pierced Jesus' side during His crucifixion was inside."

"You do know your ancient history, Adriana. Here's one for you: What were the estimated dimensions of the Ark of the Covenant?"

Her eyes opened like teacups. Placing a hand to her forehead, she removed it and said, "130 x 80 x 80 centimeters. You don't…"

"A Hebrew inscription, *Aron Habrit*, was carved on the center plank on a box with those approximate dimensions."

"That means…" Adriana was about to confirm Rance's conclusion when he cut her short.

"Other boxes of different sizes had the words, *Reliquiae*, carved atop each box. Name some of the other Holy relics associated with the Templars' rumored treasure?"

"*Reliquiae* comes from the Latin word meaning 'remains.' Of course there were rumors of fragmented remains of the True Cross."

Rance laughed. "Yes, and John Calvin said that there were so many pieces of the cross that Jesus died on scattered about churches throughout the world, that if they were gathered together, there would be enough wood to build a ship."

"How about the Holy Grail?" Tina asked.

"There's that," Adriana said. "But dozens of theories abound. Then there's Veronica's Veil, used to wipe the sweat from Jesus' face as he carried the cross. And the Holy Sponge soaked in vinegar and offered to Christ—along with Holy Nails that pinned Him to the cross. There's even talk of the Holy Prepuce," she made a face, "but I'm not going into that. Then of course there's the legend of the Seamless Robe, the garment said to have been woven by Jesus' mother that miraculously grew with Him from childhood to manhood."

"I think that's quite enough, Adriana." Rance said. "I'm sure Calvin had much to say about all of that, and more. I just don't know what is secreted away down there—and frankly I prefer it that way. Maybe no one should ever know. And my gut tells me that it's best that way.

There's way too much religious power in what might be below our feet. I seized the day—and made my decision." He looked at his friends and added, "*We* all made the decision. The right decision. I believe Brother Sebastian, the last true Templar, would agree."

Mr. Benito could be heard coming down the steps, huffing and puffing, tugging on a water hose. A.T. picked up the pickax to finish off the wooden door, and the woman helped Rance pour the dusty dry cement into the mixer with the right combination of water to cement. Mr. Benito was told that the hole was a danger and had to be filled. Someone could fall through the rotted wooden door. It was a danger. Piecing Rance's words together, he nodded in agreement, but felt that the door that fought so hard not to give up was certainly sturdy enough. But he was only the hired man.

Two hours later, the treasure hole was filled, and the remaining cement spread over the floor to make a hard surface. There remained no hint of the room below. For whatever reason, the flooring next to the tunnel door was uneven. Rance had designed it that way. The hidden tunnel door could be opened, if ever it was necessary.

MR. AND MRS. BENITO WAVED TO RANCE AND PARTY as they made their way into the private dining room of Tome's restaurant. Rance whispered in Adriana's ear. "Inform your brother to put the Benito's meal on our tab—and that their wine glasses should never be, at any time, more than half empty."

Tome's normally rosy complexion paled, and his jolly laughter appeared subdued. His loving sister would be leaving him forever in the morning, going with her new husband to his Italian villa. Yes, she would have company in the form of Mr. and Mrs. Testaccio who lived in the adjoining villa, but that wasn't really like family. He was visibly worried for his sister and sad for himself. His spirit perked up when

Rance offered to fly him to visit his sister in a few months when he and Mac returned to Italy for a visit.

Plans were made over a Spanish feast, accompanied by numerous pitchers of sangria. Rance and Mac planned to fly their friends to Italy early tomorrow morning, stay the night, then return to Castle de Molay to begin life anew. Mac was prepared to join the group working to restore Spain's castle ruins. They met in Madrid once a month. Rance, after much pondering, thought about becoming an author writing novels of international mystery and intrigue, and of course for obvious reasons, he'd use a pen name.

Arturo and Tina were happy to be going home and thrilled to have the L' Ami family living close by. Adriana was downhearted to be leaving her beloved Spain and her brother, but excited about her new role as Lady Adriana L' Ami, as her husband was now referring to her. Al had made a phone call to his villa to alert his 'flower girls' that he was now happily married and would no longer need their services. A.T., who had a housekeeper, made arrangements for her, or a friend of hers, to work for Lady L' Ami. All was well. All was prepared.

Epilogue

PAVAROTTI'S VOICE FILLED THE FLOWER SCENTED AIR surrounding the covered outdoor patio of A.T. and Tina's hilltop villa. It wasn't quite twilight and the ancient olive garden at the bottom of the green valley was beginning to produce distant shadows. Mac and Rance sipped from their glasses, relaxing and talking in hush tones to their host and hostess. Lord and Lady L' Ami had yet to arrive.

A booming and joyful *Buona sera* aroused a covey of doves as the four lounging peacefully under the red-tiled patio roof. It was Al, hand-in-hand with a beaming Adriana. Al's free hand held a full bottle of JD. "You there, round stout bald man, I hope you have a clean glass and ice for a thirsty lord—and a second clean glass of wine for my lady-love."

Arturo looked at Tina and shook his head. "Are we going to have to put up with this aggravation from now on? Maybe we should sell this place cheap to a family of gypsies and move far, far away."

"Oh, don't fret, my love," Tina said, getting up to fill Al's order. "Remember, after half a bottle, he normally mellows out."

"Passes out is more like it," A.T. said, tossing both hands in the air. Pulling up a lounger for Adriana, he went on. "For the lady of the next-door villa. You, Lord L' Ami, can stand there and lean against a column or find your own seat."

Quickly changing the subject, Mac asked, "Adriana, what do you think of your new home?"

Adriana at first appeared to be at a loss for words. "Something I wasn't prepared for. It's like living in a museum, a wonderful and beautiful museum. I've never seen ceilings so high. There's marble everywhere: the floor, walls, decorative columns, fountains, even in the bathrooms. There are eight of those," she exclaimed with amazement.

"Jist a moodest bungaloow," Al yawned. "Nothing tae guid foor ma lady." This time he attempted a Scottish accent.

"I just love Pavarotti," Adriana said, a bit embarrassed by her husband's words.

Handing a glass of wine to Adriana and a tall glass of ice to Al, Arturo mentioned, "He's my favorite, too. Tina did a good turn for him during one of his concerts, and as a return favor, at Tina's request, he came and sang at our wedding."

"Sang all night and into the early morning hours as I remember it," Rance said. "Between Mac and the Italian tenor, I got very little sleep." Mac's shoe just missed his shin.

During last evening's dinner in Tarego, and tonight, the women were showing off their femininity in spaghetti-strap sheaths. Tina in black. Adriana wore gold, and Mac was wrapped in turquoise. The men wore tan slacks and flower-patterned short-sleeve silk shirts. After an entire adventure dress in khakis, they had sworn off the Indiana Jones look.

Everyone suddenly became silent: only night sounds of birds, crickets, and an occasional tree frog could be heard. Then Rance broke the pensive mood. "Do you think we did the right thing?"

There was no doubt what he was referring to: it happened to be on everyone's mind. Slowly, five heads nodded yes. "Sometimes legends need to remain—legends," A.T. said.

"No harm, no foul," L' Ami added. "Whatever that means, it sounds about right."

ARTURO, TINA, ADRIANA, AND AL STOOD BY THE LEAR to say their good-byes as Rance, and Mac hugged their friends. With the luggage stowed and the stairway ready, tears welled in the women's eyes. The men exchanged thumbs-up. Turning to wave for one final time, Rance pulled the door hatch closed. As the engines spun and made a high whistling sound and the craft turned to taxi down the tarmac, one of the ground crew, clutching something white in both hands, ran up to the group. "*Signor Testaccio!*" he shouted to command attention over the roar. "Your friend, the pilot, told me to give one of these to each of you once the plane was about to lift off. Here," he said, distributing what looked like something inside a folded piece of paper.

With puzzled expressions, each unfolded their paper. On it was printed: 'Guardians Behold Our Keeping.' Inside the paper was a single gold coin.

About the Author

W.R. Park, author, columnist, teacher, lecturer, past president of three advertising agencies, William R. Park, Sr. has served as a consultant to some of America's largest and most successful companies and introduced at conferences as one of America's leading advertising authorities. As a nationally known and respected advertising executive for forty-two years, he has written thousands of newspaper/print ads and TV/radio scripts.

Winner of national awards in print and television, his popular 'Ad Pulse' monthly column appeared in Modern Retailer Magazine in the '70s and again in Publishers' Auxiliary in the '90s. In addition, his articles have appeared in Editor & Publisher, The Best Times Magazine, Route 66 Magazine, Atlanta Journal, Kansas City Star, and various nationwide daily newspapers.

W.R. Park's twenty published novels have been read and reviewed by a host of bestselling authors comparing his work to some of the most talented suspense-thriller writers.

W.R. Park is a Member of International Thriller Writers, Inc.

Coming Soon!

W. R. PARK'S

UNLIKELY ASSASSIN
The Shadow Master Series
Book 5

A broken man. Adam Rance, aka Rance Colby, the former president's Shadow Master, lies half-naked under the baking sun on a South Pacific beach—drunk, despondent, and in poor shape mentally and physically.

After years of covert service to his country, Rance found love and married. The fiery accidental death of his wife changed everything that was right in his life. Despondent, he refuses to abandon his hermit-like existence until he's told his wife is alive…

Avoiding numerous attempts on his life, his quest takes him from the mean streets of New York to an underground community of thugs from various countries and finally a face-to-face confrontation with an unlikely assassin—Mac and her sniper rifle.

For more information
visit: www.SpeakingVolumes.us

Now Available!

W. R. PARK'S
THE SHADOW MASTER
BOOKS 1 – 3

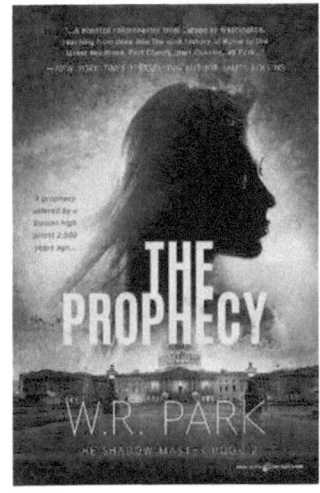 

**For more information
visit:** www.SpeakingVolumes.us

Now Available!

STEPHEN STEELE'S
THE TROUBLE WITH MIRACLES
BOOKS 1 – 3

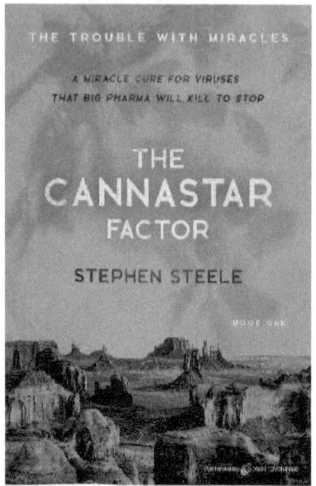

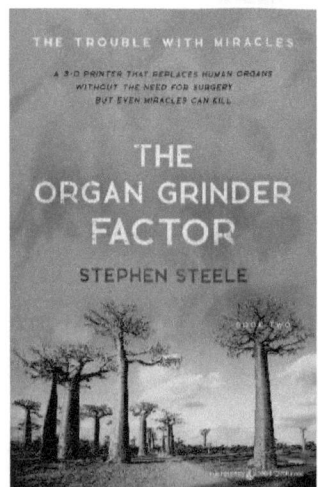

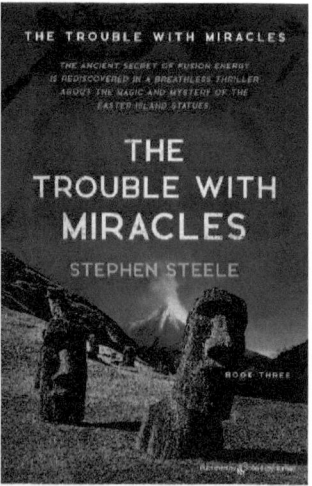

**For more information
visit:** www.SpeakingVolumes.us

www.ingramcontent.com/pod-product-compliance
Lightning Source LLC
LaVergne TN
LVHW041658060526
838201LV00043B/476